The Worst In Us

The Worst In Us

ELIAS WITHEROW

THOUGHT
CATALOG
Books

BROOKLYN, NY

**THOUGHT
CATALOG
Books**

Cover art is a derivative of "Kids, older photo" by Joe Crawford and licensed under CC by Thought Catalog Books. Designed by KJ Parish.

Published by Thought Catalog Books, a publishing house owned by The Thought & Expression Co., Williamsburg, Brooklyn.

First edition, 2018

ISBN: 978-1-945796-78-4

Printed and bound in the United States.

10 9 8 7 6 5 4 3 2 1

This is for my brothers, Dave and Joe
I love you guys
There isn't anything I wouldn't do for you

Chapter 1

Things would be OK.

That's what I kept telling myself. The July wind danced through the tall grass before me, and the evening sun was a glorious globe of brilliant orange. Color trickled across the horizon, a bleeding vein of purple and pink. The heat clung to my face and I welcomed it, closing my eyes against the fading rays.

Things would be OK.

That's why I had come here. That's why I had come *home*. I ran a hand through my long brown hair as the breeze stirred it across my face. My fingers came away slick with sweat. It was hot today, but with the approaching night, I could feel the temperature mercifully dropping. I scratched at the stubble on my chin and took a deep breath. I listened. The night bugs had already begun their gentle song. The wind rustled the swaying field before me. The old deck creaked beneath my boots, and my knuckles tightened on the porch railing.

Things would be OK.

I heard the front door open behind me. I continued to stare out at the beautiful countryside, completely enraptured by its serenity. A hand fell across my back and ran up my shoulders. A loving hand. I turned around and smiled.

"Hey, Ma."

My mother smiled up at me, her eyes twinkling. "Thought I'd find you out here, Cole."

I exhaled slowly. "I've missed this."

Ma offered me the cold beer she was holding. "This will make it even better."

I took it gratefully and drank deeply. I smacked my lips and ran a hand over my mouth. "Thank you."

Her hand returned to my back, cautious and comforting. "How you doing? I haven't had the chance to catch you alone like this since you've been back."

I let my eyes return to the dimming field. "I'm OK. It's good to be back home. It's good to be around family again."

Ma leaned against the porch railing next to me. I passed her the beer and she took a swallow before handing it back. "We've missed you. All of us."

"Missed you too, Ma," I said quietly.

Silence grew between us. It was a soft silence, filled with nothing but the moment. A flock of birds rose from the distant woods and I tracked them as they disappeared into the sun. The air smelled of dirt and heat. My mouth tasted like cold beer and sweat. My heart slowed and I let myself be filled with these sensations.

"Dave is out back firing up the grill," Ma said after a moment. "Think he's going to make his special ribs. You know, the ones with that barbecue sauce he swears is homemade?"

I chuckled quietly. "I'm pretty sure I once caught him dumping a store-bought bottle into some Tupperware. To this day, though, he swears it's a secret recipe."

"Your brother just wants to impress you," Ma said. "He always has. Ever since you two were little."

I took another sip of beer. "He doesn't need to impress me. He's always been better than me. At everything."

"All my children are perfect just as they are," Ma said, rubbing shoulders with me, "even when they run off to the city for five years."

I stared at the bottle in my hands.

Ma leaned in, smiling. "I'm just teasing, Cole. You went where your heart told you to go."

I picked at the label, peeling the corner. "My heart went with Maria. And so I followed."

Ma's hand returned to my back. "You know I love you, right, son?"

I felt a lump form in my throat. I nodded without looking at her.

"I'm so sorry about what happened," Ma said gently. "You're a good boy. You don't deserve such sadness in your life. None of my children do."

"Maria didn't deserve what happened, either," I said quietly.

Ma put her cheek against my shoulder and stared out at the dying light. "There's a lot of evil men in the world, Cole."

"I know," I whispered.

A crow cawed across the field and took flight. I drank the rest of the beer and wiped my eyes. Ma said nothing more and I was grateful. I wasn't ready to open that door again. Not yet. Instead, I cleared my throat.

"You said Joe isn't going to make it tonight?"

Ma smiled. "I'm afraid not. He's working." She sighed. "That young man needs to learn to put his feet up every now and again. It's like he feels a need to compensate for being the youngest of the litter by working the hardest."

"How's he doing?"

Ma waved a hand dismissively. "You know Joe. Doesn't take shit from anyone but will be the first to help you out of a pickle."

"Still a hothead?"

Ma snorted. "That boy was born with coals in his skull."

"I think we all were," I said, smiling slightly. "The rest of us just learned how to douse the flames."

Ma shook her head. "Not Tammy. No sir, your sister has always been the most levelheaded of the bunch," Ma laughed, "and I would expect nothing less from my firstborn."

"She was always your favorite," I joked.

Ma's eyes lit up. "You're *all* my favorite. Tammy, you,

Dave, and little Joey." She smiled sadly. "Ever since your father passed, I've realized just how special each and every one of you is."

I hugged her, planting a kiss on top of her gray head. "You know you're the best mother a kid could hope for?"

Ma giggled into my chest. "Oh, stop it or you're going to make an old lady blush."

I laughed and took her hand, twirling her across the porch. "Old? Don't make me laugh; you're just hitting your prime."

Ma smiled openly. "Still blessed with a silver tongue, I see."

I winked at her. "Gets me into trouble sometimes."

"Oh, I'm sure it does."

I released her hand and stepped back, grinning. "Hey, Ma?"

"Yes?"

"It really is good to be home."

She nodded, her face alight with happiness. "It warms my heart to hear you say so. What do you think, should we go check on your brother and see if he's ruined the ribs yet?"

I laughed. "Yeah, that sounds great. Just…give me another second out here?"

My mother's gaze lingered on me for a moment and I saw worry briefly flicker in her eyes. She simply nodded and offered me a warm smile before heading back into the house. As the front door closed behind her, I turned back to the railing and filled my lungs with the growing night.

I was glad I had returned home in time to catch summer. I had forgotten the charm it held. The special display nature expelled during these hot months. I had loved New York, I truly had, but something about this peaceful evening told me that *this* was home. This was the land that held my heart. And it always would be. I felt sweat roll down the back of my neck and I smiled. It was strange to find comfort in discomfort.

I was about to go inside and find my brother Dave when I noticed a car making its way down the winding dirt road in front of the house. I turned back to the railing and watched the trail of dust grow closer. I squinted in the fading light.

The car slowed as it approached my mother's driveway, and as it turned in, I grinned. Without waiting, I trotted down the front steps and hurried to greet the newcomer.

My sister Tammy beamed as she got out of her car. She ran to me and embraced me in a fierce hug.

"Oh, I missed you so much!" she laughed, squeezing me tightly.

I laughed with her and pulled away. "You too, Tam. It's been too long."

She was a beautiful woman. Long honey-brown hair, shining green eyes, and a smile that brought sunshine with it. I looked down at her, shaking my head.

"Ma said you were coming, but I wasn't sure," I smiled.

She playfully punched me in the arm. "Had to make sure my little brother was actually coming home. What took you so long?"

I shrugged. "You know…life."

She cocked her head back. "Ah yes, that darned thing. You look good, Cole."

I nodded. "I feel good."

She rubbed my arm. "I'm glad to hear it." She dropped her eyes and stared at her feet, growing somber. "I'm so sorry about what happened. It was a terrible thing."

I shuffled awkwardly. "I don't really want to talk about it tonight."

She smiled gently. "Of course not. I just felt like…like I had to say something."

I looked into her eyes, grateful. "I know…thank you."

"I've got beer in the car," Tammy said, cocking a thumb over her shoulder. "Wanna give me a hand?"

"Yeah, of course, but hold on a second," I said, stopping her.

She looked at me.

I stole a quick glance at the house and lowered my voice. "How's Ma been? I know she's putting on a brave face for me, but I've been worried about her."

Tammy sighed. "She's doing OK. She misses Dad, like we all do. But it's been six years and I think she's learned how to"—she licked her lips—"to live without him being here. We all had to learn how to do that."

"Yeah…" I said quietly, my mind drifting back to memories of my father. He had been a strong man. A man born to work with his hands. When he had died in the tractor accident, it had shaken the very foundation of our family. He had always been a man of few words, but after his death, they were all I craved. Just to see him smile one last time and tell me, like he always did, that if I took care of the land then the land would take care of me. I smiled. I couldn't count how many times he had fed me that line.

I shook the clinging thoughts away. "And how are you doing, Tam? Things been good with you? Have you found yourself a decent man to take care of you yet?"

Tammy snorted. "First off, there are no decent men. And second, I don't need anyone to look after me."

I balked. "Of course you don't. You could still kick my ass if you really wanted to."

She balled her fist at me, chuckling. "Damn straight. Now come on, help me with the beer and let's go inside."

"Dave's making ribs out back," I said, following her back to the car, "with that shitty BBQ sauce he's been lying about for years."

Tammy handed me a case of beer, groaning. "Oh, God, thanks for the warning. I'll make an appointment now to get my stomach pumped."

I hefted the beer onto my shoulder and we began to

walk toward the house. "Oh, come on now, the man tries."

"Yeah, he tries to kill us with his charcoal bones and pig-slop sauce."

"Boy, time hasn't dulled your sensibilities," I said, laughing.

"It's the one thing Dave does wrong, so I have to stick it to him."

We walked up the front porch, the old wood groaning beneath my boots. "He seems happy."

"He's always been happy," Tammy said, opening the front door for me. "Even as kids he'd find the positivity in any given situation."

"Oh, I remember," I said, stepping inside. "Used to drive me crazy 'cause Dad would turn to me with that look on his face and say: 'Can't you be more like your brother?'"

"The fabled 'look.'"

"I could never fault Dave for that, though," I said. "In fact, I always admired it."

"Well, don't tell him," Tammy said, "or it'll go right to his head."

"Yeah, and then this would go right to his head," I grinned, holding up my free fist. We both laughed and went into the kitchen. Ma was by the stove, stirring up something in a saucepan. She turned and smiled when she saw the two of us.

"Tammy, you made it!" she exclaimed, setting down her wooden spoon.

"Smells amazing, Ma," Tammy said, hugging our mother. I put the beer down on the counter as they started to talk. I pulled two out and headed for the back door, throwing a wink over my shoulder at my sister. She smiled and turned back to Ma.

I pushed the screen door open and stepped out into the backyard. The fields behind my mother's house were borderless, an eternal stretch of Southern earth clothed in rich grass and lonely trees.

I breathed it all in, taking the aromas deep into my memory. Smoke rose from the massive grill my brother Dave was posted in front of. He was taller than me by a couple inches but thinner. I stood for a moment watching him struggle with the ribs he was coating. To my delight, it smelled delicious. I strode to his side and placed a beer in his hands.

"Looks like you need one of these, Davey," I said, noting the beads of sweat standing out on his forehead.

He took the beer and turned to me. "Oh, look who it is! Ol' Cole-nelius!"

I rolled my eyes. "God, I just love that nickname."

He chuckled, "I know."

"Looks like you're making some progress here," I said, eyeing the array of meats sizzling on the grill.

He closed the lid. "Please…of course I am. I have always been the grill master of this family."

"Don't make me test that," I said, clinking bottles with him.

"Any time you wanna throw down, city boy."

We drank and sighed gratefully, a swath of BBQ smoke wafting across our faces. We took a step back from the heat. Dave picked up a mason jar from the ground that I had failed to see. He offered it to me.

"Eh? Want some of this?"

"Holy shit," I exclaimed, eyes going wide, "is that Dad's moonshine?"

Dave laughed. "Sure is. Only a couple jars left. I found it in Ma's basement a couple months ago while I was helping her move some stuff around."

"And you've been going through it ever since."

"Of course," he said, winking. "So you want some? It's apple pie-flavored."

"Absolutely," I said, taking the jar. I sniffed the liquid and was immediately overwhelmed with the aroma of baked apples and cinnamon. I took a hesitant sip and felt fire run down my throat. I coughed violently, wincing, laughing.

"Wow, that's some hot stuff!"

Dave went to take the jar back, but I cradled it against my chest. "Ah, ah, ah, ya greedy bastard. Spread the love, will you? You been hogging this gold all to yourself."

Dave shrugged. "I just don't want you falling on your butt. It's been a while, don't know how your tolerance is these days."

I narrowed my eyes at him. "I'll drink you under the table any day of the week."

Dave snorted. "Big talk, big talk."

"Well, I'm your big brother, so it's my right."

"Well, your head is definitely bigger—" Dave started, a sly smile plastered on his face.

"Yeah, and it's stuffed with all the brains you were supposed to get!" I laughed, wiggling my head at him. Dave threw his head back and cackled with me. After we settled down, I passed him back the mason jar.

It was way too strong for my tastes.

"Tammy's here," I said, watching Dave take a sip from the jar.

He went back to the grill and opened it. "Oh, yeah? Good. Heard Joe's working and can't make it tonight."

I watched smoke engulf my brother. "Yeah. That's what Ma said."

Dave prodded the ribs with his spatula. "Did she say anything about him?"

"What do you mean?"

Dave shrugged. "I don't know much about it, but apparently the Morrisons are really pressing to get his garage."

I blinked. "The Morrisons?"

Dave closed the lid again. "Yeah, you remember them, don't you? Derek, Mark, and Leo? Those three jerkoff brothers we grew up with?"

Slowly, I nodded. "Oh, yeah. Mean bastards if I recall."

Dave sighed. "Yeah, and their daddy is the sheriff now. I think they're into some dirty business and they've been pressuring Joe."

"What do you mean 'dirty?'"

Dave turned and looked at me. "They were always a shady family. This is just speculation, but I think the brothers are dealing hard drugs to the locals. I don't have any proof, but things have changed around here, Cole."

"Shit," I muttered, taking a swill of beer. "What do they want Joe's place for?"

"I don't know. Probably to cook in."

"Cook?"

"Meth, Cole, meth," Dave said, shaking his head. "When you spend some time in town you'll see what I'm talking about. People just seem to be…" He twirled his finger. "I don't know…hollow."

"But their father is the sheriff!" I said.

Dave snorted. "Yeah, and what better protection than to have your father keep the law off your operation?"

"I didn't know things were so bad here," I said quietly.

Dave shook his head. "Aw, they're not. I make it sound worse than it is. Joe's a stubborn kid, he isn't budging. And he sure isn't intimidated by them. The Morrisons are just a stain on an otherwise great country town." Dave looked at the moonshine in his hand. "Ah, man, look at me running my mouth." He grinned sheepishly. "Don't listen to me; I don't know what I'm talking about."

I grunted, "OK, man, whatever you say."

Dave paused. "Just…if you happen to see any of the Morrison brothers…maybe keep your distance."

"Why's that?"

Dave's smile was grim. "They're just not good people."

Before I could say anything else, the back door opened and Ma came out holding a bowl of steaming mashed potatoes. Tammy followed, carrying a tray of beer.

"Have you ruined the meat yet?" Tammy asked, placing the tray down on the picnic table. "'Cause I'm starving."

"Everyone's a critic," Dave muttered under his breath.

"Everything else is finished," Ma said, wiping her hands on her apron after she set down the bowl. "Just have to grab the green beans."

"Those wouldn't happen to be your famous garlic butter beans, would they?" I asked, stomach growling at the thought.

"They sure are!" Ma chirped, heading back inside to retrieve them.

"God, I missed the food down here," I said. Dave chuckled and began to pull the ribs from the grill and place them on a platter.

I walked to the picnic table and took a seat next to Tammy. I drained the rest of my beer as she handed me another.

"You trying to get me drunk?" I teased, popping the top.

"Doesn't take much if memory serves," she grinned, taking one for herself.

"Why do you two think I'm such a lightweight?" I asked, shooting Dave a look.

Dave carefully walked the platter of smoking meat over to the table and set it down. "Don't you remember that one time we stole a bottle of Dad's moonshine? It was Halloween and you were dressed as—"

"—as Neo from *The Matrix*," I groaned, the memory surfacing.

Tammy pinched my cheek. "You were such a dork."

I pulled away, laughing. "Oh, please! Didn't you go as Indiana Jones!?"

Tammy winked. "Sure did. Dad was not happy about that, but Ma convinced him it was OK for a *girl* to be Indy."

"Anyway," Dave continued, helping himself to another beer, "that night we snuck into the basement and stole a jar of Dad's moonshine. We came out here when we thought Ma and Dad were asleep and drank it. Cole, I remember you were borderline black-out drunk after three sips."

I threw my hands up. "I was fifteen!"

Dave laughed. "And I was thirteen, but I fared better than you did!"

"Where was Joe during all that?" Tammy asked as

Ma came back outside carrying a dish of steaming greens.

"I made him stay in his room," I chuckled. "He was only nine."

"Ooooh, I bet he was furious," Dave snorted.

"Hell, yeah he was," I said. "He threatened to tell Ma and Dad."

"But he never did," Tammy said fondly.

Ma took her place at Dave's side, attuning herself to the conversation. "No, he didn't. Your father got up to take a leak and looked out the bathroom window to see two giggling boys and one very sick girl."

"Oh, yeah, I think I threw up," Tammy chuckled.

"I ain't never seen your father so angry in all my days," Ma laughed, shaking her head. "Boy, I thought the fires of hell were upon us when he started hollering."

I picked up my beer bottle and clinked it with Dave's. "Worth it."

Dave winked. "For sure."

"Well!" Ma said, cutting us short. "Are we going to just sit around yammering all night, or do you kids want to dig in?"

Tammy picked up her fork. "I say we dig, boys."

"It really does look good," I told Dave, "despite the rumors."

"What rumors!?"

"Just shut up and eat," I chuckled, piling his plate with food.

As the sun finally set, the four of us filled our bellies with the feast before us. As we ate, we fell into fond memories, swapping more stories about our youth. The beer flowed, the food seemed endless, and laughter echoed across the calm grassland.

Yes…things were going to be OK.

Chapter 2

I said my goodbyes to everyone, the night growing late. I hugged Dave in the driveway, assuring him his ribs were truly fantastic, and then embraced Tammy. She asked if I was OK to drive and I rolled my eyes. I moved on to Ma and she squeezed me tight.

"I'm so glad you're back with us," she whispered into my shoulder.

I kissed her on the head. "Me too, Ma. I'll see you soon."

She pulled away, smiling. "You better."

I walked down the driveway to my truck, waving over my shoulder, and climbed in. I started the engine and backed down into the dusty, dirty road. As was tradition when leaving Ma's house, I honked three times and threw a hand out the window. In the high beams, I saw my family return the gesture.

I hit the gas and peeled down the road, throwing gravel in my wake. As the dark land expanded before me, I rolled the windows down and sighed happily. The air smelled sweet, an earthy, wonderful thing, and I let the wind blow through the truck. I turned on the radio and found a country station. I turned it up. Smiling, I placed an arm out the window and just drove.

In that moment, everything felt right.

I was headed back to the small apartment I was renting in town. It was a tiny thing but enough to ground me until I decided what the hell I wanted to do with myself. I had plenty in savings, so money wasn't really a concern right now. Right now I just needed to find myself again. Get centered. Feel the dirt beneath my boots, as Dad would say.

I had made it three of the six miles back into town when I heard my cell ring. I dug it from my pocket and answered.

"Hello?"

"Look who's come crawling back home!"

I chuckled. "Hey, Joe."

"Hey, yourself, man! How the shit how have you been? You still at Ma's?"

I adjusted my grip on the steering wheel. "No, just left actually. I'm heading back into town."

"Oh, perfect!" he exclaimed excitedly. "I just got out of the shop. Was wondering if you had time for a beer with your little brother before turning in for the night."

I checked the clock on the dash. "For sure, Joe. I'm not really tired anyway. Where do you want to meet?"

"Where are you staying?"

"I got a small place above the bookstore on Main Street. You know it?"

Joe grunted. "Do I know it…hell, yeah, I know it, I know every nook and cranny this shitty little town has to offer. Over the bookstore, huh? OK, there's a dive just across the street from where you're posted up called The Tin Can."

"Sure, I've seen it."

"I'll be there in twenty minutes," Joe continued. "Just driving in from my garage."

"Sounds good."

"See you soon, Cole."

I hung up, the night air whipping through the car. I turned up the radio station again and tapped my hand against the wheel. It would be good to see Joe. Real good.

As the town lights came into view, a beacon that stood out in the flat grassland, I felt a tinge of guilt. Why hadn't I come back to visit during my time in New York? Five years is a long time to go without visiting family. Too long. I sighed, memories twisting into one another. I had just been so enraptured with Maria and so saddened by Dad's death a year earlier that I had kind of wanted to just forget about this place for a while. It held too much sadness. Too much weight. I had needed to get out, a sense of claustrophobia growing thicker with each passing day.

And so I had, much to the dismay of my remaining family. But they had understood. That's just the kind of people they were. Joe had been the most outspoken, of course, but even he had come around when the day came. I remembered the hug he had given me, an almost desperate embrace. I thought about that a lot during my five-year absence. I had considered coming back, but each time I had resisted. Why had I been so terrified of this place? It was beautiful. Well...Maria had been a big part of it, too. I knew she didn't ever want to return to the town where we had grown up. She hadn't been outspoken about it, but I could see it in her eyes every time I approached the subject. And so I had stayed away.

Until the night she died.

No, I thought turning onto Main Street, *until the night she was murdered.*

I blinked and pushed the thoughts away. I turned my attention onto the humble town and slowed at a red light. Main Street was a long stretch of local businesses, a cheerful, well-kept conglomeration of local charm. There was the ice cream shop, the diner, the bookstore, a handful of hardware destinations, a smattering of humble restaurants, and finally the church at the end of the street. Its steeple rose into the night air like a trumpet to God. No doubt Ma would insist I join her for Sunday service. And I would go. I wasn't an especially religious man, but down here God was just part of your routine. I remembered Dad once saying, "If a man don't got God in his life, then what the hell use is he?" I'm not quite sure what that meant exactly, but it was something he repeated quite often.

I guided my truck toward the bookstore, the sidewalk lit by glowing lampposts. They lined the length of Main Street like soldiers protecting us from the dangers of darkness. In a way, I guess they were.

I parked my truck around back and got out. I didn't need to go upstairs to my room for anything, so I wandered out front. There were a few people still about, a handful of couples and loners, just strolling the length of the town. I watched a pair of old-timers walk hand in hand, the man's white beard matching his wife's white hair. They were across the street and headed the opposite direction, but I could still hear them laughing. The older man reached down and gave the woman a quick pinch on her behind, and she let out a delighted laugh and smacked him playfully on the arm.

I turned my eyes away from them and found The Tin Can almost directly across from where I stood. I hadn't been inside, but it matched Joe's description. A dive.

What the hell, I thought, *I think I've had my share of snooty city bars. Time to get back to my roots.*

As I was about to cross the street, I heard someone call out to me. I turned around and saw a young man of about twenty emerge from the shadows. I didn't like him on sight. His hair was thin and wispy, almost colorless. His skin was pale and gaunt, his clothes hanging loosely around a thin frame. His eyes were sunken and dark, and he dry-washed his hands as he approached.

"H-hey brother," he croaked. For a horrifying second, I thought it was Joe, but then I shook the nightmarish notion away. Of course it wasn't Joe; he didn't look anything like this.

"D-do you have a buck I could borrow?" he asked, getting closer.

I stepped away. "No man, sorry. I don't carry cash."

The man stopped and looked at his feet. He began to scratch his neck, his voice weak. "Shit…shit…O-OK…God bless, then…"

"Yeah, you too," I said and hurried away from him. As I crossed the street I threw a look over my shoulder and caught him staring at me, immobile. I quickly looked away and approached the dive bar. Gratefully, I pushed my way inside.

I was greeted by a mostly empty bar, dim lights, an enthusiastic jukebox, and the smell of grease. I paused in the entryway. Yeah…this looked like home, all right. I smiled a little and then went to the bar. I found a stool at the end and slid onto it. I scanned the crowd and counted maybe fifteen people. They all looked local. Dark tans, rough hands, and hard faces. A couple patrons eyeballed me and I turned away. Whatever. I was one of them; I just took a break for a while. I looked down the bar and saw a couple men idly flirting with the women, all sipping whiskey and dancing drunkenly to the jukebox. Yes, sir. These were real country folk. This was their paradise. Friday night, a paycheck in their pocket, and Coors on tap. The ghosts of America.

The bartender wandered over, a heavy fellow with a long black beard.

"Howdy," he greeted, his Southern accent thick. "What'll it be?"

"I'll take a Pabst," I said, digging out my wallet, "and pour one for yourself while you're at it."

"Much obliged," he said, taking the ten from my hand. He handed me back three singles and I almost died laughing. New York this was not.

The bartender retrieved my beer and set it down in front of me. I nodded to him and took a sip. I sighed, feeling completely content. Behind me, Johnny Cash sung about the ring of fire, my boots stuck to the floor, and everyone around me looked like we had entered heaven.

I had drained half my beer when I felt a hand fall across my shoulder. I turned around, expecting Joe, but found myself staring into three ragged male faces I didn't recognize. They were around my age, cheeks flush from drinking, and breath reeking as if to tattle on my suspicion.

"Hol-ee shee-it!" the biggest of the three brayed, shaking his head, a smile cracking his face. He was wearing a cutoff John Deere T-shirt and stained jeans. His arms were about as big as my legs.

"Cole!?" he asked, swaying a little. "Cole Barker, is that YOU!?"

I must have looked as confused and uncomfortable as I felt, because the three men burst out laughing.

"Oh, my gawd, you don't remember us, do you!?" the man on the left asked. He looked slightly younger, a blond ponytail tied behind his head.

"Uh, I'm afraid not," I said.

The third, probably the youngest, snorted, a Confederate bandana tied across his forehead. "Oh, man Derek, little Cole has completely forgotten about his best friends!"

The first man slapped me on the shoulder, still laughing. "It's us! The Morrison brothers! How the hell could you forget about us!?"

Ah shit, I thought.

The first man placed his hand on his chest. "Don't you remember your ol' pal Derek?" He pointed to the man with the ponytail. "And Mark?" His finger went to the guy in the bandana. "And our little brother Leo? Christ, Cole, did the city wash away your memory?"

I remembered now. And I remembered what Dave had told me about them.

"Sure, I know who you are—" I started, but Mark cut me off, his ponytail swaying.

"Those fancy city lights must have given him amnesia or something."

Leo guffawed loudly. "Or maybe he's just too torn-up over his dead girlfriend!"

I felt my fists clench at the sudden mention of Maria. Derek turned on his brother and slapped him hard across the mouth.

"What kinda manners are those, you dumb fuck!?"

he yelled. "Honestly, Pa raised you better than that!" He shook his head as Leo rubbed his cheek and looked at the floor sheepishly.

Derek threw his arm over my shoulder and leaned in close, his voice soft. "Ignore my idiot brother, Cole. He's just had one too many tonight and doesn't know how to keep his trap shut."

"Whatever," I said, wishing he'd take his arm off me.

Derek shook his head. "Don't take offense to his loud mouth." He leaned in closer. "I am sorry to hear about your girlfriend, though. Terrible thing, that. You have my condolences. Truly."

"Yeah, thanks," I said, pulling away. How the hell did they know about Maria?

Derek took his arm away and slapped the bar. "Jimmy! Get us a round of shine. The good shit you keep under the counter. I need to properly welcome my good friend Cole back into town."

"It's not necessary," I insisted.

"Bullshit!" Derek exclaimed loudly. "It most certainly IS necessary! It's not every day I get to drink with a Barker!"

"Yeah, speaking of which, Joe should be here soon and I'd really like to catch up with him," I said hesitantly as four shot glasses were placed before us.

Derek smiled slowly. "Good ol' Joe. He's a good dude, that one. Stubborn as a mule, but he's got grit."

"Yeah…he sure does," I said, begging this conversation to be over.

Derek leaned into me, his voice dropping. "And what about you, Cole? You got grit?"

I stared blankly at him, Mark, and Leo leering over their brother's shoulder.

After a second, Derek burst into laughter and pounded me on the back, almost severing my spine. "Aw, I'm just messing with you, man! Jeez-us! Lighten up, cowboy! FUCK!" He wiped his eyes, still giggling, and handed me my shot.

"You better drink it all down," Mark said, taking his. "This here is ten bucks a pour!"

"Let's see if this boy's tongue has gone soft!" Leo sniggered, reaching over his brother to retrieve his. "Or if he's forgotten what it's like to have dirt in your drink."

Derek smiled, holding up his shot. "Here's to the Barker brothers. And more specifically, to our good bud Cole."

As one, we all drained our shots. I had to fight against a hurricane of fire to keep it down, but I managed without making a fool of myself. The Morrisons laughed and applauded my capabilities, clapping and roaring with laughter.

"What the hell is this?"

I turned, wiping my mouth, and saw my brother Joe standing behind the four of us. His face was twisted in disgust as our eyes met. I coughed and tried to speak, but Leo cut me off.

"Well, well, if it isn't the runt of the Barker family!"

Joe crossed his arms. "Look who's talking, idiot."

Leo's brow furrowed, but Derek raised his hands, chuckling. "Easy there, killer. We were just welcoming your brother back to town. We missed this kid!"

Joe shook his head. "Sure you did."

"You're always so serious," Derek mused.

"You should try it sometime," Joe said. "Maybe then people wouldn't think your family is such a joke."

Angry, Mark stepped to Joe, but Derek stopped him. "OK, OK, that's enough. Calm down, Mark, he's just cranky. Ain't you, Joe?"

"Sure."

Derek stepped away from the bar, motioning for his brothers to follow. "Come on now, fellas, let's let the man converse with his long-lost family. I'm sure they have plenty to talk about." He winked at Joe.

Joe didn't move, his eyes boring into the three of them. "Yeah, get the hell out of here. Oh, and Derek? Tell your men to piss off and stop driving by my garage. It's irritating and pathetic. You aren't scaring anyone."

Derek shrugged, backing away toward the door. "I don't know what you're talking about. Maybe you're getting paranoid."

"Maybe I'm getting pissed," Joe growled. "I'm not selling the garage."

"Not yet you're not," Mark snickered. "Give it time, Joe."

Joe raised his middle finger at the Morrisons as they exited the bar, leaving Joe and me in peace. When they were gone, Joe sighed, his whole body deflating. He looked apologetically at me and then slid onto the stool at my side.

"Hey there, buddy," I said. "How you doing? You look good."

Joe ran a callused hand over his face and snorted. "I look like shit."

Fragile was never a word I'd use to describe Joe, and despite some weight loss, he still looked sturdy. He had cut his hair down to a fine stubble along his scalp that matched his unshaven face and I noticed he no longer wore his earring. I was glad about that last part. I had never been a fan. Still, though, he looked tired. Shadows hung beneath his dark eyes and his clothes were grease-stained and unkempt.

"What the hell were you doing with those assholes anyway?" Joe asked as he ordered a beer from the bartender.

"They kinda sprang on me," I said, shrugging.

Joe folded his arms across the bar. "Yeah, they do that. Fucking leeches."

I smiled. "Hey, Joe?"

He cocked his head toward me. "Yeah?"

"It's good to see you, man."

Finally he smiled and sat up, clapping me on the back. "Hell, you too, Cole." He chuckled. "I'm sorry, I get so wound up when I see those Morrison morons." He twirled a finger in a circular motion around his temple. "They really get inside my head, you know?"

"What were you saying about them hanging around your garage?"

Joe rolled his eyes. "Well, they've been trying to buy my place for a while now—"

"—yeah, Dave told me," I said.

Joe nodded. "Yeah, they won't take no for answer. They keep prodding and poking, fucking with me a little, sending people by, watching me, that kind of thing."

"That's a little concerning," I said quietly.

Joe waved a hand at me. "Ah, it's fucking hog shit. They don't scare me."

I leaned in close. "Is it true, though? Are they peddling drugs in town now?"

The bartender arrived with Joe's beer and he waited until he was gone again before answering in a low voice. "Yeah, it's true. Those bastards are ruining this town one junkie at a time. They've got a network that seems to grow bigger by the day. I see more and more people on the streets with this hollow, hungry look on their face. It's sad. Terrible. And I swear to God, Cole, I will not let them use my garage to spread that poison. I will die first."

"Why doesn't anyone do anything?" I asked. "The law? Surely they've noticed."

"Their Pa is the sheriff," Joe said, taking a sip of beer. "And he's got all the surrounding counties on the payroll."

"Oh, yeah, Dave mentioned that, too."

"Dave's got a big mouth," Joe muttered.

I lowered my voice again. "So, what, the Morrisons can just distribute this crap and remain completely ignored by the authorities?"

"Sick, isn't it?" Joe mumbled, burying his face in his beer.

I sat back on my stool, shaking my head.

Sighing, Joe cleared his throat. "But enough about all those miserable bastards. How the shit are you doing, man?"

I allowed myself a smile. "I'm doing well. Really. It's good being back here in Mill Valley. I didn't realize how much I missed it."

Joe grinned. "It gets in your blood."

"Amen."

"What'd y'all do at Ma's tonight?"

I laughed. "Dave made us ribs! Before you say anything, I thought they were pretty good!"

Joe shrugged. "Don't you ever tell him this, but I always thought they were pretty tasty. Don't know why Tammy and Ma are always giving him a hard time over it."

"'Cause God forbid a man cooks better than them," I whispered, an evil slant to my lips.

Joe snorted into his beer. "Aw, shit, Cole, don't let Tammy hear you say that. Especially knowing the way she is about that kinda crap."

"She's a proud woman," I said, smiling.

"Goddamn right she is," Joe said. "Wouldn't have her any other way."

"I feel sorry for the man that marries her," I said, snickering. "He's going to have to get used to taking orders."

"Tammy's a smart girl," Joe defended, "and whatever bum is lucky enough to wed her, well, he better listen to what she has to say."

"Absolutely!" I said loudly. "And if not, then we're going to have a little talk with the bastard."

"Oh, I'll talk to him all right," Joe snarled. He raised his beer. "Hey, here's to Tammy."

"To Tammy!"

Our glasses clinked and we drank deeply.

"So what are you doing to fill your time these days?" Joe asked after a moment.

I watched condensation drip from my glass to the surface of the bar counter. "Nothing really. Least not yet. I've only been back a couple days. I don't really know what to do with myself right now. I'll figure it out; I'm in no rush."

Joe eyed me for a second before asking, "You wanna come work with me at the garage?"

Surprised, I looked at him. "You serious?"

"Hell, why not?"

I pondered it for a moment before replying. "I don't really know how to fix cars, Joe. I don't think I'd be much help."

"Christ, I wouldn't let you touch the cars!" Joe laughed. "But there's some other projects around the shop that I keep meaning to get done. I just never have the time."

"Like what?"

Joe shrugged. "Place needs a new paint job for starters."

I turned the idea over in my head.

"It's nothing grand," Joe admitted, "but it's something. Plus we'd get to hang out."

I balked a laugh. "You just want to be my boss!"

Joe shook his head vigorously. "Hell no, I don't. I just need a hand and I'll pay you for it. The wages won't buy you a Lambo, but it'll put food in your belly."

I stuck my hand out. "Shit, why not?"

Joe's face lit up and he pumped my outstretched hand. "That's awesome, Cole. Thanks. Now, let's get some more beers, yeah?"

I laughed and ordered us another round.

The fresh beers came and we dove into them. Joe seemed to relax more and more as the night went on, our conversation remaining light. After our fifth drink, Joe settled down and got a serious look in his eyes.

He licked his lips and stared at the half-empty glass in front of him. "Hey, uh…Cole. I been meaning to say something about what happened to your girl."

The mood quieted and I exhaled slowly. "You don't have to say anything, man."

Joe jabbed a finger down on the bar. "No, I do. I do. You're my brother and I care very much about you. What happened…shit, I didn't hear much, but I heard enough." He looked up at me, his face soft. "Goddamn it, Cole, I'm real sorry. I mean that."

"Thanks, Joe," I said quietly. "I appreciate you saying that."

"Course, of course," he mumbled, looking uncomfortable.

"What about you?" I asked, changing the subject. "You seeing anyone?"

Joe waved the question away. "Nothing serious. Little bit of this and that. I'm not really the settlin' down type."

"You just have to find the right woman to put a leash on you," I chuckled.

Joe snorted. "You mean noose?"

"I mean," I said leaning forward, "that you should at least be open to the prospect. I know we're both looking for different things, but Joe I'm telling you, a man needs a woman in his life." I tapped my head. "Otherwise we start getting stupid."

Joe grinned sheepishly. "Shit, I know what you mean. I just get kind of skittish when they start talking about 'relationships.' I feel like suddenly there's all these walls closing in on me."

"Yeah, they're called boundaries and we all need them," I said, grinning.

"A boundary is still a type of wall," Joe snorted. "I'm not stupid. They wanna trap you so you can't get away."

"Maybe they just want to love you and shelter you from all the bad shit outside the walls," I said quietly.

"I don't know if I believe in something like that. Love, I mean."

"What about Dad and Ma?" I asked. "That was as real as it got."

Joe smiled sadly. "I suppose you're right."

I poked a finger at his chest. "So just…be open to the idea, OK? I want to see you with someone. I think it'd do you a lot of good."

"You think so?"

"I wouldn't lie to you."

Joe sighed and I saw something wash over him. A weariness. A fatigue that he had been secretly carrying with him this whole time. It broke my heart.

"I just got this goddamn temper," Joe said softly. "Gets me into all kinds of trouble. Anytime I start getting close to someone I feel my ears start to burn."

"Well, that's just something you gotta work on, man," I said. "At least you're aware of it. That's something."

"I don't know why I get so angry," he said, staring at the floor. "It just…bubbles up in me like a hot spring and I can't seem to control it. There were times I swear I thought I was going to kill the woman I was with."

"Yeah…they do that too, sometimes," I said grimly.

Joe sighed. "Aw hell, enough of this gooshy talk." He suddenly smiled and the life returned to his face. "Sheesh, get a couple beers in me and I turn into a contestant on the Dr. Phil show."

I laughed. "You're going to be OK, Joe."

Joe pounded his chest, slightly drunk. "Course I am! I'm Joe Barker, the best mechanic in Mill Valley!"

"Cheers to that," I said, raising my glass. We polished off the rest of our beer and set them back down, feeling the night begin to end.

After a couple moments of silence, our eyes met and we both nodded.

"Ready to get out of here?" I asked.

"I guess."

I cashed us out, despite Joe's protest to pay, and together we walked out onto the street. The night sky was vast and beautiful. The open air felt wonderful in contrast to the thick atmosphere of the bar, and I found myself sighing and closing my eyes.

"Pretty, isn't it?" I heard Joe say at my side. I also heard the familiar sound of him smacking a Marlboro out of a weathered pack.

"It's the best."

I took a deep breath and turned to Joe. "Well, it's been real, man."

Joe snorted. "It's been real…get the hell in here and give your brother a hug!" He suddenly embraced me and I smiled, hugging him back.

"It was good to see you, kid," I said, pulling away.

He nodded, grinning. "You too, Cole."

"I'll see you tomorrow? At the shop?" I asked.

"You want to start tomorrow? Hell, that's fine by me. Yeah, come on by whenever. I'll be there. I'll text you the address in the morning. Sound good?"

"Sounds great."

We looked at one another for a second longer. Joe lit his cigarette.

"Later, Joe."

"See you tomorrow, bro."

And with that, we parted ways.

Chapter 3

I rolled out of bed the following morning feeling good. Hungry, but good. The alcoholic endeavors of the previous night swashed about in my stomach, calling for food. I decided it would be wise to oblige. I showered and dressed, growing more accustomed to my new lodgings. The small apartment was humble and simple, but it suited me.

I went to the window and looked out onto Main Street. It was early still, but people were already milling about and getting on with their day. The sun was bright and I could tell it was going to be a scorcher.

I left my apartment, locking it behind me, and descended the stairs to the back parking lot. The bookstore below me was still closed and would be for a while.

I checked my phone and saw that Joe had texted me while I was in the shower. It was the address to his garage. I checked my watch and decided to go grab breakfast at the diner before heading over. I left my car and shoved my hands in my pockets, pushing out into the brilliant sunshine.

It had to be at least eighty degrees already and I grinned. In a masochistic sort of way, I had missed the sweltering Southern heat.

Whistling, I walked out onto Main Street and casually made my way down the sidewalk toward the diner. A couple pickup trucks rolled lazily down the street, exhaust filling the morning air. Shopkeepers were unlocking their stores or standing outside smoking, awaiting the first wave of customers for the day. A crow cawed overhead and I craned my neck and followed its soaring arc all the way down to the end of the street.

Without watching where I was going, I ended up bumping into someone. I jumped back, readying an apology. Instead, I stared at the woman I had just collided with, disgust rolling through me like an afternoon storm.

She was bone-thin and smelled atrocious. Her hair hung in clumps over her face and her teeth were black with rot. She looked at me with empty eyes and held up a hand that was far too wrinkled for her age.

"Got a couple bucks?" she croaked, pulling at the shoulder of her dirty shirt.

I shook my head and hurried past, covering my nose. I felt bad, but I couldn't help it. It was either that or puke. I chanced a look back over my shoulder and saw her crying, face in her hands. I stopped, hating myself.

I reached into my pocket and retrieved my wallet. I pulled out a five and made my way back to her.

"Here," I offered.

She looked up at me, surprised, her eyes brimming with tears. When she saw the money she practically snatched it out of my hand.

"Oh, thank you! Thank you!" She nearly wept.

"Look," I started, knowing it was pointless, "there are people who can help you. It doesn't have to be like this."

She smiled sadly and tucked the money into her pants. "Yes, it does." And then she left, leaving me feeling hollow.

Sighing, I turned and continued down the street.

When I reached the diner, I found it nearly full. Waitresses in blue dresses scurried about the booths filling coffee mugs, jotting down orders, and carting food to tables. A charming air of conversation floated above the whole scene and I stood at the entrance for a moment, absorbing the whole thing.

"Just you, mister?"

I turned to see a cute girl in her early twenties. Her eyebrows were raised and I hurriedly nodded.

"Uh, yes, just me."

"You mind sitting at the bar?" she asked, distracted.

"Not at all."

Before either of us moved, I heard my name shouted from across the diner. I turned to see who it was and my eyes found Dave, grinning and waving me over from the corner booth.

"You know him?" the waitress asked.

"Yeah, that's my brother," I said, waving back to Dave. "Thank you, miss, I got it from here I think."

"Suit yourself."

I walked over to Dave, passing booths filled with hard-looking men and women. They didn't look hostile but weathered. People of the earth. Overalls, jeans, work boots, Chevy hats, and cigarettes tucked behind a multitude of ears. Dirty fingernails and nicotine-stained teeth. Grease smudges and goatees. The gears of America fueling up before heading out.

I stood over Dave's booth, staring down in mild surprise. Papers scattered the table top along with pens, a calculator, and an array of charts. I cocked an eyebrow at my younger brother.

"What's all this?"

Dave spread his hands. "This is my money. I'm just trying to figure out where it all is."

I sat down across from him. "I don't follow."

Dave shrugged sheepishly. "I own this place."

My eyes widened. "What!? Since when?"

"Two years now. The original owners were putting it up for sale and I decided it was time for something different."

"Why didn't you say anything last night?" I asked, shaking my head, amazed.

Dave shrugged again. "It's just a diner, Cole."

I smiled broadly. "Are you kidding me? This is amazing, man! Look at all these people! And look at you, sitting in the corner like some kind of mafia boss! I love it!"

Dave laughed and waved over a waitress. "Oh, relax, we're just serving eggs and hamburgers."

I leaned across the table. "No horse heads on the menu?"

"I'm afraid they weren't very popular."

The waitress arrived holding a pot of coffee and a mug. She placed it in front of me and filled it to the brim, smiling. Her blonde hair fell in curls across her young face and her blue eyes radiated with youthful energy.

"You want sugar with that, sugar?" she asked sweetly.

"No ma'am," I said. "I take my coffee like I take my women."

She raised an eyebrow. "Oh?"

"Strong and smoking hot," I teased, throwing her a wink.

The waitress giggled and looked at Dave. "Is this your brother? The one who moved back?"

Dave, his face beet-red, nodded. "I'm afraid so."

She placed a hand on my arm. "Well, I only make strong, hot coffee so you're in good hands, sugar."

"You shouldn't flirt with me, I'll start getting ideas," I laughed.

She put her hands on her hips. "Oh, honey, if I'm flirting with you, you'll know."

Dave nodded.

"Now, my name's Nancy," she continued, switching modes. "What can I get for you this morning?"

"I'll take three eggs, scrambled, and a mountain of bacon," I said. "Oh, and do you serve biscuits and gravy?"

"Sweetie, we got whatever you want," Nancy said, jotting down my order on her pad.

"I'll take some of those, please," I said.

"I'll have that right out," she said, "and if you need more coffee, just holler."

As she walked away, I stared at Dave. "Well, isn't she a tall glass of water?"

Dave chuckled. "It's the real reason I bought this place."

"Seriously?"

Dave rolled his eyes. "Of course not, you pig. Now don't embarrass me anymore, please."

I reached across the table and pinched his cheek. "Awwww, I'm sorry little Davey! Did I make you blush?"

He smacked my hand away, appalled. "Hey, cut it out! Jeez, man!"

I settled back into the booth, laughing. "Don't worry, I'll behave myself. In all seriousness, though, I'm impressed. This is a really cool thing you got going on here."

Dave rubbed his cheek and mumbled, "Thanks."

"I saw Joe last night!" I announced, taking a hesitant sip of coffee.

"Oh, no kidding, where?" Dave asked, suddenly interested again.

I jammed a thumb over my shoulder. "At The Tin Can. He called me right after I left Ma's last night. He looked good! Still as…emotional as ever, but he seems to be doing OK."

Dave nodded. "He's a hard worker. He spends so much time at that garage, though, I wish he'd find another hobby besides cars. I mean, I know it's his livelihood, but he needs a break every once in a while. I don't get to see him as much as I would like."

I set my coffee down. "He offered me a job."

"Really?"

I nodded. "Yeah, helping him out and whatnot. Fixing the place up."

"Did you take it?"

"Sure did. I'm heading over there this morning."

"To work on…cars?" Dave asked, incredulous.

"No, no, just painting the place, doing odd jobs, all the things he doesn't have time to."

Dave smiled slowly. "That's fantastic, Cole. It'll do him good to be around you."

"What's that supposed to mean?"

"I just think it'll be good if you're around," Dave said, twirling a pen in his hand. "His shop is just outside of town on a small plot of land. It's…cute."

"Cute?"

"It's fitting."

"Well," I said, stretching my arms across the back of

the booth, "I guess I'll find out. Speaking of people I saw last night, I also ran into the Morrison brothers."

Dave's smile dropped. "Oh?"

I nodded. "They seem like a burly bunch these days. Can't say I've grown any fonder of them."

"They hassle you?"

"Ah, not really. Joe says they've been sending their guys over to his garage. Apparently they're really pressuring him to sell."

"Told you."

"It left a bad taste in my mouth," I said.

"And it should. They're bad dudes. They're not the simple bullies they used to be. This business they have going on in this town…it's for real."

"The drugs?"

Dave nodded. "I'm worried about what will happen if Joe doesn't cave."

"You think they'll get hostile?"

"I honestly have no idea what to think. So much of their foul business happens away from the public eye that I don't know how to gauge their capabilities. I guess that's why I'm glad you're going to be hanging around with Joe. So you can keep an eye on him."

"I'll keep two," I said quietly as my breakfast arrived.

The waitress, Nancy, dropped a pair of plates in front of me. The food smelled amazing and my mouth began to immediately water.

"Make sure you eat all of it now," Nancy instructed.

I smiled up at her. "Yes, ma'am, that won't be a problem."

"You enjoy now."

I dug in with a vengeance and Dave went back to his paperwork. The food was absolutely delicious and I cleaned my plates with enthusiasm. Finished, I sat back and wiped my mouth with a napkin, sighing happily and patting my stomach.

Dave looked up at me. "Should I drive you to the hospital now or later?"

I sipped my coffee. "That's no way to talk about your own food."

"I'm more concerned with the urgency you threw it at your face."

Nancy returned, beaming, and refilled my coffee. She took the plates away and asked if I would like anything else. I assured her that wasn't necessary. I saw Dave exhale with relief.

"You sure you don't want a slice of pie?" Dave goaded. "I'm pretty sure I can restart your heart if you want a piece."

I shook my head, laughing. "I think I'll pass. Next time though, for sure."

Suddenly, a loud voice robbed my attention and I turned to look at the diner's entrance. A massive man dressed in a sheriff's uniform was talking loudly to one of the men in the booths. They were laughing uproariously.

"Oh, wonderful, the protector of Mill Valley has graced my establishment," Dave said quietly.

"Who is that?" I asked, already knowing the answer.

"That's dear ol' Papa Morrison."

The big man looked up, removing his aviator sunglasses, and spotted Dave and myself. He grinned, a wide, toothy smile, wrinkles expanding across his clean-shaven face. He strode over, his stomach bouncing over his belt, and slapped me on the back cheerfully.

"Well, howdy, boys! How are you doing this fine morning?" he asked, his voice offensively loud.

"Hey, sheriff," Dave muttered, staring at the table.

"Hey, yourself David!" the man laughed. He looked down at me, his brown eyes wide and ugly. "And look who's here! It's Cole, the long-lost lamb! You remember me, don't you? I'm Derek, Mark, and Leo's father! I haven't seen you in ages, boy! Heard you scuttled off with some tail to the city a couple years ago. But by God, as soon as I saw your face I remembered you in an instant! You and Dave here used to play with my boys if memory serves!"

"I wouldn't call it playing...but yes, we knew your children," I said, sizing the man up.

"You visiting or something?" the sheriff asked. "Or did you get sick of the city life?" He leaned in, his enormous white teeth alarmingly close to my ear now. "Or maybe that little biddy you were hunting left you for another fella?"

I saw Dave's hands ball into fists, but I spoke before

he could. "Something like that. I actually ran into your boys last night at The Tin Can. Seems they haven't changed much."

The sheriff stood back up and swatted his chest. "Hell no, they haven't! They are as true as blue is blue! They were raised on grits and whiskey and by God they certainly show it, don't they?"

I had no idea what he was talking about, so I just shrugged.

"Yessir," he continued, "them boys are the pride of my heart. Hard workers, loyal children, and determined as hell to get what they want!" He put a hand to his mouth like he was passing me an exclusive secret. "Maybe you could learn a thing or two from them. Maybe that way you wouldn't be sitting here looking so heartbroken and sad." He blinked and then burst out laughing, slapping me on the back, his great belly rolling.

I said a prayer for the buttons on his shirt.

"I'm just teasing ya," the sheriff said, wiping a tear from his eye. "Jay-sus you boys need to learn to laugh a little, you'll live longer."

"Is there something I can help you with, sheriff?" Dave butted in, sensing my tension.

The sheriff patted his stomach. "Oh, no, thank you, David, I'm just here for some coffee before I start making the rounds."

"Keeping the town safe?" I asked a little too coldly.

The sheriff's smile dropped from his face and he

stared down at me. "Why yes son, that's exactly what I'm doing."

My irritation spread, his annoying humor lingering beneath my skin like a slow sucking tick. "Protect and serve...isn't that your code? Maybe you get out there and do just that so my brother and I can finish our conversation."

The sheriff sucked his teeth and didn't say anything for a moment. I heard Dave's jaw click from across the booth.

Finally, the big man leaned down, putting his hands on his knees, our faces inches apart like he was talking to a child. "You got a burr in your ass, son? Was the coffee not to your liking? Because for the life of me I can't figure out why you're talking to me like this."

I didn't move. "Maybe it's because your breath stinks and you've been blowing it in my face for the past sixty seconds."

The sheriff stood up, surprised. He cupped a hand over his mouth and blew into it. He sniffed and winced.

"Well I'll be damned, you're absolutely correct!" He placed a hand on my shoulder and I wished he hadn't. "My apologies. I'll get out of your hair and let you enjoy the rest of your morning, how about that?"

"That'd be fantastic."

The sheriff gave Dave a curt nod. "See you around, David."

Dave just bounced his eyebrows: *Yep*.

As he turned to go, the sheriff stopped and looked

at me. "You stay safe out there, cowboy." And then he made a gun with his fingers and shot me in the head. Chuckling, he left us, proclaiming loudly that he needed hot coffee ASAP.

"Jeez, Cole, what was that about?" Dave whispered, leaning forward.

I hunched over, suddenly in a bad mood. "I didn't like the way he was talking about Maria. Like he knows anything about me. Inconsiderate asshole."

"Yeah, I get that, but watch yourself, man," Dave cautioned. "He's as dirty as his children and he's got an arsenal of officers at his disposal. You don't wanna end up on his bad side."

"Dirty cops and a deceitful king," I sighed. "Someone bring me a bottle of Crown Royal to baptize him with."

"What the heck are you mumbling about, Cole?"

I slid out of the booth and stretched. "Oh, nothing. Just the ramblings of a madman."

"Well, watch yourself around him."

I pretended to holster a pair of pistols. "Don't worry, dear brother. I have these to protect me."

"Yeah, and your mouth working against you."

"OK, I can tell when I've overstayed my welcome," I said. "I'm out of here."

Dave softened. "Heading to Joe's?"

"Reckon I am. I'll catch you later, bro." I waved a hand at his papers. "Don't have too much fun here."

"See you, Cole."

I left the diner and walked back to the bookstore. I

rounded the building and went to my truck out back. The sun was merciless and as I pulled open the door and got in, the back of my neck was already coated in sweat. I fired up the engine and pulled out onto Main Street.

I rolled the windows down and stuck my arm out, allowing the wind to dry my damp face. The street gutted Mill Valley right down the middle and I observed with some fondness the simplicity of it all. It was a complete contrast to New York. Instead of constant noise and blaring horns, the air was filled with the gentle rumble of blue-collar life revving up for the day.

I passed the old church near the end of town and stared up at the rising steeple. I remembered going there every Sunday as a child, Dad and Ma ushering us up the steps toward the big wooden doors, hissing to behave while the preacher spoke. I kind of missed it.

The town faded in my rear-view mirror and I gave the gas pedal some generous encouragement. Two miles down the road and the countryside began to evolve into heavy woodland. The lanes went from four to two and I followed the double yellow lines down a twisting labyrinth of rising hills and plummeting drops. I slowed slightly, the engine quieting. I listened to the buzz of insects and chirping birds, all hidden from sight behind a veil of forest. The trees pressed in tight against the road and their shade was welcome. I checked my phone to make sure I was still on course and saw that Joe's garage was just up ahead.

I saw signs for the highway and slowed even more. A mile further and the trees retreated slightly, and I spotted a building on the left at the end of a long stretch. A dirty sign loomed over the construction that read "Joe's Automobile Repair."

I flipped on my blinker, approaching the garage. It was a simple lot, something you'd drive by and never think about again if you weren't looking for it. A handful of cars were parked in front of the shop, quietly awaiting their turn under my brother's wrench. There were two bays, each open, and mechanical chaos littered the yard.

As I turned into the parking lot, my attention was drawn to a cluster of people standing out front, arguing.

I stopped my truck and got out. The sound of heated voices sparked a sense of urgency in my step as I went to see what all the noise was all about. As I approached, I saw Joe standing toe-to-toe with Mark, the middle brother of the Morrison family. Mark was screaming in my brother's face, spittle flying from his lips. His face was flush, his ponytail stained dark with sweat. Two other men I didn't recognize stood behind Mark on either side of him, their arms crossed. They were big, their cut-off sleeves revealing arms the size of tree trunks.

Joe looked just as pissed and held his ground beneath the onslaught of verbal warfare. Mark waved a manila folder around like it was a passage of the gospel.

He kept trying to shove it into my brother's hands, but Joe refused to take it.

I rounded on them, brow furrowed, and Joe turned at my approach.

"Maybe you should come back a little later," he said, ignoring Mark.

"What the hell is going on here?" I asked, coming to his side.

Mark appraised me, his face a sweaty mess of rage, his eyes wide and furious. "Oh, good! Another fucking Barker! Just who I wanted to see!"

I shot him a hard look. "Shut up, Mark."

But Mark didn't shut up. He stepped toward me now, his voice a low hiss. "Maybe you can talk some sense into your thick-headed brother."

I cocked an eyebrow at Joe. "What's this about?"

Joe squeezed the bridge of his nose and shut his eyes, irritated and visibly trying to calm himself. "The Morrisons want to buy my garage. They've been hounding me for weeks about it. You know about this, right?"

"Yeah, you told me."

"Well," Joe said, shooting a look at the trio of men before us, "these clowns can't just take no for an answer it seems. They've been showing up here like this for days now, each time with a different approach and offer. What they can't seem to get through their thick skulls, though, is that I ain't selling."

Mark turned away from us, throwing his hands in

the air. "How do you not get this!?" he yelled. "We're getting this place one way or another!"

My stomach twisted as I saw the butt of a pistol sticking out of his waistband. His shirt rode up to reveal its menacing presence and then disappeared like a magic trick as Mark turned back to face us.

I shifted in the gravel, my boots kicking up dust. "Look, Mark, maybe you should just calm down a little first, huh?"

Mark shook his head, his mouth contorted into a snarl. "Stay out of this, Cole. You have no idea what's going on here."

"Seems pretty obvious," I said, shrugging. "You want my brother's garage, he doesn't want to sell, end of story."

Mark approached me, a cruel smile twisting his lips. "No, no, no, no...see, this is the part you don't understand. If your brother refuses this, it isn't the end. It's just the beginning. And what lies beyond this rejection...well...I don't think any of us want to go there."

"That sounds like a threat," I said, not budging. "And I don't appreciate people threatening my family."

The two men flanking Mark tensed, but Mark held up a hand to them. "Relax, boys. Cole here thinks he's a tough guy. I get it. I understand. You're trying to impress Joe. You want him to feel like you got his back. You're trying to make up for lost time. I get it, really I do. But this—" he held up the manila folder like Moses and the Ten Commandments. "This right here? This is the last time we try to do this transaction above-board. Do you get what I'm saying?"

Joe stepped between us. "Piss off, Mark. You don't scare me. I'm not selling this place so you can convert it into a meth den. You poison enough people without my help. Find somewhere else. Or better yet, why don't you go home and light your fucking house on fire and then take a nap?"

Trembling, Mark glared daggers at Joe, sweat dripping from the tip of his nose. "I'm telling you right now, Joe...you don't want to do this. Derek has his heart set on this place and he's going to get what he wants, one way or another."

"Is this really about the garage anymore?" Joe asked, his voice hard. "Or has this become personal? Because to me, it seems like you just can't live with the fact that a Barker is telling you no."

Mark started to slowly shake his head, his eyes bulging. "I can't believe you're this stubborn. I can't believe you'd let your ego get in the way of this."

"This isn't about my ego, moron!" Joe yelled, causing the hired muscle behind Mark to jump. "This is about my life! I love this place and no amount of money would ever convince me to sell it! So take your offer and shove it right up your degenerate asshole! Is that perfectly *fucking* clear?"

Snarling, Mark grabbed Joe by the shirt. I shot forward and shoved him away hard, tensions rising.

"Don't you fucking touch him!" I yelled, dust

swirling between us. I pointed a finger at them, voice grating between my teeth. "I know I'm fresh into town, but I'm not an idiot. Stop trying to strong-arm Joe into this. It's not happening. So clear out or I'm calling the police."

Mark looked like he was about to launch himself at me, but instead he just slowly smiled. "Go ahead, Cole…call the police. See what happens. See what side of the story they hear."

I jabbed a finger at the road. "Go! Leave us alone and don't come back!"

"Or what?" Mark sneered. "What are you going to do?"

Joe placed a hand on my shoulder. "Let it alone. It's over. These boys are leaving, aren't you?"

Mark began to back away toward his pickup, his tiny entourage following. "Sure, Joe, we're leaving." He held up the envelope. "Last chance?"

"Tell Derek he can eat it," Joe spat. "And don't come crawling back here again."

They reached the truck and right before Mark got in, he called back to us one last time. "You're going to regret this, Joe! We could have done this the easy way! We're *going* to get what we want!"

Joe threw them the middle finger and turned away. I went with him, feeling a rush of energy suddenly leave me. I realized that my hands were shaking and I forced them to steady. Behind us, Mark and the two men tore out of the lot and went roaring down the road.

"That could have gone better," I muttered, following Joe into the garage.

"Oh, don't worry about them," he said casually, lighting a cigarette. "All bark and no bite."

"He had a gun, Joe," I said, serious.

Joe stopped and turned around, exhaling smoke through his nose. He lifted up his shirt to reveal a revolver shoved into his waistband. "Yeah, so do I."

I blinked and then shook my head. "I guess I'm just a little worried."

Joe slapped me on the back. "Don't be. I can take care of myself. I think they finally understand that I'm not giving this place up."

"Yeah, but what he said—" I started.

"I'll deal with that when the time comes," Joe said, waving me off. "Honestly, don't worry about it. Those boys are persistent, but they know better than to fuck with me."

"Do they?" I asked quietly.

Joe sighed. "Look, Cole, I don't expect you to understand things. You just got back. But please, don't worry about me. I can handle myself."

"Alright," I said, dismissing the subject. I scanned the bay, absorbing the disarray the place was in. Tools lay on every surface, dust coated the walls, grease and oil stained the concrete floor, and the whole place smelled like diesel.

I wrung my hands together. "Looks like this place needs more than just a paint job."

Joe shrugged. "Probably. But you'll become blind to the mess in a couple days, I can promise you that."

"I'm not so sure," I chuckled. "This is pretty rough. How many employees do you have?"

Joe went over to the car currently resting above us on the hydraulic jack. "Zero."

"You do this all…alone?" I asked, eyes going wide.

"Sure do," Joe said with some pride. "It takes me a little longer, but at least I know I'm giving my customers the best quality of work every time. Plus, I like working by myself. No noise, no bullshit, just me and the job."

"Hey, whatever works, I guess," I said, running my eyes over the walls. "You want this whole place painted?"

"Having second thoughts?" Joe laughed.

"No, but I'm going to need to get all the dirt and grime off the walls before I even think about priming and painting it."

Joe tossed me a rag which I caught. "Have at it, bro."

I looked at him and couldn't help but laugh. "Oh, you're going to be a real ball buster of a boss, huh?"

Joe lifted his shirt to reveal his gun. "I'll let the gun do the talking if you fall behind."

I laughed harder, shaking my head. "By the end of this job I might be begging for a bullet."

And so the day began. The two of us receded to our respective corners of the garage and started to work. I found a bucket and filled it with hot water and soap.

I managed to uncover half a dozen more rags that weren't completely covered in oil and began to scrub.

The day grew even hotter and by lunch I was soaked in sweat. The garage was even more filthy than I first thought and the going was slow. But despite the snail's pace at which I worked, I found myself falling into a comfortable rhythm. I realized that I missed working with my hands, making an honest day out of some honest labor.

By evening I had managed to get two of the four walls washed. It wasn't easy, as I had to maneuver stacks of tools and equipment out of the way. Each time I touched something, Joe would bark at me to be careful. I didn't know what he was worried about; everything I shifted away from the wall was made of metal, usually doused with a generous helping of rust and grime.

As the sun sank into the sky, I heard Joe announce we were done for the day. He came to my side and observed my work, impressed.

"Looks brand new," he mused, wiping sweat from his forehead.

I threw a rag, my latest victim, into the bucket of soapy water and grinned. "Should have it finished by tomorrow and then I can start priming. This wood is old and it's going to suck up the paint like water in a desert."

Joe held up his hands. "I leave it up to you."

"We calling it a day?"

"Yeah," Joe sighed. "If I go any longer I'm going to end up here all night. See you in the morning?"

"You better believe it," I said, wiping my hands on my pants.

"Thanks, Cole," Joe said suddenly. "I'm really glad you're here and helping me out like this. I really appreciate it."

"No worries," I said. "But tomorrow bring a cooler of beer or something, I thought I was going to die today."

"I think I can make that happen." Joe grinned. "Night, man."

"Night."

I exited the garage, leaving Joe to lock up, and headed for my truck. As I walked, the setting sun spitting its final rays through the trees above, I realized I was exhausted. Sleep sounded like the most appealing thing in the world and I looked forward to sinking into the sheets. After a shower. Definitely after a shower.

I crawled into my truck, waved one more time to Joe, and then pulled away and went speeding back toward town.

Chapter 4

The trees by the road darkened under the dying light. I reflected back on the day's work and found myself looking forward to tomorrow with hesitant anticipation. I knew the job was a temporary fix, but it was exactly what I needed to take my mind off of things. Nothing purges grief better than hard work and honest labor.

As I approached town, I spotted a van pulled off to the side of the road. It was gray and almost lost in the shadow of the fading day. I slowed down and saw a man leaning against the driver's side door, his arms crossed. It looked like he had a flat.

Assuming he needed help, I pulled up behind the van and got out, raising my hand to the man, who looked gruff and not entirely happy with his predicament.

"Hey, need a hand?" I asked, drawing closer.

The man turned and squared me up, his low brow dipping lower. "Got help coming. You best move along."

"You sure?" I asked, stealing a glance at the flat. "I have a jack if you need one."

The man pointed toward the empty road. "Said I was fine. Now get going."

Shrugging, I turned to leave when a new voice called out to me.

"Is that Cole Barker?!"

I looked over my shoulder and saw Leo, the youngest of the Morrison brothers. He poked his head out of the driver's-side window, a bandana tied loosely around his neck. Our eyes met and the young man chuckled.

"Shit, Cole, I seem to be running into you everywhere."

I felt immediate irritation at his presence, like a piece of clothing that rubs your skin the wrong way. I walked back to the van, sighing.

"Hey, Leo. What a pleasant surprise."

The man leaning against the van looked at Leo. "You know this guy?"

Leo leaned on his hands and cupped his face. "Sure do. This here is Joe's older brother." The gruff-looking man just grunted.

Out of duty, I offered my services again. "You sure you don't want some help? Like I was saying, I got a jack in the truck."

Leo waved my offer away. "Naw, Daddy's coming. He should be here in a little bit."

I stared at him. "Daddy…"

Leo snorted. "What, yours been dead so long you forgot what they are?"

"OK great, well good luck, I'm leaving," I said, turning once again for my truck.

"Hey, wait!" Leo called, raising a hand to me.

I closed my eyes. "What is it, Leo?"

Leo's voice dropped low. "Mark called me earlier. Told me Joe wouldn't sell."

I stayed put. "Yeah? So?"

Leo clucked his tongue. "Hoo-wee…wouldn't want to be your brother right now. You see, Derek is the kind of man who just doesn't understand the word 'no.' He's about as stubborn as a mule and as mean as a hyena. If you care about your brother, you should convince him he's making a big mistake."

I felt something spark inside of me and I spun around, fists clenched. "What the hell is it with you people and my brother's garage? Are you so used to getting what you want you seriously can't live with being told 'no'? Why don't you just drop the bullshit, leave Joe alone, and go back to doing what you do best?"

Leo leered at me, seemingly unaffected by my rant. "Oh? And what would that be?"

My voice turned to gravel. "Fucking *off*."

Leo snickered. "Can't do that, Cole. You see, the wonderful folks of Mill Valley are depending on us. They may not want us, but they sure do need us."

I rapped my knuckles against the side of the van. "Is that what got in here, Leo? The town's *needs*?"

The gruff man pushed me away suddenly, his hackles rising. "Hey, piss off, buddy. I think it's time for you to leave."

I brushed myself off, shaking my head. "Couldn't have said it better myself."

Leo held up a hand. "Hold up, one more thing before you go."

I glared at him.

"Why'd you come back? Why the hell come back to Mill Valley?"

I met his eyes. "'Cause it's the only place left that got people I care about. Now…are we done?"

Leo grinned at me, a broken, crooked thing. "You miss her?"

I felt my jaw pop. "You take care now."

I walked to my truck and got in. As I fired it up, I saw a police cruiser coming down the road. I pulled out as it pulled in, the sheriff tipping his hat to me as we passed. I ignored him. I gripped the steering wheel and drove into town.

When I was back in my apartment, I stripped down and got in the shower. The water was hot and as steam rose around me, I found myself struggling. A knot had formed in my chest, a ball of anger and stinging memory.

Do you miss her?

I closed my eyes against the onslaught of water and exhaled.

Let it go, just let it all go.

I felt something stir in my throat, a whimper maybe, but I refused to acknowledge its existence. I washed up and got out. I toweled off and wrapped the cloth around my waist. I went to my bedroom and heard my phone ringing.

I answered. "Hello?"

"Hey, Cole, you busy?"

I smiled and suddenly the knot in my chest disappeared. "Hi, Tammy. No, I just got back from Joe's. What's up?"

A pause, then: "You mind if I come up?"

I blinked. "Are you downstairs?"

"I was driving by and saw your truck parked out back. Figured I'd see if you're free."

I shifted the phone to my other ear. "Yeah, of course, come on up. Everything OK?"

Tammy sighed. "I just came back from a shitty date and need to vent. You tired? I can leave you alone if you want."

"No, no, it's fine. Let me throw some clothes on and I'll let you in."

"The hell are you doing up there?" Tammy teased.

"None of your damn business, lady," I chuckled. "See you in a second." I hung up and quickly got dressed. I tossed the towel back in the bathroom and trotted down the stairs barefoot. Through the window in the door, I saw my sister with her arms wrapped around herself, waiting impatiently.

I unlocked the latch and waved her in. "Please, after you."

She smiled upon seeing me and I followed her up the stairs. When she entered my place, she looked around and nodded approvingly.

"About what I'd expect from you, Cole," she said, eying the décor. "Completely bland and perfectly functional."

"Pft, you don't know me," I chuckled, walking us into the living room. "Drink?"

She waved the offer away and took a seat on the couch. "I think I'm good. Help yourself, though."

"Actually, I don't think I have anything," I muttered, taking the chair opposite her.

We held each other's eyes for a moment, waiting for the other to say something. When I remained silent, she sighed wearily.

"I hope your day was better than mine."

"Can't complain," I said. "Got a good start on Joe's garage. You been down there recently? It's kinda filthy."

"Every now and again I go check up on him."

"As chaotic as it is, I can tell he's really proud of the place," I ventured. "He's never been a people person and I think he enjoys the peace and quiet."

"Yeah, I agree," Tammy exhaled.

I could tell she didn't really want to talk about Joe and so I steered the conversation back to her. "OK, sis, enough small talk; lay it on me. I can feel the waves of frustration rolling off of you."

Tammy snorted. "Ah, I feel stupid now complaining about this kind of thing to you."

I spread my arms. "I got nowhere I'd rather be right now. Let's have it. Who was this guy and what'd he do?"

Tammy sighed. "It was just another disappointment in a long line of disappointments. I swear to God, I feel like men get stupider every day."

I held a hand up to my heart. "Hey…that hurts."

Tammy finally cracked a grin. "Oh, shut up, I don't mean you."

"So who was this lucky man?"

"Just some guy who owns a farm out by Ma. His parents died a couple years ago and he inherited the place. I've seen him a time or two whenever I'm out there to visit and the last time I was there he asked me out. Poor guy. He was stuttering and stammering, rubbing his straw hat like he was afraid it'd burst into flames."

I winced. "Totally sounds like your type."

"I don't know if I felt bad for him or what," Tammy said, "but I figured what the hell. Why not? He was cute enough, in a kinda gritty way. Plus he owns some land so I wouldn't have to worry about supporting him or some nonsense. He checked off a couple of my boxes, is what I'm saying."

"Sure, sure," I agreed, "but he was as boring as a sack of flour, right?"

Tammy groaned. "Dreadfully so. I don't know if that man has ever been around another woman his entire life. He had no idea how to hold a conversation, what was appropriate to say, or how a date even works."

"Oh, boy," I grimaced. "Sounds like a real winner."

"When I said goodbye, not only did he try to kiss me, but he groped my chest, Cole," Tammy said flatly. "Like, full on, open palm, 'I want me some of that boob!'"

I burst out laughing, unable to help myself. "Jesus Christ, Tam, did you kill him?"

Tammy snickered. "No, but I did grab hold of his junk and gave it a hard tug. Told him if he ever did that again that I'd make sure his severed dick is the only piece of him the police find."

"You know, I think it's your submissive personality that makes you so...alluring," I joked, still laughing.

Tammy threw her hands up. "Well jeez, I'm sorry I'm not some doe-eyed milkmaid just begging for a man's approval!"

"Tammy, Tammy, you're perfect," I said, calming her, grinning. "And you deserve someone who can respect the woman you are."

"Are you mocking me?" Tammy glared.

"No!" I laughed. "No, of course not! I mean it, really."

Tammy's eyes narrowed even further. "Why do I not believe you?"

I playfully covered my hands with my eyes. "Ah, there we go again, that distrustful aggressiveness that scares the fellas away."

"I'm actually going to kill you tonight," Tammy growled, but there was humor in her voice.

I calmed myself, waving a hand at her. "I'm sorry, Tam, I'm just trying to make you feel better. In all seriousness, I'm really sorry you had such a bad night. You really are an incredible woman and I wish you could find someone who not only sees that but cherishes it as well."

Surprised, Tammy blinked at me and her face softened slightly. "Holy shit, Cole, how long were you out in the sun today?"

I winked at her. "Long time."

She smiled and the edges dulled. "That…was actually really sweet. Thank you. I needed to hear that. Sometimes I think I'm just this bull that maims anyone who shows interest in me."

"When you find that guy, it'll be worth the wait."

Tammy sighed heavily and ran a hand through her hair. "I know. That's what Ma keeps saying. I just…"

"What is it?" I asked tenderly.

Her voice softened. "I just really want to meet someone and get on with my life. I feel like I'm stuck in limbo right now or something. I'm not getting any younger. There's this countdown in the back of my head all the time, and I'm worried that I'm going to meet someone who is just 'good enough.' But I don't want 'good enough.' I want someone who can appreciate me and be there for me when I need them. I want to feel like I'm part of a team, ready to take on anything the world throws at us. Is that dumb?"

"Of course not," I said gently. "That's what we all

want. I think you're an incredible person Tammy, really, I do. And I want someone at your side who will unequivocally understand that. I want to know that my sister is doing OK. I want to know she's happy, that she's with someone who will treat her right. You have a big heart. The fact that you've stuck around to keep an eye on Ma, on our family, even though I know you want to get away…well…it puts me to shame."

"Don't say that," Tammy said softly. "Please don't say that. You did what your heart told you to do and I don't believe for a second that it was a mistake."

"I wonder about that," I said, staring at the floor. "I wonder about that a lot."

"Look," Tammy pressed, "we can only play the hand life gives us. For what it's worth, I'm incredibly proud of you. And I'm sorry about how things turned out. I can't stress that enough, Cole. You're a good person, a damn good person, and you didn't deserve what happened. I think about that a lot, and it fills me with such sadness sometimes. The fact that someone so good has to carry around the weight that you do. If anyone is impressed here, it's me."

Our eyes met and I smiled sadly. "Thanks, Tam. You're a hell of a good sister, you know that? I really missed you."

"I missed you, too. And despite the awful circumstances of your return, I'm glad I can be here for you if you need it. I want you to know that if you ever need to talk, or just blow off some steam, then I'm just a phone call away, OK?"

I felt my eyes misting up. "Thank you. That means a lot to me." I wiped my face and laughed. "Jesus, I'm the one who's supposed to be making you feel better!"

Tammy shrugged. "Ah, I'll be fine. Just a frustrating night."

"It sounds like it."

"I wonder sometimes if my standards are too high," she continued. "Like there's something wrong with me. As if I have these lofty expectations of the men I see. I don't know. When I was younger, I had these ideals and fantasies about what the man I'd fall in love with would be like. And the more I date, the more I realize that they were just that…fantasies. The real world isn't black and white. There are infinite shades of gray and I just have to find one that strikes my fancy. No one is perfect. No one is without loss or hardship. We all have our own shit we're dealing with, and I just need to find someone who understands mine."

"I couldn't have said it any better myself," I said. "And you will find someone, Tammy. I promise you. Someone is going to come along that really knocks your socks off. The fact that you've been so patient is impressive and should be commemorated instead of questioned. You know what you want. Don't settle for anything less. Yes, there are shades of gray, like storm clouds, but behind all that is a brilliant sun. Wait for the sun, Tam, because when you see it—*him*—you're going to be overwhelmed."

Tammy smiled gently. "I think I really needed to hear that."

I shrugged, suddenly awkward. "I think you've known it all along. That's why you're still looking for that special someone. Just keep at it and don't give up."

"I won't."

The mood settled and our conversation began to ebb toward simpler things. We stashed away the heavy topics for another time and spent the next hour catching up on the little intricacies of life: what movies we had seen, what concerts we had gone to, crazy people we had met, wild nights out, everything and anything that would begin to bridge the gap of my five-year absence.

At some point, Tammy checked her phone and decided it was time for her to be off. I hugged her tightly and walked her down to her car. I waved as she pulled away, feeling deeply satisfied and appreciative of her unexpected visit.

I marched back upstairs and readied for bed. In minutes, I drifted away on a tide of exhaustion and distant dreams.

The next morning I drove back to Joe's garage and began a new day of cleaning and scrubbing. Joe was already there when I arrived, hoisting the promised cooler of beer. I grinned and slapped him on the back.

We didn't talk much while we worked. He was always behind me, working on the cars, while I dutifully cleansed the filth from the walls. Occasionally, an idle memory would float by that I would snatch and share with my brother. Usually it was something funny we had done in our youth and we'd both have a good chuckle before comfortably reclining back into our tasks.

The day after, I began to actually prime the place. It was much more satisfying work and a lot less filthy. As predicted, the walls ate up the coat I carefully applied, but I managed to get the entire shop done by evening.

Satisfied and pleased with my progress, Joe and I shared a beer and watched the sun go down. We both stunk to high hell, but the beer was cold and the day was ending. I realized that I could get used to this kind of life. I had always shuddered away from it as a child, but the purity of the work was both rewarding and strangely satisfying. I mentioned this to Joe and he just rolled his shoulders and grinned, remaining perfectly noncommittal. I didn't blame him. I doubted he was willing to give up his sanctuary, his cove of peace.

We parted ways and soon I found myself back in my apartment, tucked away and plummeting toward sleep.

The next morning I stopped at the hardware store on Main Street and bought a couple new rollers and paint-brushes. Joe already had the paint, but I knew supplies were running low. I paid for the wares and tossed them in the back of my truck. Feeling good, I pulled out of the parking lot and accelerated for Joe's.

Fifteen minutes later as I approached the garage, I

could tell something was wrong. With the windows rolled down, I could hear Joe cussing up a storm. I rolled into the lot and got out, rushing toward my brother who stood out front, screaming and yelling like he had lost his mind.

"Jesus, Joe, what the hell is going on?" I asked, panting. I looked around, searching for another person who could have possibly riled my brother up so much. But the lot was empty.

Joe wheeled around, his face red with rage. He shot a finger over to the far side of the garage where two cars awaited their turn under Joe's capable hands. I remembered they had been dropped off at some point yesterday. Joe had gone out and seen to the customers while I continued priming the walls. The cars were newer models than Joe was used to working on, but you'd never be able to tell now.

And that was because the two cars had been obliterated. The windshields were smashed, the windows were shattered, the doors had been ripped off, the interiors were slashed, and the tires had been punctured. In other words, someone had come along and properly fucked them up.

"Holy shit," I whispered, whistling.

"What the FUCK!?" Joe howled. "I can't believe this! I just can't fucking believe this! To stoop so low, so GODDAMN LOW!"

"What the hell happened?" I asked, eyes wide.

"Those *cocksuckers* did this!" Joe bellowed.

I turned my attention to my frothing brother. "Hey, take it easy, I know this is bullshit but let's take a breath, OK?"

"Take a breath?!" Joe screamed, his face inches from mine, his eyes bulging. "Those motherfuckers are messing with my LIVELIHOOD! Do you know who has to pay for this!? Do you know how much work I'm going to have to take on just to make up the difference!? DO YOU!?"

I held up my hands. "N-no Joe, I don't. I'm sorry. I'm really sorry. Who exactly do you think did this?"

"Oh, come on, Cole, I know you're not STUPID!" Joe howled, throwing his hands up in the air. "It was the Morrisons! Who else would do something like this?!" Joe balled his hands into fists and I heard him grind his teeth together. "Those fucking bastards, I swear to God in heaven, I'm going to fucking kill them."

I swallowed hard. "You think…the Morrison brothers did this? Because you wouldn't sell them the garage?"

"Of course!" Joe yelled, a vein pulsing in his neck. "And now they're fucking with me! They can't have what they want, so now they're just going to destroy it piece by piece unless I change my mind! Well, let me tell you something: those idiots aren't going to get away with this."

I exhaled shakily, planting my hands on my hips. "Christ, Joe…what a mess." I shook my head and chanced a glance at my brother. His chest rose and fell rapidly, but he looked like he was finally calming down, if only to catch his breath. Sweat ran down his face in greasy streaks and I could practically see him thinking through his enraged eyes.

"Goddamn right it's a mess," Joe hissed, allowing himself to settle a little. "I never thought, never in a million years, that those three assholes were capable of something like this."

"Well, we don't know for sure it was them," I started, but Joe shot me a look that would have frozen hell.

"Don't be dumb," Joe said, turning his gaze back to the destroyed vehicles. "They did this, no doubt about it. I know they really want this place, but damn…to stoop this *low*?"

"I mean, look at their line of work," I said quietly. "They're not exactly good people. In fact, I'd go so far as to say they're bad people. Look at what they do to the people of Mill Valley. I've seen the evidence, Joe, seen those poor people with that awful, hollowed-out look on their faces. The Morrisons are poisoning this town. Sure enough, little by little, they are ruining the lives of the good people here. Something like this," I waved a hand at the cars. "I'm honestly surprised they stopped there."

"Yeah, this time they did," Joe muttered angrily. "Who knows how bad it'll be next time? Who knows how far they'll push me until they get what they want? Fucking animals…"

"Why not call the sheriff?" I offered.

Joe sighed. "How many times do I have to remind you that's not an option? There's basically no law when it comes to those brothers. You just need to understand that, once and for all. We're alone in this. And we got to deal with it ourselves, one way or another. Well, I do at least."

I placed a hand on his shoulder. "You got it right the first time. We. We'll deal with this. I'll help you clean up the mess and then we can figure out some way to keep this from happening again, OK? I don't know, maybe we can go to the hardware store and get a chain-link fence to put around the place. How does that sound?"

"Don't think that would stop them," Joe grunted. "But I appreciate your enthusiasm. We'll come up with something. Now come on, let's get this glass cleaned up. I need some time to think before I call the owners and tell them their rides are busted. Fuck me, man."

"Whatever you need, I'm here, man."

"Well…let's get to it then," Joe grumbled miserably.

It took the better half of the morning to clean up the damage that had been done to the cars. As we worked, I could see Joe mentally preparing himself for the phone calls he was going to have to make. I pitied him immensely. I was in just as much shock as he was that the Morrisons had done something like this. It infuriated me…and kind of scared me. I knew Joe was a hothead and something like this could really lead to something awful. I vowed to stay at his side until the storm had passed. Maybe, with any luck, this was a one-time thing. One last pathetic attempt to get Joe to sell. If they knew anything about my brother, though, they would know this would only cause him to dig his heels in even deeper. And that's where my fear stemmed from.

After all the glass had been collected and disposed of, I went to start painting and heard Joe make the first call. He was incredibly apologetic and humble, offering to pay for the damage and make things right with his customers. I admired him for that. Despite his many flaws, Joe was an honest man.

I left him alone after the calls were done, content to work in silence and let him work through his anger and humiliation without me bothering him. He disappeared inside the hood of a truck and I diligently coated the walls with fresh paint.

When night came and it was time to wrap up, I prayed his mood had softened beneath the lull of labor.

"How are you doing?" I asked gently as I covered the paint equipment, shooting a glance at him over my shoulder.

Joe finished putting his tools away and looked at me. "I think I'm staying here tonight. Just in case they come back."

I felt uneasy at this news and quickly vocalized my concern. "You sure that's a good idea? You don't know what they're capable of at this point."

Joe lifted his shirt to reveal his pistol. "Yeah, well, they don't know what I'm capable of."

The unease I felt quickly turned to worry. "Joe, come on. That's not the way to handle this. What are you going to do, shoot them?"

"If that's what it takes," Joe said casually.

"Look," I said desperately. "How about I stay here with you tonight? With the two of us here, they wouldn't dare cause any more trouble."

"You don't know that."

"Yeah, but if I leave I'm going to be worried about you all night."

"It's not necessary. I'll be fine. You go on home."

"No, if you're staying, then so am I," I said stubbornly.

Joe sighed and ran a hand over his face. "Christ, Cole, this isn't your problem."

"Are you my brother?" I asked, cocking an eyebrow.

"Yeah, so?"

"Then it's my damn problem, too," I said, "so stop fighting me on this."

Joe snorted. "Alright, alright. You win. But if you're staying then you're going to need something."

"And what's that?"

Instead of answering, Joe went to the corner of the shop and pulled open an oil-stained cabinet. He reached inside and pulled out a shotgun. Without waiting for comment, he retrieved a handful of shells and began to load them into the gun.

"Come on, Joe," I begged. "We don't need that."

"You're right," he said, still loading. "We don't. You do."

I groaned and walked to his side. "You really think this is going to solve anything?"

Joe finished loading and chambered a shell. He pushed the gun into my hands. "No, but it'll put some ice in their veins. You point that bitch at someone and they'll start second-guessing every choice they ever made. That's all we're doing here."

I hefted the shotgun in my hands, feeling uncomfortable. "You promise?"

Joe suddenly grinned and crossed his fingers. "Sure I do."

"Liar," I muttered.

Joe placed a hand on my shoulder. "It'll make me feel better if you have it, OK? Just in case they do come back, I want you to be prepared."

"I'm not shooting anyone, Joe," I said.

"I'm not asking you to. Just hold onto it and look mean. We don't even know if they're coming back tonight, OK? So quit being a pussy and just take the gun."

"God, I hate you sometimes," I muttered.

Joe grinned. "Are we brothers?"

"Yes..."

"Then we're going to hate each other sometimes. Now relax, Rambo. Everything is going to be fine."

"So you say."

With nothing more to do, we went into the back and

sat down on the old musty couch against the far wall. I leaned the shotgun against the arm and crossed my legs. Joe took his place next to me and we watched the day evaporate like colored ice cream, melting slowly across a sky of murky blue.

When full dark fell, I stirred restlessly and scrubbed my hands over my jeans. "I, uh…I saw Tammy last night."

Joe looked at me sideways. "Oh, yeah? How's she doing?"

"She was pretty upset over a date she went on. Some guy who owns a farm over by Ma's."

Joe grunted indifferently. "She's too picky."

I snorted. "Like you have room to talk."

"I'm too picky."

I chuckled. "You two are pretty similar, you know that?"

"No."

"Stubborn as hell and quick with the temper," I mused.

"Yeah, well, I was born this way. What do you want from me?"

"Nothing, Joe. Just making conversation."

Joe looked at me again. "You nervous?"

I checked my watch and saw it was almost ten. "A little."

"Not much for confrontation, are you? You never have been."

I looked at my hands and grew quiet.

Joe sighed, "I'm sorry."

"S'OK."

An uncomfortable silence emanated between us.

"Hey," Joe started, suddenly somber. "You remember that time Dad whooped your ass for breaking his tractor?"

I grunted. "Hard to forget. I figured it'd be funny to take it for a joyride through the field. I thought Dad was still in town. Stupid. Ran over a massive rock and broke the axle. Boy, he tanned my hide good for that one."

"He shouldn't have done that," Joe said quietly.

"Ah, I deserved it."

"Not like that. I remember hearing you crying…it's always bothered me. I should have done something."

I looked at him through the shadows. "You were only six, Joe."

He shrugged. "Still coulda done something. That day's always stuck with me."

"You don't have to feel bad," I offered gently.

"Yeah…"

Silence followed and together we stared out at the night through the open bay doors. Night bugs sang woefully around the garage and I watched a sea of fireflies ignite the darkness like flickering embers. Joe smoked idly, the cherry glowing like the fireflies outside.

At some point I began to grow tired. I fought against it but found myself unable to battle the anchors on my eyelids. Around midnight, I dozed off, falling quietly into a light sleep.

An hour later, Joe woke me.

I blinked in the black as Joe urgently shook my shoulder. I wiped my eyes and immediately went on full alert.

"What? What is it!?" I hissed.

Joe's face hovered like a ghost before me, his voice low. "There's a van. It's parked on the other side of the street. It just pulled up."

"Shit," I whispered, snatching the shotgun from its place. I rose with Joe and we quietly slunk to the open bay doors, hugging the walls. My heart began to race and I tapped my fingers against the barrel of the gun, anxious and afraid. I forced my breathing to steady and shot Joe a look.

He was pressed up against the wall opposite me, staring out into the lot. His mouth was a grim line in the moonlight and I saw he had his pistol in his hand.

We waited like that, the seconds ticking by, each beat amping my fear. What if they were armed? What if they came at us? What if they shot us?

Relax, Cole, they don't even know you're here.

I closed my eyes and took a long breath. When I opened them again, I heard soft voices making their way toward us. I gripped the shotgun tighter and Joe met my urgent gaze. He placed a finger to his lips and held up a hand.

Wait.

I squinted around the corner and saw the van Joe had mentioned. Like he said, it was parked across the street from the garage. When I saw it, my heart sank. It was Leo's van.

Two figures slowly approached the parking lot and I saw they were carrying something. After a moment, I realized they were holding baseball bats.

And that's when Joe emerged from the shadows and advanced on them, gun raised.

"That's far enough!" he yelled, stopping a dozen feet from where they stood. The two men froze, paralyzed at the sudden confrontation. They looked at one another and then back at Joe, unsure and taken back.

I swallowed my fear and followed Joe, placing the butt of the shotgun against my shoulder. I kept the barrel trained on the ground as I went and stood shoulder-to-shoulder with my brother. The moon was full and by its light, I saw that one of the men was indeed Leo. The other was the gruff guy I had offered to help with the tire.

"You're trespassing," Joe said darkly, keeping his revolver trained on Leo's head.

Leo shifted in place and squeezed the baseball bat tightly. "Whoa…hey Joe. W-why don't you lower that thing, yeah? Seems like we got ourselves a misunderstanding here."

Joe looked over at me and then back at the two men. "What do you think, Cole? You think this is a misunderstanding?"

"I think these boys are a little lost," I said, watching for any sudden movements, "and I think they need to get right back in their van and go home."

Leo and the man nodded. "Yeah, that might be for the best."

"I don't think so," Joe growled. My heart crawled up my throat.

"Derek sent us," the gruff man explained, his voice not quite steady.

"I bet he did," Joe continued, his voice ice-cold. "I bet he sent you last night, too."

"No, that's just it!" Leo exclaimed. "See, we heard about what happened! A-and, and so Derek sent us to keep watch over the place! So you'd understand there's no hard feelings!"

Joe ground his teeth together. "What a crock of *shit*." He cocked the hammer back.

"Joe..." I whispered. Joe stepped forward and Leo and the gruff man stiffened with fear.

"So what do we do here, boys?" Joe said softly. He slowly moved the gun back and forth between the two intruders. "Are we going to continue to have a problem here? Or are you going to leave me and my business alone for good?"

"We don't want no trouble," the gruff man practically whimpered.

Joe looked down at the baseball bats. "Clearly."

"I'm telling you, Derek sent us here for protection!" Leo cried.

"In the middle of the night?" I called. "You have to admit, Leo, this seems awfully shady."

"I know, I know," he pleaded, "it's my own damn fault. We stopped over at The Tin Can for a couple drinks and time kinda got away from us. We meant to be here before you closed, honest!"

Joe's eyes glowed beneath the moon, his voice a venomous hiss. "If you don't quit lying to me, I swear to God on high, I will blow your fucking brains out the back of your skull."

"Leo!" The gruff man whispered desperately.

"Shut the hell up, Trevor!" Leo yelled suddenly. "Just keep your goddamn mouth shut for once in your life!"

Joe smiled and pointed the gun directly between Leo's eyes. "Say goodbye, Leo."

"JOE!" I yelled, advancing. I grabbed him by the shoulder and pulled him back. "Take it easy! They're not going to bother you again!" I shot Leo a desperate look. "Isn't that right?"

Leo nodded vigorously. "No, sir, we won't ever come by here again, honest! This was a big misunderstanding, but you've made it clear to me you don't want our help and that's fine! We was just trying to mend the bridge, that's all!"

Joe lowered his gun and glared at me, then shot his eyes over to the two men. "Get the fuck off my property."

They didn't need any more encouragement than that. The two men practically scampered back to their van.

I watched as they turned it around, rubber screeching, and roared back toward Mill Valley.

As the dust settled and the symphony of night swelled around us again, Joe turned to me.

"You didn't need to do that."

I exhaled heavily. "I thought you were going to shoot him, Joe."

Joe shook his head. "No…I wasn't going to shoot him. But I wanted him to think I was. I wanted him to think he was about to die."

"You think they'll be back?" I asked, calming my racing heart.

Joe retreated back to the garage, lighting a cigarette as he went. "Who knows?"

Chapter 5

That Sunday I went to church with Ma. She only had to ask twice before I caved and agreed to go. It was strange being back in that building. As I found a pew for us, the smell of the place sent memories shooting through me like fireworks. It was like I was a kid again, kicking my feet idly, restless, praying not for my soul, but for the preacher to hurry up and finish his sermon. Church bored the hell out of me as a kid. I remember sitting there between Joe and Tammy, daydreaming, my mind soaring out of reach.

A lot of the time I would imagine scenarios. Like, what if a group of terrorists invaded the church and held the pastor hostage? Of course, I would be the hero. I would somehow acquire a gun, maybe snatch a pistol off the hip of an unaware evil agent and blast the bad guys away. Oh, how everyone would cheer for me. How brave they would I think I was. Who knows, maybe even the cute girls I stared at every Sunday would notice me. Maybe they'd think I was cool, in a dangerous kind of way. I'd shrug the killing off like it was nothing, like I was carved from cold steel.

Sitting there with Ma, reflecting on those returning fantasies, I couldn't help but chuckle. Ma shot me a look and I waved it away, shaking my head. The congregation continued to filter in, the pews filling with respectful townsfolk. Everyone was dressed up in their Sunday best, which wasn't saying much, but in comparison to the dirty, everyday look, it was an admirable effort. The men awkwardly combed their hair, shaved their beards, and the women usually tried to do something fancy with their hair, which wildly varied in success.

After the service, Ma insisted I say hello to the preacher, which I did. It was the same old man from my youth whose voice I had grown to loathe. But I shook his hand politely and told him what a wonderful sermon he had given. This seemed to please Ma, and she beamed up at the preacher and informed him that I had come back into town recently and he should expect to see my face again. I grimaced at that but kept my mouth shut, not wanting to upset my mother.

As I drove her home, Ma asked how things were going at Joe's.

I adjusted my grip on the wheel and nodded. "Things are going well. It's good working with him."

Ma smiled. "Course it is. You two are good for each other, always have been."

"Where's Dave today?" I asked, passing the diner. "I thought you said he was coming to church with us."

"Oh, him," Ma said, shaking her head. "He had to go pick up a shipment of something or other for the diner."

"Likely excuse," I muttered.

Ma swatted my arm lightly from across the cab. "Davey's not lying, he wouldn't do something like that. He comes with me every Sunday to service and this is the first he's missed all year. You should take note of that, I think some more of Pastor Barry's sermons would do you good."

"He's boring as hell, Ma," I said, smiling slightly. "Don't get me wrong; I love going with you, but he's been spouting the same nonsense for almost thirty years now."

"It's not nonsense!" Ma said defensively. "Maybe if you listened a little closer, you'd be able to learn a thing or two."

"I don't know about that, it all seems kinda…generic."

"Well, sometimes that's what you need to hear in order to activate the goodness God puts in all our souls."

"I used to fantasize about killing people in church," I muttered.

"What did you say?"

"Nothing, Ma."

She sighed and let up a little. "Look, I just want all my children to be in heaven together. Otherwise, it wouldn't be heaven."

"I'll hitch a ride somewhere," I said, grinning.

"You boys worry me sometimes," Ma said, staring out the window. "Especially Joe. That boy has some anger in his heart that only the Good Lord can heal."

"Joe's a good man," I said. "And I've really enjoyed working with him the past couple days. He's just a little hotheaded. You know this."

"I heard about what happened to his garage," Ma said without looking at me. "About the Morrison brothers."

"Oh…"

She turned to me and put a hand on my arm. "It was good you were there when they came back."

"Who told you?" I asked.

"Word travels fast in Mill Valley," Ma said ominously.

"Yeah, well, don't worry about it. The confrontation is over and has been dealt with."

"Thank God for that."

I dropped Ma off at her house and she thanked me for coming with her. I kissed her on the cheek and told her I'd see her soon. As I drove away, I realized I had the whole day free. Joe told me not to bother coming in today because he was going to get a couple parts from two towns over. Feeling content in the odd way church can sometimes make you feel, I decided to take a drive out into the country.

The day was cooler than it had been of late, and the morning sun pleasantly ignited the sky. I rolled down the window, stuck my arm out, and inhaled the aroma of earthy grassland. I kept the radio off, content to let my mind wander in the solitude of silence. I didn't think about anything particular, leaving the door open for whatever topic walked into my head. I'd examine it, pat it on the back, and usher it out the door as another waltzed in.

Time tumbled away from me in the most freeing of ways, and before I knew it the sun had reached the summit of the sky and began to laboriously trek back toward the distant hills. I stopped along the way at a roadside eatery and got myself a burger and fries. Plus a milkshake, 'cause screw it, it was Sunday.

I had driven a couple hours outside of town, the land a pleasant expanse of rising hills, abandoned farmland, and humble residences. Everything seemed so much more basic out here, the essentials of life boiled down to the most necessary of tasks. At least that's how it appeared from the outside as I passed farmhouse after farmhouse. Gone was the roar of chaotic cities, replaced by the rumble of tractors and squawk of chickens.

Headed back toward Mill Valley now, sucking on the final remains of my vanilla milkshake, I felt amazingly at peace with how I had spent my day. I had thought about nothing at all and yet everything at once. I had suffered no unexpected plummet of emotional memory, and the horror I left behind in New York had been kept cautiously at bay.

When I finally made it back into town, the sun now tucked away behind the horizon, I decided to keep driving down Main Street past the bookstore. Not knowing why, I headed back for the church.

I parked my truck in the near-empty lot and curiously approached the steps leading inside. During my daytime musings, I thought of the service this morning, and despite my complaining, I discovered that I had indeed enjoyed being back. I felt like church would be better suited if there were no pastor and the congregation was forced to sit in the pews and do nothing but contemplate their lives in complete silence. What's that saying? Take a moment to listen and you will hear God? I wasn't sure if I was quite there yet, not even sure if I actually believed in God, but the serenity the sanctuary offered was alluring if nothing else. It seemed like a place I could be open with myself and just let whatever I felt come out for examination, ironically, without judgment.

I pushed open the door to the church, the wood echoing loudly in the thick silence. I walked inside. The sanctuary was dimly lit and for a second, I thought I had the place to myself. But as I walked through the pews toward the front, I saw someone else sitting by themselves, head bowed.

Curious, I walked toward them and when I saw who it was, I smiled to myself.

"Hey, Dave," I called quietly, sliding in next to him.

Startled, Dave jumped and his head shot up. "Cole? What the heck are you doing here?"

"Just thought I'd pop in for some quiet time," I said. "That OK?"

Dave nodded. "Yeah, of course, that's great."

I stared at him and realized that his eyes were red-rimmed and it looked like he had been crying.

"Hey, are you alright?" I asked, concerned.

Dave gave me a weak nod. "Yeah, I'm fine."

"What are you doing here?"

The smile dropped from his face and he looked down at his hands. "Just talking to Dad."

A boulder rolled over my chest and I exhaled slowly. "Oh…I can leave you alone if you want."

Dave shook his head, wiping his eyes. "No, no. I was just about finished."

"You come here like this a lot?" I asked carefully.

Dave shrugged and continued to stare at his hands. "Sometimes, when I really miss him. I keep thinking that maybe, just one time, I'll be able to hear him talking back to me."

"I miss him, too," I said quietly, staring ahead.

"I just…" Dave started, struggling. "There are just some days when I think about him a lot. I think about what he'd say. About what he'd say about me, about what he'd think of my life. Would he be happy? Would he be disappointed? What would he tell me to do different?"

I reached over and put my arm around my brother. "I think he'd be really proud of you, Dave. You're the best of the bunch, ain't no question about it."

Dave barked a laugh and wiped his eyes again. "Don't be ridiculous. Joe's got the grit I don't, Tammy is the strongest woman I've ever met, and you're the most motivated of the lot. You went away and did something with your life. Where does that leave me? I own a diner in the same town I grew up in. I don't really help anyone, like Joe does with his garage, I don't inspire anyone like Tammy does, and I don't have the courage to leave like you did. To me, I feel like I don't offer this town, or this family, anything of value. I feel like Dad, if he was alive, would be pretty disappointed with how I've chosen to live."

"Hey, don't say that," I said gently, squeezing his shoulder. "You don't have to prove anything to anyone. This town loves you, your family loves you, and I love you. You have no idea how special you are to the people around you. Everyone knows you, everyone talks about you, and everyone thinks you're a great person. Hell, I went to the hardware store the other day and I swear half the people there only knew me 'cause I was your brother. When people talk about you, they do it with a smile on their face. They always have, for as long as I can remember. Maybe you don't know it, but you bring warmth to those around you in a way I never could. And that's something special, Dave, and that's something Dad would be proud of."

Dave continued to stare at his hands, his voice sad but hopeful. "Yeah? You think so?"

"Of course I do," I said. "I love you, man. Don't ever think otherwise."

Dave sniffled and smiled. "Thanks, Cole."

"You don't got to thank me; I'm your brother."

Dave looked up at me and I saw hesitation wash over his face. "Can I ask you something?"

"Yeah?"

Dave bit his lip and looked unsure. "What exactly happened to you in New York?"

I was silent for a moment, his words opening a pit I wished to never look into again.

"Hey, you don't have to talk about it," Dave said hurriedly. "Ma just told me that something bad had happened to Maria and you were coming back home."

I slid my arm off his shoulders and stared straight ahead, fighting with myself. "It's OK…I just haven't talked about it since it happened."

"If it's too painful—" Dave started.

"It's alright, Dave," I said quietly, a tide rising in my chest. "You deserve to know." I took a deep breath and steadied my voice. "We were living together. We had an apartment, nothing special, but it was in the city. Every day was an exciting step into our new life. We were scared at first. Everything was so intimidating, but we learned how to get around, how to live, and we did it together. If felt like it was the two of us versus the world. We relied on one another to get through those hard days when we felt overwhelmed by it all. It was scary, yes, but we made each other brave, you know?"

I paused, the tide in my chest gurgling up my throat. I clenched my hands into fists. "One night we went out to dinner. It wasn't in the best part of town, but it had been recommended to us by a friend. One of those places that looks terrible on the outside, but the food is good."

I stopped and took a second to breathe. Dave stared at me, his face soft and concerned. He waited patiently for me to continue.

I gathered myself, each word growing heavier than the last. "Well, after we ate we were waiting on the check. Maria wanted to go outside to smoke a cigarette so I told her to go, I'll stay and pay. Didn't think anything of it.

"Well, after about ten minutes, the waiter finally came over and I paid the check. I put on my coat, stuffed my hands into my pockets, and went outside to retrieve Maria."

I felt my eyes welling up, the memory returning with picture-perfect clarity. Dave remained silent, but the pain I felt reflected in his own eyes.

"I-I went outside," I stammered, fighting against the horrific tide. "And I couldn't find her. I didn't know where she went. It was late and there weren't too many people out in this part of town. I turned around, looking for possible places she could have gone. Well, there was this alley a couple feet away, on the side of the restaurant. I thought maybe she ducked in there to smoke." I stared down at my lap and gritted my teeth, the first traces of tears finally escaping my eyes. "Fuck," I hissed, squeezing my eyes shut.

"Hey," Dave whispered. "It's OK, Cole. It's alright." The gentleness in his voice threatened to overwhelm me, but I continued, my own voice shaking with emotion.

"I went down the alley and at first I didn't see anything. But then...but then I saw these two men over by a dumpster. They were kinda hidden behind it, and I could see they were doing something. Concerned, I walked closer, and as I approached..." I let out a quivering sob, tears rolling down my face. "As I approached, I saw Maria. They had her pressed against the wall...and they...they..." I choked a cry and shook my head. "Goddamn it, Dave...they were *raping* her."

Dave's face melted and he shook his head, horrified. "Oh, my God, Cole..."

"One of them had his hands around her throat, holding her in place, while the other one...the other one *fucked* her," I sobbed. I placed my head in my hands and leaned over. "When they saw me, they froze. Maria's eyes were closed and it looked like she was unconscious. There was a cut along her forehead, a horrible bloody thing that leaked down her face."

Dave placed a hand on my back, his voice gentle and full of pain. "Cole..."

I closed my eyes behind my hands. "When they saw me, they ran. They just let her go and she fell against the dumpster like she was garbage to them." I cried harder, every word like a razor blade across my tongue. "And I just…stood there…and watched them go. I was frozen in place, too horrified and scared to even move. My breath billowed out in front of me like smoke in their wake. When I could move again, I went to Maria and cradled her in my arms. I started to cry, the reality of what I had just seen finally starting to grip my mind. There was so much blood. It ran through her hair, down her neck, between her naked thighs…and I couldn't wake her up, Dave…I couldn't wake her up…" I sobbed into my hands, shoulders shaking with relentless grief.

Dave clutched me tightly and I heard his voice crack with the same sadness I felt. "I'm so sorry, Cole. God, I'm so sorry. It's OK. I'm here. I'm right here with you." His hand rubbed my back and I continued to cry, the tide pouring out of my eyes like a hurricane.

"They never found the men who did it," I finally croaked, sitting up. "They're still out there somewhere. They get to keep on living and Maria…she…she doesn't…" I clenched my fists through tears. "It's not right, Dave…it's just not right."

"I can't imagine going through something like that," Dave said softly, lovingly. "I wish I could take your pain from you. If there was some way I could, I would without hesitation."

I looked at him and smiled, vision blurred. "You already are."

A hole opened between us, a swirling vortex into

which we both emptied our grief. Neither of us spoke for some time, allowing the absence of conversation to speak a language only shared by brothers.

I gathered myself, wiped my eyes, and righted the mental discomfort running through my psyche. I collected the memories I had just spilled and clumsily shoved them back into the far corners of my mind. After the exposure, I found that they fit just a little easier.

"Thank you for sharing that," Dave finally said.

I simply nodded, not looking at him. Dave smiled sadly. It was enough.

I went to stand, and as I did I felt my phone buzz in my pocket. Welcoming the distraction, I dug it out and answered.

"Hello?"

Joe's voice came in muffled and not quite right. "Hey…Cole. I need you to pick m-me up. If you're not…you know…*busy*."

I looked down at Dave and cocked an eyebrow. "Are you drunk?"

Joe snickered on the other end, his voice slurring. "Maybe a wee tad bit. Why? You goin' a call the cops?"

"Where are you?" I asked, running a hand over my flushed face.

"Tin Can."

"Christ," I breathed. "OK, yeah, I'll be there in a few. I'm just down the street at the church."

"Church?"

"See you in a minute, Joe." I hung up.

"Was that our dear brother?" Dave asked from the pew, smiling kindly.

I nodded. "Yeah, sounds like he's pretty plastered. He needs a ride."

"Want me to get him?" Dave offered.

"No, I got it. Appreciate it, though."

"Yeah."

I leaned down and grasped his shoulder. "Thank you, Dave."

Dave nodded, still smiling. "You, too."

I left my brother in the pew and retrieved my keys from my pocket. As I walked out of the sanctuary, I felt as if I were leaving something behind. Something that had been perched on my shoulders for a very long time, its claws digging deep into the fibers of my soul. I still felt the pain, I still cringed at the blood, but the source had seemed to vanish, if only for a little while.

The night was calm as I walked to my truck. I swung into the cab and headed for The Tin Can, thoughts of one brother departing only to be replaced by another.

A couple minutes later as I approached the local bar, I spotted Joe standing outside. He was leaning against the wall, idly smoking a cigarette. When he spotted me, he attempted to heave himself away from the wall, caught himself, steadied his balance, and approached as I pulled up alongside the curb.

He pulled open the passenger's-side door and

crawled inside, reeking of beer and smoke. He burped offensively and slung his eyes over at me.

"Thanks, man," he said with some effort, squinting. "I appreciate the lift."

"You OK?" I asked, half-amused, half-exhausted.

He nodded confidently. "Never better. You know…" he exhaled. "I've been doing some thinking."

"*Have* you now?"

He turned back to me, eyes slivers of glass. "Don't condescend to me, Cole."

I shrugged defensively. "Was just a question. What have you been thinking about?"

He scratched the stubble beneath his chin. "About this whole…Morrison situation."

"Oh?"

"Mhmm."

"Care to elaborate?" I pressed, checking my side mirror and pulling away from the bar.

"Well, maybe it's time to bury the hatchet," Joe said quietly, rolling down his window and lighting another cigarette.

I let him inhale before answering. "You think so?"

"Mhmm." Exhale.

"Are you talking about selling your garage?" I asked carefully.

Joe snorted. "Hell no. Would never give that place up. But"—inhale—"maybe they meant well when they stopped by the other night. Maybe Derek did send them, you know? It's most likely bullshit, I know that, you know that, but shit"—exhale—"Leo is a dumb kid. Maybe he did come by to offer protection. I asked the bartender, Jim, back at The Tin Can if he had seen Leo that night. Sure enough, he had."

"So what are you going to do?" I asked, gripping the wheel.

Joe ashed his cigarette out the window. "Drive me to Leo's. I want to take him up on his offer, see what he says."

I coughed violently, partly from the smoke, mostly out of disbelief. "What, *now*?! You want to go...now?"

Joe waved in my direction. "What better time than when I'm kinda fucked up? Might not have the fortitude tomorrow. Look, Cole, I don't want to spend the rest of the summer looking over my shoulder or wondering if my cars are getting busted up every second I'm not there. I want to settle this. Even if it's just a superficial gesture. I want them to know that I'm done fighting. I'm not giving up the place, but I need to offer some kind of truce."

"Jeez, I don't know. You sure about this?" I asked.

Joe nodded. "Yep. Take a left up here, I'll show you where Leo lives."

"You're just going to forgive and forget all this?" I asked, still not convinced.

Joe sighed wearily and took another drag from his smoke. "Look, man...I don't got a whole lot in this world. I need to make sure the little I do is protected.

Even if that means swallowing my pride and offering peace."

"I gotta say," I said, turning, "I'm impressed."

Joe stared out the window. "Yeah, well, don't get used to it."

I followed Joe's occasional grunt and gesture down the dark road, the single lane taking us deep into the woods away from Mill Valley. We rose up a rocky cliff side and then plummeted back into the claustrophobic forest. Joe mumbled to himself from his seat and I wondered what he would possibly say. My brother was a lot of things, but apologetic he was not. But as I watched him, I saw that his face had taken on a peaceful hue, around the drunkenness, and I felt honest pride that he was taking this step forward. I just hoped it was a truthful expression.

Ten minutes later we rolled down a long gravel driveway that snaked through a cluster of dark trees. An owl hooted somewhere in the distance and out of the gloom rose a shack, illuminated by dim yellow light.

"Stop here," Joe said, about fifty yards from the house. "And shut your lights off."

"Why?"

"'Cause I don't want him coming out guns blazing," Joe said, tossing his cig. "Let me walk the distance so I can at least talk to him without staring down the barrel of a gun."

"OK."

I turned off the lights and switched the truck off. The

house looked to be in rough condition, an old porch hanging from the front door like it was on life support. Garbage cluttered the front lawn, if you could call it that. Car parts littered the driveway. A stack of tires stood obediently by the stairs leading up the rickety porch.

Joe got out and looked at me. "Wish me luck. And keep your window rolled up. This is humiliating enough without you poking in."

"Be careful and be smart," I said as he got out, licking smoke from his lips.

"My head only got room for one of those," Joe said, winking.

I watched him approach the house, my own heart racing. He was a dark shadow that glided down the driveway, his boots crunching over the gravel. About ten yards from the truck, he froze. I sat up, alert, and saw a big black dog slink quietly from the porch and approach my brother.

"Shit," I hissed, debating whether to get out or not. The dog began to growl.

Joe stayed his ground and outstretched his hand to the animal. Despite my brother's instruction, I rolled down the window, eyes adjusting to the dark. I heard Joe speak quietly to the dog as it lurked closer. He kept his hand outstretched toward it. He slowly crouched down to its level.

I exhaled with relief as the dog reached Joe and began to nuzzle his hand, its growls subsiding.

Joe reached into his boot, pulled out a long hunting knife, and slit the animal's throat, ear to ear.

My eyes went wide and my mouth dropped open. I blinked in the cab, mind reeling at the sudden act of cruelty. *What the hell?!*

The dog let out a gurgling whimper and collapsed to the dirt. Joe held its head back and I saw blood as dark as midnight coat his hands. He stared into the dog's eyes as it died, a pitiful, pathetic departure from this world. When the animal stilled, Joe finally stood back up. He stared at Leo's shack, then back at the corpse. Still gripping the bloody knife, he returned to the truck.

"What the *fuck*!?" I hissed as he slid back inside the cab.

"Drive," he said darkly, staring straight ahead.

"Joe, what the hell just happened?!" I pleaded, bringing the truck to life.

Joe wiped the blade of the knife across his pants. "Changed my mind."

"You just killed his dog!" I cried, slamming the truck into reverse, turning around. I gunned the engine and took us roaring down the driveway back toward Mill Valley.

Joe looked at me from across the cab, a crooked smile on his lips. "I sure did."

He lit up another cigarette.

The blood from his hands turned the cigarette paper red.

Chapter 6

We were getting close to Mill Valley before I found my voice again. I simply could not believe what I had just witnessed. My mind tumbled over the sudden violence and I was horrified. I looked over at Joe who flicked his cigarette butt out the window and lit another.

"Why?" I asked, shaking my head. "Why the hell did you do that?"

Joe inhaled deeply, the blood drying on his knuckles. "Because someone has got to hold them accountable."

The wind ripped through the cab and I felt my eyes watering. "And so you thought the best way to get even was to kill Leo's dog?!"

"Seemed fitting."

I turned my attention back to the road. "Joe, you just kicked the hornet's nest. Do you really think they're just going to stop now?"

"They don't know it was me."

"Right," I said loudly, "just like you don't know it was them that busted your cars up."

Joe let the comment go unanswered and worked on

his cigarette. His face was calm and his eyes traveled across the landscape with mild disinterest.

"Jesus, man," I continued. "I honestly don't even know what to say to you."

"Finally."

"Oh, cut the SHIT!" I yelled, suddenly angry.

Joe turned to me, a darkness in his eyes. "I'm tired of being pushed around by them, Cole. This has been going on since before you came back. And it's time to dig my heels in and show them they can't keep doing this. I'm sick of it."

"And you really think *this* is the end of the line?" I cried. "Are you stupid?"

"No, Cole, I ain't stupid," Joe growled. "I'm fucking *mad*."

"You have no idea what you're doing, do you?" I asked, appalled.

"Thought I was headed back into town with my brother," Joe snarled. "But apparently I'm being taken to church to confess my sins."

"This isn't about morality!" I said, voice rising. "That's a whole other can of worms we're not even going to get into! This is about the repercussions of what you just did!"

"Enough of this," Joe said, turning back to the window. "I don't need a lecture from you right now. What's done is done. Just wish you'd have my back."

"Of course I have your back!" I stressed. "I will always have your back, no matter what, but please,

please try to keep your temper in check. I know it's not easy getting your cars smashed up, I get it, but doing this…it's not going to solve anything. OK? That's all I'm saying. I have no idea how Leo is going to take this, probably not well, but I'm there for you. Just…don't do something like this again."

"Sure."

I looked over at Joe frustrated but let the conversation die. He was angry and still kind of drunk. I had made about as much headway as I was going to tonight. I rolled down my window and exhaled heavily as we entered town.

We passed the church and I quietly sighed. "Hey…you're going to stay with me tonight."

I expected some pushback, but Joe just shrugged. "Fine."

"We'll pick up your truck at The Tin Can in the morning before we go to the garage for the day. Sound good?"

"That's fine, Cole."

"Alright."

We made it to my apartment without further conversation, the night growing long. Wearily, I parked my truck and headed inside and up the stairs with Joe in tow. We didn't say much when we got inside, but I pointed to the bathroom and suggested a shower. He complied without resistance. While he washed, I gathered a pillow, some blankets, and prepared the couch for him.

I went into my bedroom, feeling exhausted, and heard Joe turn the shower off. A couple minutes later he trudged out of the bathroom. Without saying a word, he collapsed on the couch and pulled the blankets over himself.

Satisfied, I climbed into bed and did the same. Sleep came easy and I sank into a dreamless slumber, a cool expanse of empty darkness.

I awoke the next morning to my phone ringing. Barely conscious, I pawed for it on the nightstand and brought it groggily to my ear.

"H'lo?"

My sister's voice chirped in my ear. "Cole? Are you still asleep? Did I wake you?"

I rubbed my face with my free hand. "What time is it?"

"It's nine-thirty."

"Shit."

"Did you oversleep?"

"Not really. What's up?"

"I'm taking Ma to the doctor this morning, but we're going to stop in and have breakfast with Dave at the diner first. You want to meet us there?"

I blinked at the clock and saw that it was indeed nine-thirty. "Uh…yeah. Sure. Is everything OK with Ma? Why is she going to the doctor?"

"She's fine, it's just a checkup."

"Then why are you going?"

"Just to make sure."

"Make sure of what?"

"That everything is fine, Cole. Go splash some water on your face and wake up. We'll see you in a little bit."

"OK. Bye."

I hung up and put the phone down. I lay on my back and stared up at the ceiling, gathering my thoughts for the day. I craned my neck and looked out the bedroom door. Joe remained asleep on the couch. Good.

After a moment, I heaved myself up and padded into the living room. I stared down at Joe and nudged his leg.

"Hey."

Joe stirred and creaked his eyes open. "Huh? What's up?"

"Tammy and Ma are going over to the diner. Wanna come? We can pick up your truck after at The Tin Can."

Joe rubbed his eyes. "What time is it?"

"Nine-thirty."

"Shit."

"That's what I said. Now, you coming?"

Joe groaned. "Sure, sure."

"Then get up."

"I'm up."

"I'm looking at you and you're definitely not up."

"Oh, piss off, will you? Give a man a second to open his eyes. Shit."

I turned away. "After we pick up your truck I'm going to follow you back to the garage. It's time I finished that paint job."

"You sure you want to?" Joe asked, sitting up and staring at the floor.

"Why wouldn't I?" I asked, walking back into the bedroom. I began to dress. I needed some coffee.

Joe shrugged from the couch. "I dunno. You seemed pretty mad last night."

I pulled on my socks. "I don't want to talk about last night."

"Suits me," Joe mumbled, reaching for his boots.

When we were ready, we marched downstairs and out into the sunlight. I winced against the bright rays and shielded my eyes with my hand. Joe lowered his head and strutted across the street toward the diner. I followed, half-walking, half-trotting.

We reached the other side of the road and went inside, the doors expelling delicious aromas as we opened them. I scanned the tables for my family and saw Dave sitting in his corner, a cup of coffee in hand. His face lit up when he saw the two of us, and we walked over.

"Weren't expecting to see you guys this morning," he smiled as Joe and I slid into the booth.

"Cole twisted my arm," Joe said, looking around.

"Tammy called," I explained. "Figured we'd grab some breakfast before heading over to the garage."

"Oh, yeah? And how's that coming?" Dave asked, taking a hesitant sip from his mug.

Joe waved a waitress over before answering. "Not bad. Place is shaping up."

"Got a ways to go," I said. "But we're making progress."

Dave's eyes shifted between Joe and myself. "No, uh…further problems with the Morrisons?"

Before I could answer, Joe curtly shook his head. "Nope." I let the statement lie on the table for Dave to examine as he saw fit. The waitress hustled over and Joe ordered a pot of coffee for the table. After doing so, we heard Ma and Tammy arrive. I turned and waved to them and they joined us in the booth.

Ma beamed as she sat down, sliding in next to Dave with Tammy. "What a surprise it is to see both of you!"

"Hi, Ma," Joe said, smiling sheepishly.

She reached out and grasped his hands in hers. "It's good to see you, dear. I feel like it's always too long."

Joe shrugged and almost blushed. "Ah, you know how it is at the garage. Can never seem to pull myself away."

"Well, you should make more of an effort," Tammy scolded, pouring a cup of coffee for Ma and herself. "There's no excuse when you live just a handful of miles away."

"Oh, it's OK," Ma said, smiling softly and staring across the table at Joe and me. "I'm just glad all my children are here right now."

"Did you order yet?" Tammy asked across the table.

I shook my head. "Nope. We were waiting for you two."

"Because you're such a pair of gentlemen," Dave chuckled.

"We try our best," Joe said.

"When's the last time you shaved, Mr. Manners?" Dave goaded.

"Watch it, buddy," Joe warned without any real weight.

The waitress came back and we all ordered. Our conversation flowed back to the garage and all the progress we were making. Joe and I were careful to avoid mention of the Morrisons or the dark deed last night. I finally steered us away from the topic around the time the food came and we all dug in. Forks clanked, toast crunched, and ice-cold water was slurped down through clear straws. It felt good to eat a meal with my family, with everyone present. It was comforting, in a way, knowing that everyone I cared most about was gathered before me at one table. I smiled at that thought and stuffed down the last of my eggs.

"I don't know where your cook learned to make eggs," Joe said, pushing his plate away and burping offensively. "But it sure wasn't from you, Davey. That shit was fantastic."

Dave rolled his eyes. "I think you'd have a stroke if you ever said anything nice to me."

I placed a hand on Joe's arm, my eyes wide. "Hey…go easy…the boy is sensitive." Tammy snickered and I saw Ma grin behind her napkin.

Joe's voice was dry. "Oh, my God…I had no idea…how long has he had it? The sensitivity?"

I exhaled dramatically. "His whole life, I'm afraid."

"What a tragedy," Joe said gravely. He looked at Dave, who had his face buried in his hands. "I didn't know…I'm very sorry. Are you on anything for it?"

"Yeah, I give out one of these twice a day," Dave said, flipping us off.

Tammy laughed and reached out to squeeze his shoulder. "Oh, don't be sore, these two idiots are just jealous you get to work in the air conditioning all day."

"Is that part of his condition?" Joe asked.

Dave puffed his chest out proudly and ran a finger slowly across his forehead. "Not a single bead of sweat can touch this handsome brow."

It was my turn to laugh as Dave smiled and deflated. "You know, Dave, for as much shit as we give you, you sure do take it in stride."

"That's because he's a sweet boy," Ma said, patting Dave's leg.

Dave grinned evilly. "That's right, Ma…keep spreading that rumor. One day Cole and Joe are going to wake up to me holding a pillow over their faces."

"If you're going to do it, make it soon," Joe said, draining the rest of his coffee. "'Cause I got shit to do."

"You're so *tough*," Tammy laughed. "Where do you keep all that courage, Joe?"

Joe reached under the table and grabbed his crotch. "I manage to stuff it into my pants every morning."

Ma threw her hands up. "OK, that's enough! Gross! Can we please refrain from that talk at the table?"

I laughed and playfully smacked Joe across the back of the head. "Yeah, what's wrong with you?"

"His stones are only outweighed by his vulgarity," Dave mocked.

"Boys!" Ma pleaded.

Tammy lightly pounded the table. "OK, cut it out, you bunch of animals. I gotta take Ma to the doctor."

"Everything OK?" Joe asked, suddenly concerned.

Ma rolled her eyes. "Oh, yes, I'm fine. No one's dying today. Just going in for a checkup and your sister thinks I'm going to pass out on the way like the frail mermaid that I am."

"Mermaid?" Tammy asked, cocking an eyebrow.

Ma turned to her. "Oh…oh no…that must be the dementia kicking in…I'm confusing my analogies again."

Dave laughed and I joined him. Even Joe cracked a smile. Tammy slid from the booth and Ma followed. Before any of us could stop her, she threw down a stack of twenties.

"Ma, come on, you don't need to do that," Dave said, taking the money and holding it out for her.

"Of course I do!" Ma said, brushing bread crumbs from her shirt. "I ate, didn't I?"

"Yeah, but—" Dave started.

"It's OK, David," Ma said, smiling warmly. "Take the money."

Dave bashfully curled it back into his fist.

"Now," Ma said, standing straight. "You boys have a wonderful day and I'll see you all soon, OK?"

"Absolutely," I said.

"Of course," Dave chimed.

Ma turned to Joe. "Right?"

Joe looked up at her and almost blushed. "Yeah, of course, Ma. Take care, OK?"

Ma beamed and looked at Tammy. "Shall we?"

"Yeah, come on," Tammy said, taking Ma by the arm. As they walked out, Tammy looked back at us and I mouthed a thank-you to her. She winked as she opened the door for Ma, taking them outside.

"You two lowlifes headed out as well?" Joe asked.

"I reckon we should," Joe said, stretching. "You ready, Cole?"

"Yeah, let's go," I said, pushing Joe out of the booth.

Dave looked up at us. "Alright, see you guys."

I tipped an invisible hat to him and followed Joe out of the diner. Joe decided to just walk down the street to retrieve his truck, and I assured him I'd meet him at the garage in a little bit. I ran across the street and pulled my keys out. I unlocked my truck and got in, bringing the engine to a grumbling start. I looked at myself in the mirror and when I was satisfied, I pulled out onto Main Street.

As I passed The Tin Can I spotted Joe approaching his vehicle and gave him a wave he didn't see. I cranked the window open and leisurely rolled down the road, belly full and successfully energized for the day. The events of the previous night seemed like a bad dream, and the cheerful breakfast washed away some of the lingering anxiety I had about the whole thing.

The town peeled by like a poorly made comic strip, and soon I was through it and zipping down the single-lane street. The trees threw shade across the windshield in thick columns of shadow. Cicadas sang loudly from all sides and the glaring sun winked down at me between a blanket of forest overhead. By the time I reached the garage, the collar of my shirt was damp. It was going to be humid today and I felt the familiar wetness in the air as I parked my truck. Joe pulled in soon after and I met him amidst a swirl of dust and grime. He wiped his hands on his jeans as he got out of his truck and appraised me.

"Thanks for sticking with me on this," he said suddenly.

No explanation was needed and I simply nodded. Satisfied, he went to the bay doors and unlocked them for the day's work. I followed him inside and went to my corner of paint supplies. I began uncovering everything, taking stock of what I had and how I was going to proceed for the day. After a couple minutes, the two of us were lost beneath the lull of physical labor.

Chapter 7

I stumbled wearily up the stairs to my apartment. I checked my watch and saw that it was a little after eight already. I had almost finished painting the entirety of the garage, and the exhausting crawl toward completion had left me drained. I fumbled with my keys and pushed my way inside. I went to my bedroom and peeled off my shirt, tossing it carelessly to the floor. Content to leave it off, I exited the room and went to get a glass of water from the kitchen sink.

As I entered the living room, I froze. The shadow of a man sat in the chair across from me, his features hidden. Paralyzed, I didn't move, my heart leaping into my throat.

The man stood slowly, his voice soothing in the dim light. "Hey there, Cole."

My hand shot out and flicked the light switch on.

Derek.

My stomach turned in on itself and I remained motionless, frozen by his unexpected presence. Derek stood across from me, his hands resting casually at his sides. He had on a ball cap that was pulled high up on his head. His eyes twinkled merrily as they met mine.

"Didn't mean to scare ya, chief," he said softly, grinning, "but I figured I'd wait for you up here where it's a little cooler. Hope you don't mind."

I finally found my voice again. "W-what the hell are you doing here?"

Derek hooked his thumbs in his pockets and rocked on the heels of his boots. "Why, I was waiting for you, just like I said."

"What do you want?" I stammered, trying to calm my racing heart.

Derek took a step toward me. "Hey, relax, would you? Shee-it, you look like you've seen a ghost or something. Well, take a breath, I ain't no ghost. Least I don't think I am." He cracked a grin. "Wouldn't that be something though, huh?"

"Yeah, I guess it would," I agreed, not knowing what else to say.

"You want a drink of water or something? I really didn't mean to startle you like that. I won't be here long; I just needed a word with you."

"OK…yeah, some water," I said. Derek smiled and walked into the kitchen. I followed, feeling like I was in a dream. Something tickled my spine and I sensed the danger behind it.

Derek filled up a glass at the sink and slid it across the counter toward me. "There you go, chief."

I picked up the glass and drained the contents. I

placed it back down and wiped my mouth, looking up at the intruder, waiting.

"Better?" Derek asked soothingly.

"Sure."

Derek nodded. "Good. That's good." He slowly pulled his shirt up to reveal a pistol stuffed into his waistband. In one smooth motion, he took it and placed it on the counter. My knees locked up and despite the water, I felt my mouth go dry.

"Don't mind that," Derek said casually. "It was just getting a little uncomfortable resting against my jewels."

"What the hell do you want?" I said carefully.

Derek kept his hand on the butt of the gun as he spoke. "We need to talk about a little incident that happened at my brother Leo's house last night."

I tried to keep my face neutral. "Oh?"

Derek eyed me as he scratched his chin. "Uh-huh…you see, somebody came along and killed his dog. Slit the poor thing's throat and left it in the driveway to die. Awful thing. Really awful thing."

"That's terrible," I said quietly. "Sorry to hear that."

"Mhmm," Derek continued, his finger rubbing the grip of the pistol. "I appreciate you saying that. You see, though…there's this one thing that just bugs the tar out of me and I can't seem to shake it."

"And what would that be?"

Derek looked directly at me. "Who would do something like that?"

I focused on breathing. "I don't know, Derek. I really don't."

"'Cause you see," Derek plowed on. "The only person I know who has anything against Leo would be your brother Joe. I mean, even you have to admit, there's no love lost between those two firecrackers."

"Joe wouldn't do something like that," I said firmly.

Derek smiled but it never reached his eyes. "Of course he wouldn't."

"Look, I think you should probably go," I insisted.

Derek continued to rub the gun on the counter, his fingers tracing the length of it. "Cole...I've always considered you the smart one of your family. Sure, Tammy's smart, but shit, she's a woman."

"The fuck does that m—" I started, but Derek held up a hand, silencing me.

"Hold up. Let me finish."

I waited.

"Tammy ain't the type to think with her head. She thinks with her heart. Your brother Dave...well...that boy's about as soft as mashed potatoes. And Joe? Shit, I don't need to say anything 'bout him. But you, Cole...you seem to be the glue that keeps everyone together. Your family looks up to you and listens to you. That's why I'm here, talking to you, instead of asking Joe himself. Because you know how to look out for your family, not just with your heart, but with your head, as well."

"So what?" I said quietly. "What are you saying, Derek?"

"I'm saying, I'm giving you one chance, and one chance only, to 'fess up. Did Joe kill Leo's dog last night?"

"Of course he didn't, why w—" I said quickly, but again, Derek cut me off.

"Before you answer…let me tell you something. Something you aren't going to want to hear, but I reckon you need to. I don't want you to talk, so just listen." Derek straightened and his eyes grew dark. "Your brother Joe ain't a nice guy. I know you been gone a while and you might be clinging to the memory of him as you left him. But he ain't the same anymore. Now, I see the doubt in your eye, I do, so let me explain. Did he ever tell you how he came about that garage? No? I didn't think so. Well, let me inform you.

"Three years ago—after you left, of course—my brothers and I were fixing to start a life. An honest life. We had been bumming around doing odd jobs for folks and we were sick of it. We wanted to do something that was ours. That we could own. That we could control. What we wanted was that garage. We had seen it up for sale and before your brother even approached the owner, we were set to buy it."

"So you could cook in it?" I interrupted.

Derek glared at me. "No, Cole, not to cook in. Let's not bullshit here since it's just you and me. I'm going to be straight with you. This was before we got into that business. We were clean and we were looking to make an honest life. That's why we wanted the garage. And everything was going smooth as butter before your brother Joe came along. You see, he wanted it, too, but the owner had practically promised it to me first. Well, Joe couldn't handle that, oh no. He wasn't about to be outdone by a Morrison. That'd just be too much salt in the wound for him. Your brother never liked us, and with good reason. I'm not an idiot, I remember the bully I was as a child as I'm sure you do. But shit, Cole, that was years ago. We were kids. Kids do stupid shit. Everyone grows up and leaves that in the past where it belongs. But not Joe. No, not ol' Joe. He hated us. He always has. I understand that. Some people can't forgive. That's fine, I wasn't asking him to. All I was asking was that he stay out of my business and let me and my brothers get on with our lives and try to make something of ourselves.

"Obviously we don't own the garage presently, so what happened, Cole? Just what the hell happened?"

I shrugged, eyes growing hard. "I don't know, Derek. You messed it up?"

Derek smiled widely. "Not this time. No sir, not this time." He stepped forward and suddenly the pistol was in his hand. "No, you see, what happened was Joe got in the ear of the owner. Oh, he whispered all kinds of awful things about us Morrisons. Told them we were into drugs, that we were violent people and nothing but trouble. What a busy little bee Joe was, buzzing with all kinds of lies and filth about me and my brothers. And you know the kicker? The owner believed him. He fucking believed him. The next day he notified me that our offer had been rejected and the garage had been sold. Guess who bought it?" Derek suddenly slammed the pistol down on the counter, causing me to jump. "Ding ding ding! You are correct, sir! Why, it was your good brother, Joe! How about that shit, huh? How-about-that-shit."

I slowly took a step away from Derek. "Look, even if that's true, it's just bad luck. Hell, how do you even know Joe spoke to the owner?"

The smile was gone from Derek's face. "How? I'll tell you how. Because a few days later I caught wind of a rumor floating around town that my brothers and I were selling drugs. Can you believe that? Can you fucking believe that? You drop a juicy lie into a small town dying of thirst and they will drink it all up and vomit it back out. I started noticing that people were giving me dirty looks on the street. People were avoiding me. People were treating me different, Cole."

"You sure that wasn't paranoia?" I asked, keeping an eye on the gun.

Derek shook his head, eyes burning. "No, Cole, it wasn't paranoia. It was hatred. Hatred for my brothers and hatred for me. Our family name got dragged through the mud and your brother was holding the rope. So what the hell was I supposed to do? I never went to college; hell, I never even finished high school.

I didn't have a lot of options and the one I had been counting on got taken away from me. Not only that, but where were we supposed to get work now that we'd been labeled as bad news? Nowhere. No one would hire us. Well, let me tell you, it ain't a pleasant thing staring down the barrel of life and knowing that forces outside your control had already cocked the hammer back.

"But you know what we did, Cole? You know what we did instead of curling up and crying about it?" Derek gripped the gun tightly. "We became the thing they accused us of. Shit, the damage was already done, why not make a buck from it? My brothers were in just the same position as I was and it didn't take much convincing. We knew people and it wasn't difficult jump-startin' our new enterprise. In six months' time, we were in business. And man…business was good."

"That doesn't make it right," I said quietly.

"Course it don't," Derek said darkly. "But it makes sense."

I cleared my throat. "So what is this all really about? All this bullshit with the garage, all the threats and back-and-forth. What do you expect to happen?"

Derek advanced on me and poked me hard in the chest. "I expect your brother to make this right."

"What's done is done, Derek, let it go," I said, standing my ground. "Nothing good is going to come of this if this spat continues."

Derek leaned down into my face, a slow smile parting his lips. "Oh, you couldn't be more right. Because

Joe just can't let sleeping dogs lie. He's got to grab them by their ears and slit their fucking throats, too."

"He didn't do that," I hissed. "And even if he did, your brother smashed his cars."

Derek's face towered over mine. "Do you know who bought Leo that dog? I did. I got it for him when it was just a little pup. Cutest damn thing in the world. Leo loved that animal, as did I. Oh, how he loved that animal. But now it's dead and Leo is in pieces about it. Someone came along and cut out a piece of my brother's heart and it's left him devastated."

"Get to the point," I said, steeling myself.

Derek's breath hissed between clenched teeth. "Your brother started something that is now out of my control. I came here tonight hoping to get a straight answer from you, but I can see that ain't happening. Because you and me? We're the rocks of our family. We hold a degree of influence over our siblings. But after my talk here with you tonight, I see no reason to say anything positive to them about you or your family. So Joe's just going to have to deal with that."

"Are you threatening my brother?" I growled.

Derek leaned away from me finally, but his eyes remained ablaze. "Joe hurt my family. He hurt them bad. We all are feeling the repercussions of his actions. I think it's time for Joe to hurt, too."

We glared at each other like mountains in the night.

Derek stuffed his gun back into his pants. "I think it's time for me to leave."

"What the hell are you going to do?" I demanded.

Derek pushed past me and opened my apartment door.

"Stop!" I called after him. "What the hell are you going to do?"

Derek paused at the door and looked back, his voice heavy with hatred. "Watch yourself out there, Cole."

And then he was gone, the door slamming loudly in his wake. I stood for a moment, chest heaving. My ears rang from Derek's departure. My throat tore beneath my breath. Then a singular thought exploded through my head like dynamite.

Oh, shit.

I went for my cell and called Joe. I paced back and forth across the living room, praying my brother would answer. After a moment, he did.

"Joe!" I almost yelled.

"What's going on, Cole?"

I ran a hand through my hair and then down my face. "I think shit is about to hit the fan."

"What are you talking about?"

I anxiously rubbed my chin. "Derek was just here. He was in my apartment. He knows, Joe."

A pause, then: "How?"

"Come on, did you ever expect otherwise?"

"Did you say something?"

"Of course not!"

Joe sighed heavily. "Goddamn it."

"You knew this was going to happen."

"What did he say?"

I adjusted the phone against my ear. "That he's coming for you. You're not safe, Joe."

"You sure he was serious?"

"You should have seen his eyes," I said, still pacing. "He was serious."

"Why the hell was he at your place?"

"He said he wanted to talk. He wanted me to confess to killing Leo's dog. Or rather, that you did it. Obviously, I denied it."

"But he didn't buy it?"

"No, he knew. He knows." I stopped walking and lowered my voice. "Joe, why didn't you tell me about the garage? Is it true?"

"Is what true?"

I chose my words carefully. "That you...*convinced*...the original owner that the Morrisons were into some bad shit? Did you lie so you could buy the place instead of them?"

I could almost hear Joe bristle. "Of course I didn't lie. Jesus, anyone who's known them for five minutes knows they're nothing but trouble. All I did was remind the owner of that fact before he sold out to them."

"Oh, Jesus, Joe," I whispered, closing my eyes.

"Don't get fucking righteous with me," Joe growled.

My eyes snapped open. "Did you ruin them?"

"They ruined themselves a long time ago. People just seemed to forget that fact and so I reminded them of it. Christ, whose side are you on?!" Joe yelled.

"Yours!" I yelled back. "But what the *fuck*!?"

"They didn't have to get into the drug business after their deal went south. That was their choice. People suffer bad luck all the time; that doesn't mean they have to start breaking the law and ruining people's well-being."

I let that statement hang in the dead air between us.

"What do you want from me, Cole?" Joe finally asked, sounding tired.

"I want to keep my brother safe," I said quietly. "What's done is done. I just wanted the whole story."

"Yeah, well, sorry for being such a huge disappointment," Joe mumbled.

"I'm not here to judge you," I sighed. "You're my brother and I'm with you. I'm just worried about your safety right now. The Morrisons are pissed, and you're the source of their rage. That's not a great combination. I want you to come over to my place for a couple days."

Joe exhaled heavily like he had a great weight on his chest. "Yeah…that's probably a good idea."

"Want me to pick you up?"

"No. I'll come over tomorrow. It's late, they're not going to do anything tonight. If at all. Shit, what a mess, huh?"

"Yeah," I said quietly. "What a mess."

"You think we should tell everyone else?"

"You mean the rest of the family?"

"Yeah."

I nodded. "It's probably best we do. Ma is going to

be so worried. Let's wait until we can see them face-to-face. We'll meet up with them tomorrow."

"The County Fair rolls into Mill Valley tomorrow morning. I'll tell Ma, Tammy, and Dave that we all wanna go. We'll break it to them there."

"Perfect."

"I'll see you tomorrow then," Joe said.

"Yeah, tomorrow. Stay safe. If you suspect anything, please call me right away, OK?"

Joe chuckled suddenly. "And what would you do, Cole?"

"Whatever I had to."

———————

Mill Valley was a bustle of activity the following morning. The police closed Main Street to traffic around noon as the County Fair set up shop. I watched from my apartment window as booths were built, food carts were rolled out, and tents were popped. The whole town seemed to be abuzz with anticipation, and I couldn't blame them. Nothing exciting really happened around here and the arrival of a fair was big news. I watched as an array of rides were carelessly built by bored-looking crew members. A small Ferris wheel, a Whiplash, and a merry-go-round among them. Cotton candy machines were parked, balloons were inflated, and the festivities stretched down the length of the street.

Children stood by their parents and watched from behind the police barrier, their eyes wide. They bounced excitedly and pointed at all the things they wanted to partake in later that night. I checked my watch. They wouldn't open the rides until around five, and it was only two now. I opened the window and breathed in the aromas below. Grilled hot dogs, charcoal, sugar, and popcorn. The smell brought back a flurry of memories that I allowed myself to examine.

Dad had taken us to the fair once. It had been strikingly similar to this one. Cheap rides, greasy food, blinking lights, and the scream of delighted children. I smiled to myself. I remembered Dave had gotten sick on the Whiplash and thrown up his ice cream cone seconds after he got off. Joe and I had laughed uproariously, while Tammy comforted him and scolded us. Dad and Ma had been on the Ferris wheel at the time, oblivious that their son was puking his guts out below.

I remembered how Dad and Ma held hands almost the entire evening.

I remembered Joe grinning, his lips coated blue from cotton candy.

I remembered buying Dave another ice cream cone and telling him it was OK that he had thrown up.

I remembered winning a giant stuffed dog for Tammy at some sideshow.

I sighed and turned away from the window, heart heavy.

That was a long time ago.

I needed to call Joe.

We ended up meeting my family around seven that night at the door of my apartment. Joe arrived last which made me nervous. He strolled around the building and was greeted with enthusiasm. I hugged him a little tighter than the rest.

Dave seemed the most excited about the fair as the five of us walked onto Main Street into the thick of things. Parents hollered at their kids, excited squeals of delight echoed from the rides around us, and the road stretched out like a buffet of cheap delights. I couldn't help but share some of Dave's boyish wonder as I walked shoulder-to-shoulder with Ma and Tammy. Joe was ahead of us with Dave, the two of them pointing to the lights and food stands, allowing themselves to get lost in it all.

Ma lovingly placed a hand on my back. "This was a wonderful idea."

At my other shoulder, Tammy laughed. "How often does the fair come into town? We'd be crazy to miss it. Do you see that Ferris wheel?"

"Oh, I see it," I smiled, staring up at the rickety construction as it lazily spun in place. Green and yellow lights blinked from the swaying gondolas and I said a silent prayer that the ride wouldn't collapse.

The sinking sun fell behind growing clouds and the

night glowed neon as the fair illuminated the street with a rainbow of color. A little girl bumped into me as she chased her brother toward the Whiplash, giggling and begging him to slow down. I smiled and Tammy nudged my shoulder with hers.

"Look familiar?"

I placed my hand around her shoulders. "No way. I always waited for you."

Ma chuckled at my side. "Not the way I remember it. You and Joe were so excited when we went all those years ago that you left your poor sister in the dust. Took your father the better part of ten minutes to find you in the crowd."

"I don't remember that," I said, grinning. "Where were we going?"

"Standing in line to get cotton candy," Ma said, throwing me a wink.

"You know what I think the best part of all this is?" Tammy said fondly.

"What would that be?" Ma asked.

"The music," Tammy snickered. I laughed with her and beneath the rumble of noise, I picked out a depressing circus tune that whined above the crowd like a grouchy toddler.

"Yeah, I think I need to get this track," I stated, shaking my head.

"It wouldn't feel the same without the music," Ma said gently. "It really brings back some good memories. Memories of your father."

I tenderly put my arm around my mother and squeezed her close. "Some of my best ones."

We continued to stroll down the street, still following Dave and Joe. Despite the grim news I had given him last night, Joe seemed oddly at peace. Almost happy. They stopped eventually at an ice cream stand and Dave bought us all chocolate cones. Joe insisted that he get sprinkles on his.

Content and licking away at the sweet cream, the five of us stood in a circle as the crowd flowed around us like a current of sugar-charged electricity.

"How are those sprinkles?" Dave asked.

Joe took a satisfying lick. "Wouldn't want it any other way. You all are animals eating that shit plain."

"They don't add any flavor," Tammy stated, rubbing shoulders with Dave and me.

Joe's eyes widened. "You take that back."

"I'm with Joe on this one," Ma laughed. "I'm kind of regretting not getting any on mine."

Joe wiped his chin and quickly stuck his cone out to Ma. "Here, take mine. I think I've had enough anyway."

"Oh, no honey, you go on ahead," Ma said, shaking her head.

Joe plucked Ma's cone from her hand and replaced it with his. "I insist, Mother."

Ma took a nibble and her face bloomed with happiness. "Thank you, Joey."

A breeze stirred the air as Joe made eye contact with me.

I licked chocolate from my lips and sighed wearily. I did not want to ruin this night. I looked up and Joe continued to stare at me expectantly.

"What's going on?" Ma asked, sensing the change.

Tammy looked from Joe to myself, her brow furrowed. "Yeah, what just happened? Why the sudden long face?"

"Joe and I need to tell you something," I said.

"OK…?" Tammy said confused.

"Should I tell them or do you want to?" I asked Joe. Joe looked at his boots.

I sighed and looked around the circle of faces. Each one held worry and anticipated fear. I lowered my voice and began to explain what had been going on. I told them about the cars getting smashed. I told them about Leo arriving the next night. I explained the confrontation and how they were pushing Joe to a breaking point. I heavily favored my brother as I went through the events of the days prior. As I did, I saw my mother's face tense and then practically crack with concern.

And then I told them about the dog.

But I twisted the story just slightly. I told them that on the way up to Leo's house, the dog had attacked Joe and he had no choice but to kill it. Joe didn't look at me as I explained this.

Dave's ice cream cone sat forgotten in his hand, chocolate rivers running down his fingers as I recounted the night at Leo's and how we had driven off in a panic. Tammy shook her head, muttering under her breath. Her brow furrowed and I could tell she was worried.

"But that's not the end of it," I continued quietly. "Derek came to my apartment last night."

I saw Tammy's fists clench. "He didn't hurt you, did he?"

"No, he just wanted to talk."

"What'd he say?" Dave asked softly.

I took a moment and studied their faces. "I think they're going to try and hurt Joe."

"Oh, Lord, watch over us," Ma whispered, her fingers nervously twiddling.

"I'm staying with Cole for a while," Joe finally said, looking up. "Just to be safe. I don't know how serious they are about doing me harm, but there's no sense in taking chances."

"Good," Dave said, nodding. "That's good. With the two of you together, especially right here in town, I don't think they'd try anything."

"That's the idea," I said. "And over the next few weeks I want all of you to be careful, as well. This spat is between Joe and the Morrisons, but I wouldn't put it past them to start screwing around with you all. I'm not trying to scare you, but you should be cautious."

"I'll stay at Ma's for the rest of the week," Dave volunteered. Ma lovingly smiled at him.

"What about you?" I asked Tammy.

She glared at Joe. "You sure you didn't have any choice but to kill that dog?"

Joe met her eyes. "That thing was going to rip my throat out, Tam."

Tammy looked at me and I nodded, hating myself. "I was there. The thing was rabid."

"Alright...God, how the hell did it get to this?" she asked, sounding tired.

I placed a hand on her shoulder. "Do you want to stay with me and Joe for a while? Just to be on the safe side?"

Tammy shook her head. "No...I been thinking about taking a trip up north for a while. Maybe New York. See what all the fuss is about. Seems like as good a time as any."

"That'd be good," I said. "Leave soon."

"I will."

"Can't we go to the sheriff?" Ma offered, her voice pleading.

I shook my head. "And tell him what? Nothing has happened."

"Derek broke into your home!"

"It's my word against his. And who do you think he'll side with?"

"It's just not right; someone has to hold those boys accountable if something happens!" Ma cried. I could tell she was beginning to fray, the thought of her son in danger tipping her mental scales.

"I'm going to be with him," I assured. "He'll be safe. And like I just said, nothing has happened. Maybe nothing will. This could all be over by tomorrow once tempers have cooled. We're just being careful."

"But the police have—" Ma started, but I cut her off.

"They're useless to us, Ma. It's not right, but that's how it is. We all know it. Sure, the sheriff and his police force might keep order around town, but when it comes to his boys, he might as well be blind."

"He's right," Dave said softly.

"Goddamn it," Tammy muttered, biting her lip.

Joe suddenly stepped into the center of the circle, eyes downcast. He cleared his throat and addressed us all, his voice thin. "I'm sorry about this. I didn't mean for shit to get so out of hand."

Ma went to him and hugged him tightly. "You have always sniffed out trouble, Joey. But you always get yourself out of it. Everything is going to be OK. You'll see. This will blow over and in a couple weeks it'll be like nothing happened. The Morrisons aren't the kindest family, but they're not stupid. What happened was an accident. They have to understand that. And if you need anything at all, we're here for you. Remember that."

"Yeah, we got your back," Dave said, sliding an arm around Joe's shoulders.

"You call me if you need anything, Joe," Tammy said, hugging him.

Joe looked up at me and an unspoken darkness passed between our eyes.

My voice turned to gravel. "We're going to see this through to the end."

Chapter 8

Four days passed. They felt like the longest days of my life. At every moment, I felt as if someone was watching me, studying my life. I felt as if my own shadow would turn on me. Every night I would wake up, sure I had heard someone break in. I'd jolt out of bed, heart racing, and listen for any sound. But always, nothing.

I couldn't even imagine how bad the paranoia was for Joe. We didn't talk about it during those four days. What little conversation we had was about the garage or our family. We never addressed the vultures that circled overhead behind the clouds. We continued to work at the garage because we had to. Because life couldn't just come to a screeching halt. With the paint job done, I began to power-wash the exterior. With every car that pulled up during those four days, I expected the Morrisons along with a crew of their people. But they remained ghosts in our lives. It was unsettling. I hadn't encountered or even seen any of the brothers since my conversation with Derek. I had seen their father, the sheriff, a couple times, but always in passing. He never even looked at me.

On the fifth day, a Saturday, Ma invited us all over for dinner. She insisted. So after Joe and I finished our work for the day, we drove over together. The night sky had grown cloudy as a summer storm stirred the air. A warm wind rustled the grassland and the trees cried out, a creaking wail beneath the first flashes of heat lightning. The road hummed beneath my truck as Joe and I silently drove into the night. Joe looked tired. Dark bags hung beneath his eyes and he hadn't shaved in a couple days, giving him a ragged look. He chain-smoked all the way to Ma's, never saying a word.

When we pulled into Ma's, the lightning overhead began to grumble. Rolling walls of thunder echoed ominously from the horizon and the wind continued to stir up dust. I shielded my eyes from it as I got out of the truck and walked to the front door. Joe heeled the butt of his cig and followed, hands shoved deep into his pockets. I reached the porch and looked back at my brother. He stared at the ground and walked slowly, his mouth pulled down into a frown. He reached my side and looked up at me.

"You cool?" I asked.

Joe looked out across the dark fields. "Yeah…I'm cool."

The two of went inside, shutting the front door behind us. Dave and Ma met us with morbid smiles and tender hugs. The house was lit up against the storm outside, but despite the glow, this sanctuary lacked the warmth it once held for me. The smell of food from the kitchen tickled my nose, but my stomach rolled at the thought. Everything felt off. Everything felt…silent.

"Did you two have a good week?" Ma asked, leading us into the kitchen.

Joe mumbled something and took a seat at the kitchen table, his legs splayed out in front of him. Dave handed him a beer, which he sipped absently. I thought about sitting but decided I would feel restless if I did. I stood by the fridge and Dave poured me a shot of whiskey. He offered one to Joe, who declined with a shake of the head. I drank mine gratefully.

"When did Tammy leave?" I asked, the liquor burning in my chest.

"Three days ago," Ma said from the stove.

"She ended up going to New York?"

Ma never turned from the stove, but I heard her voice tremble slightly as she spoke. "I think so. When we parted ways after the fair, I could tell she was deeply bothered by this whole situation. She's been with me here her whole life. I always knew she wanted to get away from this town and that I was holding her back. I'm glad she went."

Joe drained the rest of his beer, shadows falling across his face.

"Things have been OK here?" I asked Dave.

He nodded. "Yeah, no problems. I haven't even seen the Morrisons this week."

"Neither have I."

Joe suddenly looked up at us, his eyes hollow, his voice low. "Can we please not talk about the fucking Morrisons tonight?"

That earned him a look from our mother. But instead of disapproval, Ma's face bled with concern. She offered Joe a smile.

"Of course, Joey."

And that's when a knock came at the front door.

Dave and I exchanged glances and Joe sat up straight. Ma wiped her hands on a dishrag and looked at the three of us, her brow knitted with concern.

"You expecting someone?" I asked quietly.

The knock came again, more urgent this time.

"No," Ma whispered.

"Jesus, everyone relax," Joe said, standing. "I'll get it."

I motioned for Ma to remain where she was and then followed Joe to the door. He walked carelessly, his footsteps loud and deliberate. When he opened the door, his face filled with mild surprise, as did mine.

The sheriff stood before us, his hand raised for another assault. He offered an apologetic smile and lowered his fist.

"I'm sorry to interrupt your evening," he said.

I looked behind him to see if anyone else had come, but his squad car was empty. I stepped into the doorway next to Joe and crossed my arms. My stomach twisted and something tickled the back of my neck.

"The hell do you want?" Joe asked, his voice rumbling like the distant thunder.

The sheriff looked down at his hands and then back up at us. "I was headed for Cole's place when I saw his truck on Main Street. I just followed you here. I uh…I have something for you. Something you need to see."

"Something for us? What are you talking about?" I asked. I heard Ma and Dave behind me, listening.

The sheriff reached into his back pocket and pulled out a small manila envelope. "This was anonymously turned into the police station last night. It had my name on it."

"What is this?" Joe asked, reaching for the envelope.

The sheriff pulled away. "Hold on now, boys. Before I give this to you, I need you to know we're doing everything we can about the situation. This here is a copy. My men are still going over the original." He stepped forward and unexpectedly put a hand on Joe's shoulder. "We're going to make this right, Joe. One way or another."

"I don't understand," I said, feeling a deepening unease. "What situation?"

The sheriff handed me the envelope, his voice grim. "Y'all are going to want to brace yourselves before you open that." He looked from Joe's face to mine. "I'm deeply sorry about all this. And rest assured we will get to the bottom of it."

"What did you do?" Joe whispered suddenly, his eyes dark and full of venom.

The sheriff turned to go but stopped. He leaned into Joe, his words thick. "No, Joe…what did you do?"

And then he trotted down the porch and climbed back into his car. He waved to us as he pulled out of the driveway. Joe and I stood motionless in the doorway and watched him speed off down the road.

After a moment, I looked down at the envelope in my hand. It felt far heavier than it should have. I met Joe's eyes and saw the same dread in them that I felt in my chest.

"What was that all about?" I heard Ma ask. Joe and I turned to them and closed the door.

"What did he give you?" Dave asked, pointing to the envelope.

"Open it," Joe whispered, not looking at it.

I looked at Ma and saw she was clutching her apron, her knuckles white. She looked into my face and I had nothing to offer her.

With hands not quite steady, I tore open the envelope and pulled out the contents.

Inside was a single disc. In black marker it read: **For the Barkers.**

"What is that?" Dave asked.

Joe took the disc from me and examined it. He looked up at the rest of us. "Is there a DVD player here?"

"Underneath the TV," Ma said, pointing. "Boys, what is going on? What is that?"

Wordlessly, Joe crossed the living room and

crouched by the TV. He found the player and opened the tray. Before putting the disc in, he turned back to us.

"Ma…maybe you should go into the kitchen."

Ma's voice cracked with rising worry. "Why? What's happening? Joey, don't scare me, what's on the DVD?"

Dave, his face pale, placed a hand on Ma's shoulder. "Please, Ma. Maybe he's right. Why don't you go pour yourself a drink, yeah?"

Close to tears, Ma nodded and went into the kitchen. My heart went with her.

Joe looked at Dave and me, his face grave.

"Play it," I whispered.

Joe inserted the disc, turned on the TV, and stepped back. My heart thundered in my chest like the sky outside. Lightning flickered through the windows and I curled my sweating hands into fists as the video started.

As the first image appeared onscreen, my breath left me in a crushing wave and my knees turned to liquid.

It was Tammy. She was naked and bent over a table, her ankles and wrists tied to the corners, forcing her into a standing position, her stomach pressed flat against the surface. Tears rolled down her flushed face, blood dribbled from her nose, and her lips quivered.

A single light source dangled unseen overhead, casting her in a spotlight, shadows crawling across the floor at her feet. I could see nothing beyond the walls of darkness surrounding her, no clue as to where she was or who else was there. The video was grainy and the unseen cameraman circled our sister, taking in every angle of her nudity. Tammy whimpered and sobbed, bound and motionless, desperate pleas fluttering from her lips.

The camera completed its circuit and then stopped by her face. It dipped down so that Tammy's face filled the screen. Her eyes were red and wide, terrified.

I had never seen terror so real in all my days.

"Oh, my God," I heard Dave whimper. "Oh, my God…oh no…no…"

Joe stood by my side, his body tense as stone.

The voice of the cameraman filled the speakers. "Say hi, Tammy! Say hello to your family!"

A bolt of horror ran through me like hot fire. I recognized that voice.

Derek.

A black-gloved hand extended into view and gripped Tammy's chin, forcing her to look into the camera. She gritted her teeth, weeping, and tried to turn away, but the hand jerked her back.

"Say hello," the voice commanded.

"I don't think she's cooperating," another voice echoed from the darkness around the table. Joe began to quiver at my shoulder as we both recognized the second voice.

Mark.

"Maybe it's time we loosened her tongue," came a third voice we all knew. Leo.

"Not yet," the cameraman, Derek, instructed. "Not until she says hello to her brothers."

The camera dipped closer and almost pressed against Tammy's face. A gloved thumb reached out and wiped a tear from her cheek.

"You don't need to cry," Derek cooed. "Not yet."

Tammy reared her head away from the camera, sniffling. "Fuck you."

The camera tilted to follow the movement of her head. "What was that?"

Tammy glared into the camera, her tear-stained face killing me. "I said fuck you."

Leo's voice rang from the darkness. "Oh, I do love a woman with a dirty mouth. You're not doing yourself any favors, Tam."

"Don't call her that," I heard Joe whisper, almost unheard. "Don't you fucking call her that."

Dave crouched down, hands over his face, his skin pale as snow, staring at the screen between his fingers. Tears poured between them and his chest hitched as he cried.

"I don't think she's going to comply," Mark said from the wall of black.

The camera rose and stared down at our sister. "Maybe not yet. But she will. First, though, she needs to know why this is happening." Suddenly the view rotated and a man's face covered with a black ski mask filled the screen.

"And more importantly, *you* need to know why this is happening," Derek said to us.

"Oh, Christ, no…." Dave cried, shaking.

My throat had gone dry and I felt as if my stomach would devour itself in terrified horror. I gripped the top of the couch for support, my world reeling beneath a wave of nausea.

Derek continued, his masked face absorbing the view. "This is happening, Tammy, because your brothers aren't good people. They have lied to me, lied to the town, and robbed me and my family of everything. Our future, our names, our dignity, and even our dog. If it wasn't for your brothers, you wouldn't be here right now. Do you understand what I'm saying?

The camera swung back to Tammy stretched across the table.

"Don't think she does," Mark stated from the shadows.

"You wouldn't be here," Derek said, beginning to circle the table again, "if your brothers weren't murderous liars. I'm not just talking about Joe, either. Cole is as much a part of this as he is."

I felt a roar of guilt rocket through me and I choked back a growling sob between my teeth.

"I tried to fix this," Derek continued, training the camera across our sister's naked body. "I went to Cole and tried to resolve this man-to-man. But do you know what he did?"

The camera swooped down toward Tammy's face.

"He lied to me. He lied right to my face. He told me that he and Joe had nothing to do with killing Leo's dog. Can you believe that? Here I am, trying to make things right, and he had the balls to stand there and bullshit me like I was some kind of idiot."

"Goddamn you," I croaked, tears budding in my eyes, bile churning my stomach. "God damn you…"

"Well," Derek said, standing and taking the camera with him. "Let me tell you something. My brothers and me? We're sick of the *lies*. We have been molded and pushed around by *lies*. We have been forced and fucked over by *lies*. And you know what? It's time for someone to be held accountable for that."

Suddenly, Leo and Mark emerged from the shadows. They wore ski masks and black gloves as well, like they had been bred from the black. They towered over Tammy, who cried helplessly from the table.

Derek's voice hissed behind the camera. "It's time for your brothers to understand that lies can fucking *hurt* those we care about. And that harsh lesson starts right now. But don't worry, we're not going to kill you. We're not murderers like your brothers are. We're just going to keep you here until your brothers' sentence is up. So Tammy? I think you should get comfortable."

Derek stepped back and the camera took in the whole table. Leo circled around behind Tammy and ran his gloved hands over her naked back, and then gripped her ass, chuckling as he did so.

"You certainly are a fine piece of work," he said,

pressing his crotch against her. "It's a real shame you haven't found yourself a husband. Who knows? Maybe after tonight...or tomorrow...or the next day...maybe we'll make some kind of connection."

Leo unzipped his fly.

"Fuck," Joe hissed, his voice shaking. "Oh, fuck..."

Tammy thrashed on the table, screaming, as Leo pulled his pants down.

"Yeah, keep hollering," Leo laughed, taking his cock in hand.

Tears ran down my face, my head a hurricane of repulsion and agony.

The camera didn't move as Leo began to rape her.

Dave turned away, weeping, mucus running down his face. "Stop it, oh God, please stop it..."

Tammy's quivering cries climaxed into unchecked, broken howls. I cried as I watched, unable to look away. Joe's face flickered as the screen illuminated his shocked paralysis. His eyes were wide, his mouth a thin line, his jaw popping.

When Leo finished, Mark went next.

Dave went into the kitchen, his cries enveloping us all. I turned and to my horror, I saw Ma watching from behind me. Her face was a portrait of frozen agony.

I tried to say something to her, beg her to turn away, but the words were lost beneath the ocean of suffering that echoed out from the speakers.

I turned back to the screen, feeling like I was going to

pass out. Tammy, her body rocking, vomited onto the table.

A sob escaped my throat, a pathetic, frail thing.

"She's got a tight li'l cunt!" Mark howled enthusiastically. "I think she was saving it for me!"

And that's when Joe broke down. He sank to the floor, covered his face with his hands, and began to weep. I could do nothing but stand uselessly before the screen, shell-shocked, until it was over.

When Mark stepped away, Tammy was only barely conscious. Derek chuckled behind the camera and then spun it so we were looking directly into his masked face.

"Until next time, boys," he said darkly, and then the video ended.

The room descended into darkness as the TV transitioned into a sheet of midnight. Joe was on his knees, hands pulling at his hair, his hoarse cries full of pain. Tears ran down his cheeks and his eyes rolled wildly as he searched for something, anything to cope with the shocking scene we had just witnessed.

I felt a bog gurgle in my gut, a bubbling, poisonous thing. My legs threatened to give out and my mouth was a desert of hopelessness. I felt dizzy, sick, and grossly disoriented. I ran my bloated tongue across dry lips, raindrops pouring from clouded eyes. I needed to say something to Ma, something that would make sense of this horrific violence.

I turned to her, mouth opening and closing, head

shaking back and forth meaninglessly. She looked into my face, her own face bloodless and dripping with sorrow. She closed her eyes, went into the kitchen, and began to sob.

I halfheartedly followed, one hand outstretched as if to take away her pain. I stopped at the threshold by the dining room table and watched as Dave went and embraced her in a hug. He put his head on her shoulder and together they wept.

"J-Joe?" I called, searching as the blackness soared for me on shadowy wings.

Joe remained where he was, kneeling before the TV. He had stopped crying, but his eyes bulged and he stared at nothing. His face was coated in grief and shame and fear, and I wanted to scream as I looked upon it.

Wiping my eyes, nose running, stomach lurching, I stumbled into the bathroom and gripped the sink for support. I felt like vomiting but my body wouldn't allow such a release. I turned on the light and looked into the mirror and I screamed. I screamed and sobbed and pounded on the porcelain until I felt the pain and terror enter my knuckles and infect my flesh. I closed my eyes and silenced my throbbing throat. I leaned into the sink and whispered a prayer I didn't feel.

Please...not *again*.

My mind unlocked and I felt a barrage of familiar agony engulf me. Agony I had fought so hard to keep contained. All the pain, misery, guilt, and sorrow I had fought against after Maria's death returned now in a new form, a heightened, deadlier form. Pictures of that night in the alley flashed before my eyes and melded with what I had just seen. Tammy…Christ. The two danced their dark dance and laughed at me, a pawn in someone else's play of nightmares. They spit on me, goaded me, slapped me with their brutal cruelty. They burned with a fire that threatened to wink out my existence.

Not this. Not again.

A knife forged of blazing coal twisted into my mind and heart and laughed at me. It was all I heard, all I felt, all I could see. And I was helpless agains it.

Trembling, I raised my eyes to the mirror. "Please…" I cried, "not this…"

Tammy…

Maria…

Grief…

Pain…

And there I was, standing on the outside looking in. Looking in at the reckless, pointless violence of others. Pissed on and mocked for being too weak to do anything about it. Broken and emptied as those I loved were torn apart by the sickness in others.

"Tammy," I sobbed. "Goddamn it…goddamn it all…I'm sorry…I'm so sorry…"

"Cole."

Through tear-streaked eyes, I turned to see Joe standing in the doorway. His eyes were red-rimmed and his skin was sickly white. His voice was thin and his teeth clacked together as he spoke, a horrible, human plea.

"Help me," he croaked.

I stared deep into his eyes, sniffling and gathering myself. I heard Dave and Ma weeping still from the kitchen. I gripped the edges of the sink and wiped my face, gasping for breath.

"Please," Joe begged.

I shut my eyes and took a slow, deliberate breath. The storm of sadness overwhelmed me and tossed me about in its careless claws.

But through it all, I anchored myself to something beneath it. Something that roared and howled and gnashed its razor-sharp teeth.

I looked into the mirror and let it rise.

Rage.

I plunged my hand beneath the surface of grief and grasped for it, pulled at it. I let it come. I let it emerge. I drank it down, filled my body with it until it tingled through my fingers and ate at my heart.

I placed a hand on Joe's shoulder and leaned into his ear. I whispered something through gritted teeth. My brother's eyes went wide and then turned to cold steel. I pulled away and looked into his face.

"Yes," he muttered.

He turned, wiped his eyes, and went into the basement. I allowed myself a moment longer to collect myself. I shoved the grief away, pushed the sadness aside, and filled my head and heart with the darkness.

I left the bathroom and joined Ma and Dave in the kitchen. They hugged one another tightly by the sink, falling deeper and deeper into the reality of what we had all seen. I gently placed a hand on Dave's arm and pulled him away.

He blinked at me, his eyes wide and full of glittering pain.

"I need you," I said softly.

Ma looked up into my face, her voice strained and breaking. "What is happening, Cole?"

I hugged her gently and kissed the top of her head, tears threatening once again. I viciously burned them back, grinding my teeth together so hard it echoed through my skull.

"We're going to get her back," I whispered.

Ma stepped away, lip quivering. "Why would they do something like that? How could they do something so awful? Tammy...my baby girl..." She covered her face with her hands and I tenderly pulled them away, forcing her to look at me.

"Where do you keep Dad's guns?"

She stared at me, confusion spreading. "Upstairs in the closet...but...why?"

"We're going to need them," I said, looking at Dave.

"Cole...please..." Ma begged.

I turned away and went upstairs. I heard Dave comforting our mother as I reached the second floor of the house. I went into Ma's bedroom and threw open the closet. I pushed aside some old clothes and found what I was searching for.

Dad's old shotgun leaned against the back wall. I picked it up and placed it on the bed. I went back to the closet and crouched down, knocking shoes away until I located an old shoebox. I tossed the lid aside and felt something stir in my stomach once more. Anger. Bitterness. Memory...

In the box, a pistol lay amidst a heap of bullets. I took it out and emptied the ammo on the bed next to the shotgun. A handful of red shells spilled out across the comforter along with the others. I loaded them into the shotgun. Next, I loaded the pistol. I remembered Dad teaching me how to shoot when I was only seven. I hadn't forgotten much.

With both guns loaded, I stuffed the pistol into my waistband and hefted the shotgun. I gathered the remaining ammo into my pockets and left the bedroom. When I reached the stairs, I stopped and steadied myself against the railing, squeezing my eyes shut.

Jesus...

I focused my thoughts, shook haunted images away, and then descended. When I reached the kitchen, I saw Ma sitting in a chair. Dave was pouring her a drink. I took it from his hand and emptied it down my throat.

I needed the burn.

The fire.

"What are you going to do with those?" Ma asked weakly from the kitchen table, pointing to the guns.

"Whatever I have to," I muttered. Dave eyed them fearfully. I looked at him, hard.

Joe emerged from the basement, carrying a duffel bag. He slung it over his shoulder and I offered him the pistol. He took it without a word.

His face was no longer grief-stricken. Instead, I saw the hard anger that blazed through me. His jaw was set, his eyes chiseled from stone, and his mouth compressed to shelter a snarl.

"Boys, wait, stop this," Ma said, standing, shaking her head, tears escaping down her cheeks. "Slow down, please. What is happening? What are you going to do?"

"We're getting Tammy back," Joe growled, adjusting his grip on the duffel bag.

Ma bit her lip. "We…we need to call the police, we need to get help…we need…" She trailed off miserably.

"The police gave us that video," I said, holding the shotgun in one hand.

Dave stepped forward. "Yes, but…but you saw what was on there…they can't do that, Cole! They can't get away with that!"

"They're not," Joe rumbled, chest heaving.

"You need to be with us on this, Dave," I said. "We can't do this without you."

Dave looked at Ma and then back at us, hands fumbling nervously. "I…shit…*shit*…yeah…yeah, of course."

"Take your car," I instructed. "We're going to have to find her first. I doubt she's at one of the brother's houses, but we have to try."

Joe stepped forward. "Cole and I will go search Mark and Derek's house. They're only two miles apart from one another. You go to Leo's. If you see any lights, any movement, anything at all...you call us. Do not go inside; do not be seen. You understand?"

Dave just nodded, tears threatening.

"Be strong," I hissed, a great weight settling over my chest. "You have to be strong."

"This isn't happening," Ma sobbed into her hands.

I softened slightly and walked to her side. I leaned down and kissed her on the head. "When we come back, Tammy is going to be with us. I promise."

Ma looked up into my face, eyes bloodshot. "You're a good boy, Cole. Go get my daughter."

"You ready?" Joe asked Dave. He nodded.

As we headed for the door, Ma called out after us, "I'll pray for you!"

"Don't bother," Joe said darkly. "I don't think God's coming with us on this one."

Chapter 9

The road rumbled beneath us. Joe knew the way so he drove my truck. I sat in the passenger's seat, watching the town go by. I felt like I was caught in someone else's dream. I felt like I was floating above the world, waiting to wake up. I felt sick to my stomach.

Joe planted a cigarette between his teeth and lit it. He glanced at me and then offered me the smoke. I took it without hesitation. Joe lit a new one for himself. I inhaled the nicotine and coughed, uncaring.

"I'm worried about Dave," Joe said as we passed the church on Main Street. Dave, who had been trailing us, turned off the stretch of road, his headlights sparking shadows through the cab.

"There he goes," I said, watching through the rear-view mirror as he headed for Leo's house.

"He's terrified," Joe went on.

"So am I," I said.

Joe looked at me hard. "You're with me though, right?"

"Of course."

Joe exhaled smoke through his nose. "Whatever it takes, Cole…"

"Hey, Joe?"

He turned to me.

"Please stop talking."

He turned away. "Yeah…"

I let the night take me. I filled my head with its noise, with its quiet, with its chaos. The shotgun leaned against my knee and bullets twisted in my pocket.

We were going to make this right.

One way or another.

Eventually, Joe turned off Main Street and guided the truck down a long dirt road, deep into the woods. We silently crept through long miles of looming forest, the sky continuing to flash with lightning. The storm was almost upon us now, the leaves overhead swaying violently in the wind. Thunder called to us and the thudding in my head called back.

After another couple minutes, Joe slowed. "Almost there."

He turned down another road and leaned forward in his seat. He pointed ahead of us, the outline of a house growing from the dark surroundings. "There. Derek's house. Looks like no one's home."

"Figured," I muttered.

"You think we should check it out?"

"No. He's not here. He's not stupid. Let's try Mark's place."

Joe put the car in reverse and turned around. "Probably not going to find anyone there, either."

"We have to try," I said, staring out into the wall of night.

We bumped our way down another dirt road for ten minutes and then Joe slowed once more. An old house stood vacant ahead. Again, it was dark. There were no signs of life to be seen.

"Fuck," Joe hissed, hitting the breaks. The truck idled beneath us.

I gripped the barrel of the shotgun, frustrated, angry, desperate. I knew she wouldn't be here, but some part of me begged to be wrong. I ran a hand over my stubble and listened as a blast of sudden thunder rattled my ears.

"Call Dave," I said, glaring at the house, willing a light to come on. "Maybe he's had better luck."

As Joe pulled out his phone, it began to ring. We looked at one another, and then he answered.

"What's up, Dave?" Joe paused, listening, and then sighed. "Shit…"

"Not there?" I said, already knowing the answer.

"No."

"Shit."

"Hold on, Dave," Joe said, pulling the phone away. He looked at me. "What now?"

I shot a look at him. "I don't know…" I stared out the windshield, feeling the anger rise. I suddenly slammed my fist into the dash, furious, scared, confused. "FUCK!"

Joe slowly put the phone back to his ear. "What's that, Dave? Say that again." He covered his ear and strained to listen. He glanced at me, his voice lowered. "Dave says their dad has a hunting lodge a couple miles from here up in the mountains."

"Does he know where it is?" I asked, panting, hoping, seething.

"You know where it is?" Joe relayed. He listened again. "Yeah…yeah, OK. Yeah, I know where that is. We'll meet you there. Don't do anything until we get there, OK? Alright, see you soon."

Joe hung up and slammed the truck into reverse, peeling us around and back the way we had come.

"How far?" I asked as Joe hit the gas, the truck lurching forward.

"Maybe twenty minutes."

"You know where it is?"

"I think so."

"Hurry, Joe."

He leaned forward, the truck picking up speed. "I am."

The lightning turned aggressive as the tires spat gravel in our wake. Thick bolts now lit the sky and the wind began to throw rain against the windshield. Joe turned onto another dirt road and threw on the high beams. I rolled up my window as the road began to ascend.

I drummed my fingers against my leg as we climbed. Derek…Mark…Leo…Tammy…Maria…

"You find some good stuff in the basement?" I asked, kicking the duffel bag at my feet. It clinked loudly on contact.

"Enough," Joe said, concentrating.

"Good."

"You think we're going to need it?"

I watched the rain streak against the window. "Depends on who we find."

We went silent again, the weight of the night compressing around us. The wipers scraped water from the windshield like rubber claws, throwing handfuls of rain aside. Joe went fast, jerking the truck ahead. I didn't know how he could see, but I kept my mouth shut.

I looked at him, his eyes locked on the road.

"Joe?" I said quietly.

"Hmm?"

I held the bitter words on my tongue for a moment and then decided to eat them. "Never mind…"

"You can say it," he said softly.

"There's nothing to say."

He bit his tongue over his teeth and closed his mouth.

"Let's just get her back," I muttered.

"Yeah…"

After another couple minutes, the road leveled out and the trees retreated. Joe accelerated, taking off down the open stretch of rocky terrain.

"Close now," he said.

He slowed and turned off the road down a narrow, winding path. It was barely visible and I wondered how he had spotted it. The truck lurched down the single lane, the woods returning and pressing close. Branches reached out from rain-soaked darkness and clawed at the windows.

"There's Dave's car," I said, pointing. It was parked almost completely in the woods. The cab was dark.

Joe pulled up behind it and looked at me. "Where is he?"

I jumped suddenly as a knock came at my window. I spun toward it and saw Dave's face staring in at me. I quickly rolled down the window, calming my racing heart.

"Jesus, you scared me half to death," I exclaimed, rain pouring into the cab.

"Sorry," Dave apologized. "The cabin is just ahead." Water ran over his face in tiny streams and he blew it from his lips.

"And?" Joe asked.

Dave gripped the windowsill. "Someone's there. There's a light on."

I closed my eyes for a moment, exhaling and expelling all the tension I had been holding onto. I picked up the shotgun and opened the door. I stepped out into the rain and joined my brother. Thunder crashed loudly overhead. Joe grabbed the duffel bag and stepped out into the storm with us. We quietly closed the doors and I looked to Dave.

"Lead the way."

The three of us crept down the dirt road, wet grass clawing up through the packed earth. The woods threw sheets of rain down over us and soon I was soaked to the bone. We rounded a bend in the road and stopped. A cabin stood before us, small, quiet, but alive with light. The storm made it impossible to see past the windows and so we crouched down and approached it from the side, hugging the edge of the woods. A lone van was parked out front by the stoop. A van I recognized all too well.

"Let's go around back first," I said, spitting rain from my tongue.

Joe and Dave nodded. We continued to circle the cabin through the woods, keeping to the trees. My eyes poured over the windows, waiting for movement. My heart thundered in my throat and I forced myself to remain calm.

We reached the backyard and paused, squatting down to take in the surroundings. Lighting lit the sky and Dave pointed to a small structure beside the cabin.

"Looks like a shed," he said.

"Let's go," I growled, pushing ahead. Masked by the storm, we slunk to the shoddy structure and pressed ourselves against the wall by the door.

Joe retrieved his pistol from his belt and looked at me. I nodded, readying the shotgun. Taking a deep breath, Joe tried the door and found it unlocked. He inched it open and peered inside. After a moment, he stepped through, gun raised.

More lightning crashed around us and briefly illuminated the interior. In that flash, we saw an empty room with a single metal table standing at the center of the space. It was clothed in blood, dark stains streaking the bare surface.

"She was here," Joe snarled, taking in the aftermath of the video we had seen. I felt my stomach squirm with rising pain, but I forced it back down. Yes…she had been here…with them…

"Let's try the house," I said.

We left the shed and slid between the rain toward the back door. I tried the handle and found it locked. I pressed my ear against the wood and listened, but the storm denied me any clue as to what was inside.

"Anything?" Joe asked, wiping rain from his face. He adjusted the duffel bag over his shoulder and blinked at me through the pouring rain.

"Can't hear shit," I muttered.

"What do we do?" Dave asked.

Joe handed him the bag. "Take this."

Dave accepted it and stepped back, his voice urgent. "What are you doing?"

Joe looked at us. "We're going in."

"Do it," I said, locking the shotgun into my shoulder.

Joe braced himself and then booted the door aside. It

gave way in a shower of splinters and sudden noise, the impact rocking it back on its hinges.

I quickly stepped inside, gun raised, sweeping the barrel across a dirty kitchen. Immediately, I spotted Leo lounging on the couch in the next room, his feet propped up on the coffee table. His eyes went wide and his face paled as he saw us.

Joe shouldered past me and charged the youngest Morrison brother. Leo let out a panicked cry and dove for the hunting rifle propped against the couch. The toe of Joe's boot reached him first, brutally catching Leo beneath the chin.

I heard his teeth rattle as his head whipped back. Joe grabbed the rifle as Leo collapsed onto the floor, dazed. Dave walked in behind us, his face slack, his eyes nervously ticking around the house. Joe held out the rifle to him.

"Take this."

As Dave hesitantly went to retrieve it, Leo lunged for Joe. I pumped a chamber into the shotgun and pointed it at Leo's face.

"Sit the FUCK DOWN!" I screamed, advancing. Leo froze, one hand reaching for my brother. I pressed the cold circle of steel against his temple and saw his eyes flicker as they filled with fear.

"You don't gotta do this," he mumbled. "Please, you don't gotta do this…"

Dave took the rifle and stepped back. He slid the duffel bag off his shoulder and it fell with a clank to the floor. The noise caused Leo to jump, his attention divided.

Joe leaned down, pistol in hand, and grabbed Leo by the hair. "Where the fuck are your brothers?"

"P-please," Leo winced. "Just take it easy…this…this is a mistake."

Joe's eyes flared and he brought the butt of his pistol down across Leo's mouth. Blood exploded from his lips as they split, his neck whipping back only to be jerked forward by Joe's iron grip.

"WHERE ARE THEY?!" Joe roared, readying another blow. I curled my finger around the shotgun's trigger, heart pounding.

"They ain't here!" Leo pleaded, raising his hands to protect his face. "They left!" Suddenly Leo's eyes widened, realizing what he had just said. "B-but they are coming back!" he sputtered. "They're coming back real soon!"

Joe looked up at Dave and me. A silent conversation passed between the three of us.

"Where's Tammy?" I growled, looming over the sniveling man.

Leo licked his bloody lips. "Aw shit…"

Joe crouched down so he was eye level with him. "Yeah, Leo…aw *shit*." He cocked the hammer back on his pistol and pressed it against Leo's eye. "Where the fuck is she?"

Leo began to whimper. His mouth remained sealed,

fear coursing through him like currents of electricity. Blood dripped down his chin, but he said nothing.

"Oh, you don't want to give us the cold shoulder," I snarled. "That's a really, really bad idea."

"Where is she, you useless FUCK!?" Joe roared, digging the gun deeper into Leo's socket.

Leo groaned but still kept his tongue locked behind his teeth.

I pointed at Dave. "Get the rope."

"Seems like my brother is done being patient," Joe leered, standing. He dragged Leo up by the hair. Leo sniffled and whined, stumbling forward as Joe pulled him into the kitchen. Keeping the gun trained on his head, Joe shoved him into a chair.

Dave retrieved the rope from the bag and handed it to me. I passed him my shotgun and went to Leo.

"Keep your gun on him," I instructed. "And Joe? If he so much as twitches, shoot his fucking cock off."

Leo practically turned into a pillar of salt as I bound him with the rope, tying him to the chair. When the knots were tight, I stepped away and stared down at him.

My shadow covered his petrified face. "Do you watch a lot of movies, Leo?"

Leo just cowered beneath me, silent.

I knelt down and ruffled my hand through the duffel bag. "Because I watch a lot of movies. Well…I used to when I was a teenager. You know what kind of movies I liked?"

Leo began to cry, a pathetic whimpering whine.

My fingers ran over the tools in the bag, searching. "I liked the really fucked-up ones. The ones with all the gore. I couldn't get enough of it. I think I watched every single one of those flicks. Torture, murder, cannibalism, they were all fair game."

I heard Dave move behind me and stand at Joe's shoulder as I continued. "Something about those movies...I can't really tell you what it was. They scared me, for sure. They disgusted me, of course. There were so many times, so many scenes when I wanted to turn away, but I wouldn't. I didn't. Not a single time did I look away. I have seen dozens and dozens of people get tortured on screen. But you know what always bothered me? What almost annoyed me?"

I snapped my fingers under Leo's chin. "Hey, are you fucking listening to me?"

Leo nodded, tears running down his face.

I reached out and pulled his chin up to look at me. "What annoyed me most about those movies were the actors' reactions while getting tortured. You see...I never bought it. I was never convinced they were actually suffering. Sure, they'd scream...but they never *screamed*. I remember watching those movies and thinking to myself, 'Wouldn't that hurt more than that?'"

I suddenly pulled out a mallet hammer from the bag and towered over Leo, my voice a growl. "So, Leo, how about you tell me if this actually hurts as bad as I think it does?"

I went into a batter's stance and brought the hammer down as hard as I could. It shattered his knee on contact, the bone crunching loudly.

Leo buckled in the chair and screamed, tendons standing out on his neck as he arched back, his voice cracking and howling. Foam and spittle leaked from the corners of his mouth as he rocked against his restraints, eyes bulging.

I patiently waited for him to settle down.

It took longer than I would have guessed.

When he returned to a sobbing mess of agonized whimpers, I leaned down, my voice hard. "That was better than I expected. Now where the fuck is our sister?"

"J-Jesus Christ," Leo wept. "You-you-you fucking broke my knee…"

I stood up, rage building.

Joe stepped forward and snatched the hammer from my grip, his voice a grating command. "You have one second to tell me where Tammy is before I break your other knee."

Leo's head whipped up, panicked. "OK, yes I'll—"

"One."

Joe swung the hammer into Leo's other knee and split the bone. Leo went into shrieking hysterics and screamed so loud I almost covered my ears. Blood ran down his shins and splattered onto the floor as Leo thrashed wildly.

"Just tell us! Please!" Dave cried, his voice frail.

"In the outhouse!" Leo howled. "She's in the old outhouse!"

Joe stepped forward and grabbed Leo by the throat. "Where the fuck is the that!?"

Tears streamed down Leo's slobbering face, his words escaping through pained gasps. "Round the side...of the house...please...no more...I can't...take it..."

Joe released him and sprinted for the back door. Dave and I followed, leaving Leo.

He wasn't going anywhere.

We entered the rain-soaked night once again, our boots churning through the mud as we bolted toward the opposite end of the cabin. As we rounded the corner, a fang of lightning lit the world to reveal a small wooden outhouse standing alone by the woods.

The three of us ran for it.

We're coming, Tammy...

Joe reached it first and threw the door open. As he did, another flash of lightning split the sky and Dave let out of pained sob.

"Tammy!" he cried, lunging between Joe and me.

Tammy was naked and strung up like a piece of meat left out to dry. Her head drooped across her chest, her eyes closed. Her feet dangled into the open toilet and blood ran down her broken skin as the tight rope bit into her wrists.

"Jesus Christ…" Joe exhaled, the air leaving him.

At the sight of her, I felt the familiar, horrible helplessness return to me. The awful, staggering weight that threatened to crush me right then and there. My head spun and dizziness rocked me. I reached out and grasped Joe's shoulder for support, my legs weak.

"Oh, my God…" I cried. "Oh, my *God*…"

"Help me with her!" Dave sobbed, grabbing her bruised legs and lifting her up to take the weight off her wrists.

Joe pulled a knife from his boot, snapping out of his paralysis. He cut the rope that held Tammy with a flick of the blade. Her body fell like a sack of sand and Dave caught her, assisted by Joe. Together they pulled her feet out of the toilet and brought her outside into the rain. Tears ran down Dave's face and his lip quivered as he knelt, cradling her in his arms.

"T-Tammy?" he cried, gently brushing her hair out of her eyes. "Tammy, it's me, Dave. Please…God…please wake up. Please wake up…"

I put a hand to my mouth, my eyes welling with pools of sorrow. A boulder of unstoppable pain rolled through me and I was helpless against it. I choked out a sob and sank to my knees in the mud. Joe stood over us, his eyes wide, his face twisted in shock.

"Tammy, please wake up," Dave cried, hugging her as the rain beat against us.

I clenched my fists into the earth, unable to rip my bloodshot eyes off the horrific sight.

Wake up...please wake up...

The words crashed through my mind like cannon-balls, splitting every mental scab I had and spilling their blood across my exhausted, frayed mind.

Suddenly, Tammy's eyes fluttered open.

"Dave?" she called weakly.

Dave let out a relieved cry of joy and wiped Tammy's face clear of the rain. "Yes! Yes, it's me! I'm here, we're all here with you."

Painfully, Tammy turned and looked at Joe and me. "Joe...? Cole...?"

"We're getting you out of here," Joe croaked, his voice dripping with pain.

"You're going home," I said tenderly, wiping tears from my face and taking her hand in mine. "It's over...it's all over. You're going to be OK now. You're safe."

Tammy's face melted in a sudden, pained memory. "They...they..." she began to cry and she buried her face in Dave's chest. "They *raped* me..." Her voice shook shamefully.

"Oh, Tammy," Dave cried, his shoulders rocking. "Oh, God, Tammy..." He clutched her desperately to himself, and together they wept in the rain.

Sniffling, I stood up, shaking the agony from my mind as best I could. "Come on," I said gently. "We need to get her to the car. You have to take her to the hospital, Dave."

Nodding miserably, Dave adjusted his grip on Tammy.

Joe quickly stepped forward and picked her up, taking her in his arms.

He did so with overwhelming tenderness.

Tammy buried her face into his shoulder and began to cry again, thunder booming in the distance. As we slowly walked to the car, I saw Joe's mouth twist with sorrow. He whispered gently to her, kissing the top of her head as we splashed through the rain-soaked earth.

We trekked back to Dave's car, the storm a relentless monster above. When we reached it, Dave quickly opened the door and Joe bent his knees and slid Tammy inside. I took off my shirt, wet as it was, and covered her nakedness. After a moment, Joe did the same.

"We'll be right behind you," I said softly as Tammy curled my shirt against her. She brought her knees up to her chest and squeezed her eyes shut, tears pouring down her cheeks.

I stepped aside to let Joe lean in next, his voice laden with love. "We'll see you real soon, OK?"

He stood and quietly closed the door. He turned to face Dave and me.

"God *damn* it…"

"Get her to safety, Dave," I said, placing a hand on my brother's shoulder, "and call Ma, let her know Tammy is alive."

Dave nodded. "What about you two?"

Bare-chested, Joe and I exchanged looks in the storm.

Rainwater hissed from between my teeth. "We're not done here yet."

Chapter 10

Joe and I stood shoulder-to-shoulder in the gale, watching Dave's taillights disappear around the corner. The look he had given us right before departing had been one of hesitant fear. The ice in my eyes had negated any further conversation and silently, he had left us.

Left alone with my brother, I turned back to the cabin. Joe placed a hand on my shoulder, stopping me. I looked at him, rainwater running down his face in great currents.

"What?" I said flatly.

"We doing this?"

"Is that a question?"

"I guess it is."

"Is it one you really need to ask?"

Joe nodded, surprising me. "Yeah, Cole, it is. I know how you want this to end tonight. Shit, I do, too. But if we go through with it, then we're going to have to follow that hell to the very end."

I stepped into Joe, lowering my voice. "They don't

get to walk away from this, Joe. None of them do. That was decided the second that fucking video started. That choice was made the moment our *mother* had to watch it." I poked him in the chest, nose to nose. "As soon as they touched Tammy, it was over."

Joe hardened. "I know that, Cole. But I'm not asking if they get to live or not. I'm asking if you want to leave."

"And why the hell would I want to do that?"

Joe pointed to the cabin. "Because I started this. And that piece of shit in there? He's my problem. I'm offering you a chance to walk away clean. I'm going to finish this one way or another. No need for you to get even more mixed up in this. There's no point in getting your hands as bloody as mine are about to get. You've been with me every step of the way, and I owe you. You walking away, right now? That's me paying you back."

The rain thundered down around us. My fingers twitched at my sides as memory swirled through me like cold adrenaline.

My hands balled into fists. "I *need* this."

Joe looked at me, his face blank.

"I get it," he said quietly. "Come on. Let's go."

A chill ran through me, my bare torso drenched in the downpour. Together, we turned for the cabin and marched back inside. Dripping, I closed the door behind us and made sure the drapes were pulled shut. I stepped into the kitchen and heard Joe lock the door behind us.

Leo remained in the chair, a sniveling, crying mess.

A tiny pool of blood had formed around his feet, the aftermath of his broken knees. When he saw us, he began to cry.

"Shut the fuck up," I muttered, standing before him.

Whimpering, he stared at the floor.

Joe came to my side and knelt by the duffel bag. He casually dipped his hand inside, searching. His eyes never left Leo, his jawbone clenched.

"Did you think you could get away with this?" I asked coldly.

"It wasn't my idea," Leo sniffled. "Derek made me do it…said it was the right thing to do. Eye for an eye."

"I killed your fucking dog," Joe said, his voice stone. "You raped our sister. That's a deadly tip of the scales, you cunt." He stood and pulled a hacksaw out of the bag with him. Leo's eyes bulged with horror.

Joe grabbed Leo by the hair and yanked his head back. "And what's worse is you sent that video for us all to see. Like it was some school project you wanted to show off. Our mother saw that. The most important woman in our lives had to watch you monsters do that to her daughter. Her fucking *daughter*." Joe's voice shook and I saw rage building in his eyes. "I should have killed you back at the garage."

Joe raised the hacksaw and placed it underneath Leo's nose, teeth up.

He gave Leo a second to anticipate the pain.

And then he pulled the saw through the flesh. It took three pulls of the blade to sever Leo's nose. Leo screamed as blood exploded like a fountain from his face. Great spouts of red ran down his chin and dripped onto his chest. His nose fell to the floor with a wet squish.

Joe stepped away and I felt a tremor of unexpected repulsion run through me at the sight of the ruined man before us. He thrashed in his chair, losing himself in pain.

He deserves this...

I knelt down and reached into the duffel bag. After a moment, I pulled out a heavy wrench. I hefted it in my hands and waited for Leo to stop screaming.

Remember what he did...

When Leo's cries had receded some, I stood in front of him and leaned into his face, my breath hot and bitter. "You pushed us into this. You made us do this to you."

Leo sobbed, the hole in his face a bloody pair of alien slits.

"But I need to know you feel some semblance of honest-to-God remorse for what you did," I continued, a torrent of anger and grief clashing in my chest.

Leo nodded pathetically, lips working soundlessly.

I gripped the wrench. "Say you're sorry. I want to hear you say how sorry you are."

Leo rushed to speak, a babble of eagerness. "Yes, yes, I'm sorry! Oh, God help me, I'm so sorry! It was a mistake! I see that now! I wasn't thinking clearly...oh, God, please, I'm so sorry…" He paused, catching his breath, wincing through the pain.

I stared at him a moment longer and felt a sickening twinge of sympathy for the man. Not out of guilt, no, but because of how utterly helpless he was right now. I didn't pity him…

I *hated* him.

"Jesus, Leo," I said, my voice cracking. "How did we get here…?"

"I wasn't thinking…I wasn't thinking…I swear…" Leo wept, blood dangling from his chin through strands of saliva.

Suddenly, I was quivering with anger, a storm of fury sweeping through my body like a tornado.

I grabbed him by the hair and jerked his head back so he was looking into my eyes. "You did that to my sister without *thinking* about it? Is that what you're telling me? Didn't you see how scared she was? Didn't you hear her screaming?"

"I'm sorry…" Leo gurgled.

I looked at Joe, his face dark. "Well, Leo…just like you…the only people who can hear you screaming right now don't give a *fuck*."

And then I brought the wrench down into his jaw.

It whipped his head to the side and threatened to topple him in his chair. I saw his eyes go cloudy and he let out a stunned *oomph*!

Before he could recover, I smashed the wrench down a second time. I heard his jaw crack.

The third blow dislocated it and sent him crashing to the floor.

Blood flowed from Leo's mouth and his teeth clattered across the floor like crimson Tic Tacs. Still bound to the chair, his head drooped to the tile and I saw his left hand begin to shake uncontrollably as shock took him. He didn't scream but instead let out a series of moans that crawled up from deep inside his chest.

Panting, I dropped the wrench and towered over the broken man. His jawbone split away from his mouth and hung in a state of severed ruin, held to his face only by his skin.

"He doesn't have much left," Joe stated, arms crossed over his bare chest.

"He's got enough to know he's dying," I said. I stooped for the wrench, but Joe stopped me. Our eyes met and I stood back up.

Joe went to the bag and pulled out a hatchet.

"End of the road," he said grimly.

I watched, unflinching, as Joe went to Leo and raised the hatchet.

With a sickening crunch, he brought it down into the back of Leo's head, killing him instantly.

Joe righted himself, leaving the hatchet buried in the corpse.

He looked at me. "I want his brothers to find him like this. I want them to have to dig the blade from his skull."

I nodded wordlessly and picked up the duffel bag. After a moment, I dropped it to the floor.

Fuck it.

Slowly, Joe and I made our way to the door, the roar of the storm outside filling our ears. We exited the house and my bare skin was soon coated in rain once more. My boots splashed over the mud as Joe and I walked to my truck. We said nothing as lightning whipped through the sky with great lashes of thunder.

I slowly regained my breath and felt my pulse begin to slow. My adrenaline faded and reality oozed its way back into my mind. I looked at my hands. They were shaking.

And I couldn't seem to get them to stop.

By the time we reached the truck, I was freezing. I wrapped my arms around myself and climbed into the passenger's seat. Joe took the wheel. Before he turned on the engine, we exchanged a look in the dim cab.

"We just killed a man," I said, emotionless.

Joe turned on the truck and pulled out onto the road. I leaned my head against the window and watched the raindrops flail against the glass. As my mind slowed, it began to fill with what we had just done. Images fluttered across my eyes as from a projector. I looked down at my hands and saw they were still trembling. I tried to shake the sensation away, but it didn't help. Joe glanced at me. He pulled out a cigarette and held it out.

"Smoke it," he said. It wasn't a question. I obediently

took it and slid the butt between my teeth. I fumbled with the lighter and then finally got it right. I inhaled, coughed, and felt my eyes water. Joe lit one of his own. Thunder rolled overhead like an avalanche.

Halfway through the cigarette I began to feel sick. The nicotine churned my stomach and I couldn't seem to stop shivering now. Teeth chattering, I wrapped my arms around myself, my bare skin like a sheet of ice.

Joe turned on the heat and finished his smoke. I looked down at mine and then discarded it out the window. I felt like I was going to throw up. I pressed my eyes closed and held my hands against my face, digging my fingers into my skin.

I couldn't stop thinking about how Tammy had looked.

"Are you OK?" Joe asked, sparing me a glance.

I leaned my head back against the seat again, the temperature in the cab now making me claustrophobic. I rolled the window down, finding it hard to breathe. Joe turned off the heat. He cast me a second look and I ignored it. I felt anxious stirrings in my chest, and then in my arms and fingers. A tingling, desperate nervousness. My stomach buckled and my skull expanded with pain. I ran a hand across my forehead and found that I was sweating.

"Pull over," I said.

"What?"

"Stop the car, I need to get out," I said a little more urgently.

Joe cocked an eyebrow but slid the truck off the road. Rain beat against the hood, a thousand wet bullets shot from heaven.

I pulled the door open and stumbled outside. I felt my chest hitch as I sucked in air. I couldn't seem to get enough, each pull of oxygen weaker than the last. I bent down and put my hands on my knees and stared at my boots, begging myself to calm. Rainwater streamed off the tip of my nose and I followed it to the earth through blurred vision.

I broke Leo's jaw with a wrench.

Joe got out of the truck. The telltale flick of his lighter informed me he was making his way to my side. Despite the rain, I smelled smoke as my brother carelessly nursed a cigarette. A hand found my shoulder.

"He deserved it," Joe said quietly.

"I know he did," I panted. "Christ, of course he did."

Joe said nothing, but the hand remained. I closed my eyes.

They put her in the outhouse like she was wasn't even human...

"Fuck," I spat, blowing rainwater off my lips.

"We gotta get moving," Joe said, exhaling.

"I know, just give me a second."

"OK."

I slowly stood, craning my face up toward the sky. I took a long, deep breath. Blood and crunching bone filled my head. My ears ached from all the screaming.

Joe's cigarette turned my stomach. I scraped my tongue across my teeth and steadied myself.

"Let's go," I said.

Joe nodded and tossed his smoke into the mud. We got back in the truck and continued down the mountain. I didn't feel any better. My throat felt clogged, my head cluttered. Everything had just happened so fast...so goddamn fast...

We rounded a corner and were suddenly blinded by headlights. Joe squinted as we passed the vehicle, the windows darkened by night. It was headed toward the cabin.

"Shit," Joe muttered.

"What? Was that them?"

"I think so."

"Derek or Mark?"

"Does it matter?"

"Shit..."

"I was hoping we'd have more time."

"Once they see Leo, it's over."

"So what's the call here?" Joe asked.

"What do you mean?"

Joe looked at me. "What do we do now, Cole?"

I took a moment and forced my head to clear. "I don't know...shit. Hold on, just...just fucking hold on." I let my thoughts settle, a sinking ship in a dark pond. "In a very short time there's going to be two bloodthirsty brothers on our tail. Not to mention the entire police force. And I have no doubt we'd be shot on sight."

"We should go back and kill them now," Joe muttered.

I ran my hands through my hair. "Goddamn it…"

"The sheriff isn't going to let this go, either."

I gripped handfuls of my own hair. "I know. But we need to regroup…we need to get Dave. Maybe Ma, too."

"What are you thinking?"

"That none of us are safe right now."

"We could go back," Joe said again.

"No," I insisted. "No, the police are going to be crawling all over this mountain once they find Leo. I don't want to get trapped. We need to go to the hospital. We're going to need Dave."

"For what?"

"To help us," I said. "And so I know he's safe. Tammy is surrounded by medical staff. I think she'll be OK for now."

"Dave isn't going to help us," Joe said darkly. "You saw him at the cabin. He could barely look at Leo, never mind hurt him."

"He's coming with us," I pressed. "We need another person."

Joe lit another cigarette. "I guess we can try. Seems like a waste of time to me, though."

"Jesus, Joe," I croaked. "What do you want me to say?"

"That you're with me on this."

"I am! But things are spiraling out of our control at a rate I can't keep up with!"

"So you want to run?"

I bit my lip, fighting nausea. "We're not running. We just need to figure out what to do next."

"We need to finish this."

"We will."

"When? How?"

"I don't know," I exhaled, frustrated.

"Cole."

"I don't KNOW!" I yelled. "Goddamn it, how the FUCK did this happen!?"

Joe looked at me in the darkness. "I think you're having a panic attack."

I readied a retort but slammed my teeth shut instead. I forced myself to breathe. I focused on my heartbeat and counted to five in my head.

"I'm fine," I muttered.

Joe was silent for a second before speaking. "So…the hospital?"

"Dave should be there with Ma and Tammy."

"You wanna go now?"

I checked my watch. "Yeah. We should have some time. Just a little."

"You sure about this?"

"Hell if I know," I said softly.

"OK…"

"After we talk to Dave, we leave the hospital."

"Where?"

"Anywhere that's not there, Joe."

He sighed a heavy, weighty breath. "Jesus…"

I drummed my fingers against my leg as we drove. Thoughts flew through my head at a thousand miles an hour and I tried to sort through the chaos. My throat felt dry. My chest heaved. My shoulders were tense and pain pulsed through them. I rubbed my hands over my face, trying to clear out the mess in my mind.

The worst part of it all was that nothing felt resolved. Tammy was still broken. She would never be the same. Leo was dead. But where had that gotten us? What good had that done? I remembered the rage I had felt in the bathroom after watching the video. The hatred. The anger. How I had let it control me. How it had allowed me to torture Leo. I had never felt such a powerful desire to hurt someone in all my life. Not even after Maria.

A few minutes later and we were down the mountain. Joe turned the truck in the direction of the hospital and gunned it. The rain was relentless and I silently begged him to slow down. I looked across the cabin and saw a shadow cover his face. And in that shadow…was nothing.

"Oh, shit," I muttered suddenly.

Joe glanced at me. "What is it?"

"We forgot the guns."

Joe nodded at my feet. "No, we didn't. I grabbed them before we left. Look, they're right there."

I looked at the floor in front of me. Sure enough, the pistol and shotgun were there. My boots rested over them. How had I not seen or felt them?

"Are you OK?" Joe asked.

I leaned down and picked up the pistol. I turned it over in my hands as the sky grumbled above.

"Cole?"

"What?"

"Are you OK?"

I looked at him. "Yes…no…I don't know. *Fuck*…"

"Just breathe, man."

I looked at the pistol in my hands. "Did we do the right thing?"

Joe stared out the windshield. "Shit if I know. Felt right."

I held onto the pistol the rest of the way. Somewhere out there, in the violence of the night, Derek and Mark were discovering their dead brother. Again, I thought about the rage I had felt in the bathroom. Is that what they were feeling at this very moment? An overwhelming desire to do harm?

A shiver ran through me.

They're going to kill you…

I jumped as a police siren exploded around us. Lights flashed in the mirrors and I turned around in my seat, heart thundering. A cruiser roared up on our tail, engine screaming.

"Shit," Joe hissed. I gripped the pistol tighter, eyes wide.

But to our relief, the police car went zooming past us and I was temporarily blinded by red and blue. Rainwater splashed against our truck and Joe slowed.

"Thought that was for us," I gasped, watching the tail lights fade.

"Not yet," Joe said quietly.

We reached the hospital ten minutes later. As Joe parked the truck, I realized that both of us were still shirtless.

"We can't go in there like this," I said, scrounging around the cab for clothing I knew wasn't there.

"Let me call Dave," Joe said, pulling out his cell. "He can bring us our shirts back. I'm sure Tammy has her own by now."

Just the image of that sent a spike of pain shooting through me. I imagined our sister in a hospital bed, fading in and out of consciousness as our mother cried at her side. I exhaled and exhaustion took me.

Joe had a quick conversation with Dave over the phone and then hung up. He turned to me, his eyes weary.

"He's coming out. Tammy is being taken care of."

"Jesus Christ…"

Joe ran his hands over his face. "I know…"

Not long after, we spotted Dave trotting toward the truck. The hospital loomed at his back, a massive brick of light and sanctuary. Thankfully, the rain had finally stopped. Joe and I stepped out into the parking lot as Dave approached.

"Here," he said breathless, handing us our crumbled, wet shirts.

He then froze as he took in our appearance. "Holy Jesus…what did you do to Leo…?"

"You don't have to worry about that," I said, snatching my shirt from his hand.

He touched his cheek. "Cole…your face…"

"What about it?"

"Look in the mirror…"

Hesitantly, I ducked down and peered into the truck's side mirror. The left half of my face was splattered with blood. Somehow, the rain hadn't reached it. My eyes looked huge and terrified as they rolled across my stained skin; the mirror held an unwavering image.

I quickly began to scrub my face, almost desperately. My damp shirt swallowed up the evidence of our violence in seconds, a maw of black fabric that consumed the crimson.

"He's dead, isn't he?" Dave asked, his face pale.

I opened my mouth to answer, but Joe cut me off. "Yeah. He's dead, Dave."

Dave swallowed hard and shook his head slowly. "God…oh, God…"

I pulled on my shirt, the fabric sticking to my skin. "You need to come with us."

"What are you talking about?" Dave asked, looking sick.

"You're in danger," Joe said, sliding his own shirt over his head. "We all are. You need to come with us."

"Come with you…?"

"Mark and Derek aren't going to be far behind us," I

said slowly. "Not to mention the police. You were there with us, Dave. I'm sorry, but you're a part of this now and we need you."

"I can't leave!" Dave cried, taking a step back. "What about Ma?"

Joe shook his head. "Ma should come, as well. And once Tammy is on her feet…well…"

Dave covered his face with his hands, his voice dropping to a whisper. "What have you done…?"

I took a step toward him. "Come on. I need to go pick up some things from my place."

"What about my car?" Dave asked, sounding dazed.

"I'll take it," Joe said. "I'll meet up with you and Cole at the garage. We'll figure it out from there."

Dave's face was a blanket of misery. "You guys have no idea what you're doing, do you…?"

"We need to go," I insisted, "before the Morrisons catch up with us. Or the police. As soon as either lay eyes on Leo's corpse, they're going to be gunning for our blood."

"Why didn't you bury him?" Dave asked. "Why did you just leave him for them to find?"

"You think it would have mattered?" Joe asked, suddenly cold. "You think if Leo just vanished without a trace that they'd leave us alone? Our doors would still be the first they kicked down." Joe advanced on Dave. "And then they'd torture us like they tortured Tammy. So to answer your question…I left him for them to find because they deserve to see what we did to him."

Dave closed his mouth, the night swallowing him up.

"Where's Ma?" I asked gently.

"Inside. With Tammy."

"I need to talk to her real quick, see if she'll come with us. I don't want to leave her here."

"Why don't you leave Ma out of your bullshit?" Dave said, a sudden spark in his eye.

"What the hell is that supposed to mean?" Joe growled.

Dave looked at him. "It means that if the police come calling, I don't want Ma to have to lie to them. And if you think she's leaving Tammy right now, you're crazier than I thought. The second coming of Christ wouldn't be enough for her to leave Tammy's side."

I looked at Joe, who deflated after a moment. "Shit…"

I ran my hands through my hair. "I can't just leave without talking to her…I need to explain what happened…I need to…to tell her why we did what we did…"

Dave looked at the pavement. "Just leave her alone. She's been through enough tonight."

"I'm worried about her safety," I urged. "I have to talk to her."

"You should have thought about that before you fucking killed Leo then," Dave snapped. "This would have never happened, any of it, if you two had just made peace with them!"

"This was out of our hands," Joe growled. "We just did what we had to."

"What a load of shit," Dave spat. "You let your ego get the better of you."

Joe stepped forward and grabbed Dave by the shirt, snarling. "Oh, yeah? You saw what they did to our sister, right? How did that make you feel? How could we just let someone do that to her?"

Dave didn't move, his eyes boring into Joe's. "Yeah…things are so much better now."

"Fuck you, Dave," Joe hissed, pushing him away.

"Both of you stop it!" I yelled. "We're wasting time we don't have. Dave, come with me. I'll call Ma from the road. Joe, take his car and go to the garage. We'll meet up with you there, OK?"

Joe glared at Dave for a second longer before nodding. "Fine. Give me your keys."

Dave dug them out of his pocket and slammed them into Joe's open palm. "It's parked around back."

I opened the door of my truck and grabbed the shotgun. I quickly looked around the parking lot and then handed it to Joe. "Take this with you. Just in case."

The sight of the gun melted Dave's anger almost instantly, his face drooping, his shoulders slumping. "God…what the hell are we doing?"

"See you soon," I said, gripping Joe's arm.

"Keep your eyes open," he whispered.

He turned to go but stopped as Dave called out to

him. Joe looked over his shoulder and after a moment, Dave went to him.

He embraced Joe in a hug, his voice low. "Just stay alive, OK?"

Joe grunted and wrapped his arms around Dave. "Yeah…"

They separated and Joe walked briskly across the parking lot, his boots clicking against the tar. He stuffed the shotgun down his pant leg and covered the butt with his shirt.

When he disappeared from sight, I turned to Dave. "You ready?"

He looked one last time at the hospital. "This doesn't feel right leaving Ma like this…"

"Nothing about tonight feels right."

Dave turned back to me, his tongue heavy with emotion. "Why'd you do it, Cole? Why'd you have to kill him?"

I struggled to answer, to come up with some justification beyond revenge, but the words never found my lips. I looked at my boots, tension building in my shoulders.

"I don't know. Everything is so fucked right now. That video…after I saw it, I just needed to make something right again. I thought killing Leo might do that."

"Did it?"

I turned to the truck. "Let's go."

Chapter 11

Dave remained silent as we drove to my place. He didn't look at me. He didn't speak. His face looked worn, and I could tell he was feeling the same dreadful weight that I did. Guilt oozed from my mind like an ulcer. I wanted to say something, to do something that would make things right. But as the town blurred by, I knew there was nothing I could offer my brother. He had descended into a quiet, morbid acceptance of our circumstances.

I pulled out my phone, keeping an eye on the road, and called Ma. I readied unknown words on my tongue, each ring blasting through my skull with deepening shame.

On the third one, she answered. "Cole?" Her voice was weak, and it sounded as if she had been crying.

"Hey, Ma," I said gently.

"You got her back," she said softly.

"How is she?"

"She'll live. She's so strong…" Her voice trembled. "But Cole…the damage they did…"

"I know, Ma. I saw."

"How could they do something like that?"

I sighed sadly. "People are monsters."

"Where are you? Where's Joe?"

"Ma, I need to tell you something."

Silence greeted me.

"Ma?"

"What happened?" she asked, her voice barely a whisper. "What did you do?"

I gritted my teeth, chest heaving. "We did a bad thing."

I heard her brace herself. "You hurt them, didn't you?"

I forced the words from my throat. "Only Leo."

Still a whisper: "Is he dead?"

Dave looked at me.

I exhaled painfully. "Yeah…he's dead."

"Good." The venom in my mother's voice caught me off-guard. "Good boy. Thank you, Cole."

"Ma," I struggled. "Leo's dead, but Mark and Derek are still out there. I think they found their brother. They're going to be coming after us now."

"Where are you?" she asked, concerned now.

"I'm with Dave," I said, shooting him a look. "We're heading to my place and then Joe's. I don't know how much time we have before the shit hits the fan, especially with the sheriff around. It won't be long until he's after us, too."

I heard her collect herself for a moment before saying, "What are you going to do?"

"I don't know," I said wearily. "We haven't gotten that far yet. But we don't have much time. I think you should come with us. I just want to see that you're safe."

"I'm not going anywhere," she said fiercely. "I'm not leaving my daughter alone here."

"Ma, please…"

"It's not happening, Cole. If they want to come here and confront me, let them try. What have I done? What could they possibly do to me?"

"Use you to hurt me and Joe," I said solemnly. "I just don't think it's safe there."

"I'm not leaving."

"Shit, Ma…"

"I'll be OK," she pressed. "You take care of yourself and your brothers right now. When you get to Joe's, call me. I'll be worried."

"I will."

"How's Dave?"

I looked at him. "We've all been better."

She sighed faintly. "I can't believe this has happened to our family…"

"I have to go now…"

"OK…I love you. Be careful."

"I love you, too."

I hung up and focused on the road. Dave glanced at me.

"She's not leaving?"

"No. You were right."

"You think she's going to be alright?"

"I don't know, Dave."

He turned away and stared out into the darkness.

We reached my apartment and I parked. In the distance, we heard police sirens howling. They made me nervous. Dave followed me upstairs and we quickly packed up some things. We kept the lights off. With each passing moment, I felt as if some horrible creature was lumbering closer, claws raised, fangs exposed.

After stuffing the last of my belongings into a bag, we left the apartment. I had an awful feeling that it was the last time I'd see it. Dave had remained quiet through the whole ordeal. I noticed he was actively avoiding eye contact, too.

We hurried back downstairs and climbed into my truck, tossing the handful of bags into the bed. In seconds, we were back on the road.

I made sure to stay under the speed limit as we slid down Main Street. The pistol lay between Dave and me, untouched. I felt better with it there. My nerves were frayed and my thoughts came in broken pieces. As I drove, I fought with them. I needed a plan. I needed a light at the end of the tunnel.

I needed a way out of this mess.

You know how this ends...

I looked at Dave. He was staring out the window, a worried look on his face. I could see him thinking. I could see him struggling. His hands were balled into fists and he bit his lip. His brow was furrowed.

"Hey, Dave," I said quietly as Mill Valley peeled by.

He glanced at me.

"Thanks for coming with me," I said.

"Didn't really have much of a choice," he muttered grimly.

I searched for something to say. "Yeah, well…we're going to get through this. All of us. Somehow. This isn't the end."

"Whatever you say, Cole," Dave said, turning back to the window.

"I know things are screwed up right now, but Joe and I…and you…we're going to make things right. We have to. We owe it to Tammy."

"This would have never happened if you hadn't come back," Dave whispered suddenly.

His words pierced me like a knife. I felt a sadness rise in my throat, a guilty, horrible bile that burned my tongue.

Dave exhaled. "I'm sorry. You didn't deserve that. This isn't your fault."

"I'm sorry," I said softly.

Dave looked at me. "I know you're just trying to look out for Joe. I know that's what you've always done. But…Cole…how could you let things go so far?"

"I'm not going to make excuses," I whispered. "But Dave…Leo deserved to die for what he did. They all do."

"And that's for us to decide?"

I wrapped my fingers hard around the steering wheel. "Who else is going to hold them responsible?"

Dave sighed. "I know this has been especially hard on you, considering what happened with Maria—"

"Don't bring her into this," I snapped. "This has nothing to do with her."

"Doesn't it?" Dave pressed.

I glared at him. "You saw what they did to Tammy."

Dave held my eyes for a moment and then dropped his gaze. "Yeah…" he covered his face with his hands. "Shit. What a nightmare."

Without warning, the cab was suddenly illuminated with red and blue light. My heart leaped into my throat as I checked the mirrors.

"Oh, fuck," I hissed.

A police car trailed us and was signaling for us to pull over.

Dave's face turned white as he craned his head around. "Oh, no…oh, no, no, no."

"Stay calm," I instructed, heart clapping in my chest. The road had just narrowed to two lanes and dark forest surrounded us. The police car flashed its lights and I slowed.

"What are we going to do?" Dave asked, beginning to panic.

"Let's just see what he wants," I said quietly, pulling the truck off to the side. "Maybe they don't know Leo is dead yet."

"But I thought you said—"

"Stop it," I barked.

"If they know," Dave croaked, "then we're dead men."

"Just shut up and let me talk," I ordered. I parked the truck but kept the engine running. My hand found the pistol and I shoved it under the seat. I tried to calm myself as the silhouette of a police officer crawled out of the cruiser and came into view. He walked toward us slowly, his figure backlit by the high beams.

I rolled the window down as he approached. I forced myself to breathe. The officer looked about my age, and despite the darkness, he kept his aviators on. He looked into the cab and appraised Dave and me for a moment before speaking. On sight, I felt threatened by his presence.

"Where you fellas headin'?" he asked with a deep Southern drawl.

"Out of town," I said as calmly as I could. "Heading up north for a couple weeks."

The officer placed his arms on the window sill and leaned on them. "Going for a little vacation?"

"Something like that," I stuttered.

He sucked his bottom lip for a second and then nodded at Dave. "Who's he?"

"He's my brother," I said.

"He talk?"

Dave forced his eyes over to the cop. "Sure do, officer."

The man sniffed. "You got your license and registration?"

Dave fumbled with the glove box and began digging through the mess of papers. A few of them dropped to the floor. His hands were shaking and I silently cursed my brother.

"Take your time," the officer said slowly.

"You can never find these things when you need them," Dave mumbled, his voice cracking.

The officer directed his shaded gaze back to me. "This your truck?"

"Yes, sir. Um…can I ask why you pulled us over?" I ventured.

"We'll get to that," he said casually. Dave finally found the registration and handed it to the cop. He took it and glanced down at the paper. Then, slowly, he removed his sunglasses and glared directly at me.

"I-is there a problem?" I fumbled.

"Seems to be," he said, his voice hard.

I swallowed. "I know it's out of state, I moved back here not too long ago and I keep meaning to get it changed, but—"

"That ain't the issue," the officer said, leaning into the window.

I felt my pulse drumming in my ears. "Oh?"

The cop lowered his voice. "I'm still waiting on that license of yours."

Relief practically exploded through me. "Oh! Oh, yes, of course. Duh. Sorry." I leaned forward and reached into my back pocket. I felt the heel of my boot kick the pistol beneath my seat.

I dug out my wallet and slid my license from it. "Here you are, sir."

It hung between us, but the man never took it. He just stared at me, his eyes dark.

"Something else you need?" I asked. I could practically feel Dave's panic attack from my seat.

Slowly, the officer reached across his shoulder to his radio. He thumbed the receiver. "Officer Riley here. Sheriff? I think I found two of those boys you're looking for."

He said it without breaking eye contact and I felt my world rock to a halt. The blood drained from my face and I suddenly had a hard time breathing. My fingers twitched in my lap and my ears buzzed insistently.

A squawk of static and then a voice like burning thunder. "Where are you?"

The officer continued to stare directly at me. "Tail end of Main Street, headin' northbound. Right at the tree line."

Static, and then the voice of the sheriff. "Keep 'em there. Derek and Mark are on their way."

The officer smiled. "Will do."

Before I could react, I was suddenly staring down the barrel of a gun. The cop stepped away from the open window and cocked his head. "Get out. Both of you. And no sudden movements, or I will fire."

"Cole!" Dave cried, his voice a strained whisper.

Shit, oh shit, shit, shit...

"Get the hell out of the truck," the cop demanded. "I ain't asking again."

Hesitantly, I reached for the handle.

"He's going to kill us!" Dave whimpered, almost silently.

"Quiet," I whispered, my throat dry.

Miserably, Dave opened his door, stealing the officer's attention for a half-second.

I dragged the pistol out from under my seat with my boot. As I inched the door open, I leaned down and snatched it up. Hiding myself with the door, now with one foot out, I stuffed the gun behind my back and into my waistband.

I dropped my hand as the cop snapped his eyes back to me. I exited the rest of the way out of the truck and shut the door. Dave walked to my side, his brows knitted in fear, hands raised.

"Now you two just stand there," the cop instructed, still pointing his gun at us. "You got company on the way."

"Don't do this," Dave pleaded. "We haven't done anything wrong."

The cop snorted. "I think Leo Morrison would say otherwise. If he was still alive, that is."

"He raped our sister," I hissed, keeping my hands up. The pistol dug into the small of my back.

"Tell yourself whatever you need to," the officer

retorted. "But murder is murder. Now you just shut your mouths and wait for Derek and Mark."

"They're going to kill us," Dave cried.

"Shut up," the cop growled.

Dave looked at me out of the corner of his eye. He silently begged me to do something. I knew we didn't have much time. Once the remaining Morrison brothers arrived, it would be too late. I had to act. I had to get us out of this.

But I didn't want to have to shoot this man. As corrupt as he was, he had nothing to do with this. Besides pointing a gun at my head. My fingers twitched at my sides. The wind blustered between the three of us. Dave's hands shook as he nervously clenched and unclenched them.

"Where's the other one?" the cop asked, unmoving.

I looked at him. "What other one?"

"Your brother. Joe Barker. Where is he?"

I shrugged, trying to act more at ease than I felt. "I don't know."

"That's a load and we both know it," the officer growled.

"We really don't know," Dave whimpered, lying.

The cop adjusted the pistol in his grip, swinging it between Dave and me. "Well, even if you're lying, once Derek and Mark get here I'm sure you'll wanna start talking. They ain't too happy 'bout their brother, as you can imagine."

Do something, Cole. You have to do something.

I cleared my throat. "If I tell you where Joe is, will you let Dave here go?"

The cop closed one eye as he stared at me. "Thought you said you didn't know where he was."

"Yeah, well, I was lying."

"Cole!" Dave whispered, eyes wide.

I shot him a glare.

"Well, that is an interesting proposition," the officer mused. "But I'm not sure it's one for me to decide. I'll let Derek do that once he gets here. Any minute now."

I balled my hands into fists. "What's wrong? Aren't paid enough to think for yourself?"

I heard Dave inhale sharply.

"You better watch that mouth," the cop snarled.

"Or what?" I ventured. "You can't do shit to me until your masters get here and give you a bone like the good little bitch you are."

The cop gritted his teeth, face going red. "Shut the fuck up."

"Hey, Dave, I think he's crying," I sneered, bluffing. Dave looked appalled at what I was saying.

Just play along, I thought, practically shoving the thought toward my brother.

"Stop talking! I'm warning you!" the cop yelled.

"Must be nice having the sheriff there to tell you how to put your pants on in the morning," I continued, heart racing. I was pushing it, and I knew it.

I plowed on regardless. "Does he give you a treat every time you ignore the law for the sake of his sons?

Does he pat you on the head and tell you what a good boy you are? What a good obedient little slut you are?"

"I'm going to blow your head off if you don't shut the fuck up," the cop hissed, advancing, pistol trained at my head.

My heart drummed in my ears. "Does he pinch your ass if you're a good boy? Ain't nothing wrong with that. You know that, right? You don't have to be afraid. I bet you dream about him all day, huh?"

The cop was now standing directly in front of me, the barrel of his pistol kissing my forehead. "One more word," he spat. "Please."

"STOP!" Dave cried, reaching out for the gun.

The officer looked away from me for a split second and it was all I needed. In one quick motion, I grabbed the barrel of his pistol and shoved it away from me while simultaneously retrieving my own from behind my back. I shoved my gun against the cop's thigh right as he turned his attention back to me with a surprised look.

I didn't hesitate as I shot him in the leg.

He screamed and went down, his grip loosening on his revolver. I yanked it out of his hand as he fell to the road, clutching his bleeding thigh. Dave jumped at the noise and backed into the truck.

The cop lunged for me, an enraged snarl burning up through the pain. I stepped into him and booted him across the face. He went sprawling, exhaling heavily. I advanced and stomped down on his hand. I heard his fingers break. And then I heard him scream.

He clutched his hand to his chest and rolled onto his back. I knelt down and planted a knee in his chest. I put my gun to his head, sweat beading off the tip of my nose. I felt like I couldn't breathe. The cop stared up at me, his eyes suddenly huge and very afraid.

"I should kill you for what you are," I said very quietly, "but unlike you and those sadists you work for, I'm not a monster." I raised the butt of the pistol and smashed it down across his face, knocking him unconscious.

I stood, panting, and looked at Dave. He was paralyzed against the truck.

"I thought he was going to shoot you," he whispered, looking sick.

"So did I."

"Did you kill him?"

I shook my head. "No. But he won't be out for long. Come on, we need to get out of here. Now."

Dave nodded and walked around the truck to the passenger's door. I slid into the driver's seat once again. I couldn't seem to get my pulse to slow. That had been too close.

I looked outside to see the cop, immobile on the road. The lights from his cruiser illuminated his still figure. How many more would come...?

"You OK?" Dave asked, closing his door.

I looked at him, centering myself. "I think so. We need to get to the garage."

"They're going to be after us," Dave said, looking over my shoulder at the unconscious officer. "All of them."

"I already know that," I muttered, allowing myself a second to breathe.

Dave continued to stare. "There isn't an end to this, is there, Cole?"

"There's always an end," I muttered, closing my eyes. "We just have to find it."

I looked up and put the car in drive. As I pulled out onto the road, I heard Dave inhale sharply. Before I could ask what was wrong, I saw another pair of headlights in the rear-view mirror barreling down the road toward us.

"Oh, no," I whispered. I gunned the engine and the truck leaped forward.

"It's them!" Dave cried, turning around in his seat. "Oh, hell, it's them!"

"Hold on!" I yelled, applying pressure to the gas. The truck groaned and we began to pick up speed. I glanced in the mirror again. The approaching vehicle drew closer. I gritted my teeth, willing my truck to move faster. I floored it now, praying. I checked the mirror once more. It wasn't enough. They were almost on us. I could hear the engine roaring. I could feel the rage of the driver.

"Go, Cole, GO!" Dave yelled as headlights flooded the interior of the cab.

They were so close now, a dozen yards behind us.

And they weren't slowing.

"SHIT!" I screamed, bracing myself.

A second later and they plowed into us. I felt my body whip aggressively and my forehead smashed against the steering wheel. Dazed, I blindly jerked the wheel, fighting to regain control as the truck began to fishtail wildly.

It wasn't enough, and I felt the truck begin to rotate, spinning me right into their path. I looked up, eyes wide, and realized I was about to get T-boned.

"FUCK! HOLD ON!" I howled, turning away from the imminent collision.

They hit us hard, the impact rattling my teeth. I closed my eyes as pain erupted along the left side of my body, the sound of crunching metal exploding loudly in my ears. The world spun and the sound of shattered glass erupted along my face. I tasted blood on my tongue and the truck flipped over on its side, and then I was upside down. In the spinning chaos, I could hear Dave screaming.

Two more rotations and we landed roughly against a tree, the truck shuddering violently as the pillar of wood halted our roll.

Gasping, ears ringing, I felt pain crease through every part of my body. Dizzy, hurting, I heard the squeal of tires along the road and then the roar of an engine as it was slammed into reverse.

Get…out…of…here…

Panting, I opened my eyes and saw I was lying on the roof of the cab. We had landed upside down. I winced and looked up to see the floor. Broken glass rained down around me and fell into my hair. Moaning, I dragged my eyes to Dave, who lay twisted beside me.

I reached out and shook him, voice hoarse. "Hey…hey, get up…!"

Coughing, groaning, Dave opened his eyes. He looked at me and I saw a long bloody gash running down the side of his face.

"Move!" I cried, fighting to regain some semblance of clarity. "We have to get out! GO!"

On the road, I heard the truck screech to a halt.

They're coming.

"MOVE!" I yelled, the word ripping at my damaged throat.

I shoved Dave ahead of me, out of the shattered passenger's-side window, toward the woods. Wincing, hissing painfully, Dave complied and dragged himself out of the wreckage. His legs scraped against the ruined window. As he rolled out onto the grass, I saw him paint the shattered glass a deep red, leaving behind strips of torn cloth.

Bracing myself, I was forced to follow. My hands shook as I reached out and groped for something to pull myself through. Pain flared through my ribs, but my adrenaline insisted I ignore it.

Chest heaving, I slid through the window and out onto the grass next to Dave. Behind us, I heard doors slamming.

"Get up," I croaked, grabbing my brother by the back of the shirt. "Come on, get up!"

Panting, the two of us stumbled to our feet and lurched for the woods. I chanced a glance behind us and my heart froze in my chest.

Derek and Mark were out of their truck and marching down toward us, their faces contorted with raw fury.

And in Mark's hands was a hunting rifle.

"Run!" I gasped, grabbing Dave by the arm and pulling him along behind me into the woods.

Three steps into the trees and a gunshot rocked the night. Something whistled past my head, so close I felt the hairs on the back of my neck stand up. The tree ahead of me exploded in a shower of splinters and I jerked Dave to the left, deeper into the woods.

"We're dead," Dave groaned, hobbling next to me. He slung his arm across my shoulders and leaned heavily on me for support. I gritted my teeth, heart thundering, pulse roaring in my ears.

We needed help.

Foliage crunched beneath our boots as we waded further and further from the road. I could hear Derek and Mark behind us, the thud of hurried footsteps thumping through my skull.

"Faster, we have to move faster," I pleaded, heaving Dave up and adjusting my grip around him.

"I think I'm really hurt," Dave groaned, stumbling along, chest hitching.

An edge of horrific desperation lined my voice. "No, no, no, you're OK, man, you're OK. Just keep moving. We can lose them."

Another gunshot echoed across the night.

I heard the bullet rip through the air, terribly close. Another tree sprayed us with ruined wood and I frantically adjusted our course once more.

The woods towered around us, a snagging, merciless beast. Underbrush clawed at my knees, rocks rose to trip me, and branches lashed out from the darkness with dangerous intent. In minutes, I felt a hundred stinging cuts burning across my exposed skin.

At my back, Mark screamed my name.

He wasn't far behind.

"Shit, oh shit," I trembled. "Come on, Dave, you have to help me, please, MOVE!"

"I'm trying," Dave breathed, his teeth clenched.

They're going to catch you.

"Fuck," I cried pathetically, terrified.

And then a thought blasted through my head.

Joe.

Wheezing, limping, I reached into my pocket and pulled out my phone. The screen was cracked, but it still worked. Dave looked down at it through a haze and continued to stagger forward as best he could. One-handed, I called Joe.

He answered immediately. "Cole?"

"You have to help us!" I cried, listening to Mark crash through the woods behind us.

"What's going on? Where are you?" Joe asked urgently, sensing the panic in my voice.

"In the woods, a couple miles down the road from you!" I gasped, pressing Dave to move faster. He grunted painfully, clinging to me.

"What happened?" Joe urged.

"Derek and Mark…" I sputtered, lungs burning beneath Dave's weight. "They're here. They smashed up my truck…Joe, hurry! Please!"

"Oh, Christ," Joe whispered. "OK, I'm coming! Just find somewhere to hide!"

"We don't have much time," I coughed, wincing as a branch raked across my mouth.

"Don't let them catch you," Joe said desperately. And then he was gone.

I tripped and dropped my phone, lost beneath the underbrush. Dave almost took us both down as his body jerked and then he righted himself, his face twisting in pain.

Behind us, Mark's voice echoed loudly through the night. "You can't run from this! We're gonna catch you!"

Dave's breathing was ragged now, a weak wheeze that

took way too much effort. I felt him slowly sinking into me, his strength fading.

"Oh, no," I whispered, voice cracking. "Oh, please, stay with me, Dave."

Dave's eyes began to flutter. "I can't…Cole…"

And then he was falling over. The arm slung around my shoulders yanked me to the earth and I collapsed on top of him. Slivers of cracking pain shot through me, and the air was knocked from my lungs.

I fought to regain my feet, but I knew Dave couldn't stand again. His eyes rolled back and he fell into unconsciousness. I shook him frantically, a whining plea on my lips.

A sudden snap of wood caused me to look up, fear seizing me.

Derek towered over us, his face darker than the night.

"You're mine now," he growled.

A fist plowed into the side of my head and darkness took me.

Chapter 12

My head thudded, a long, painful drum across my skull. In the darkness, I winced against it. Thoughts came slowly, like lumbering images from a filthy mirror. It was hard make sense of them around the ache between my ears.

A voice called to me, but I couldn't understand it. I moaned and tried to find my eyelids so that I could open them. Something dug into my wrists. My stomach rolled with nausea. Exhaustion draped itself around my shoulders, pressing me down.

The voice called to me again and this time I heard my name.

"Cole."

I slowly lifted my head, some of the fog clearing. I opened my eyes, failed, and then tried again. Color leaked into my world and blurry images shifted and then aligned into focus. I felt drool dripping from my chin. My hair hung in my eyes. My chest rose and fell with concentrated precision.

"Hello, Cole," Derek said, his face inches from mine.

I squeezed my eyes shut and then pulled them open again. Derek grinned, but there was no humor in the expression.

"Glad to see you're back with us," he said darkly, that horrible smile still stretching across his lips. Dark bags hung beneath his bloodshot eyes. His breath blew rancid across my face and I could smell dirt and sweat on him.

"Your brother just woke up," Derek continued. "I think he wants to talk to you."

Derek stood and stepped back, allowing me to take in my surroundings. As I did, I felt my stomach buckle and the pulse in my head quicken.

Oh, God…

I was bound to a chair directly across from Dave, who faced me and was restrained in a similar fashion. We were sitting in the kitchen of the Morrisons' hunting cabin. Leo's blood still stained the floor beneath my boots, though his body was nowhere to be found. I craned my head around and saw the front door closed and the drapes pulled.

I pulled my eyes back to Dave and saw Mark standing behind him, arms crossed, his eyes red. He looked like he had been crying.

Dave weakly stared at me, lost in pain. Blood leaked from his nose and mouth and grime smeared his face. His blinked heavily and snot dribbled down his face.

"Cole…" he gasped, his voice barely audible.

Instantly, Mark slugged him across the back of the

head, his fist rocking my brother in his chair. Dave grunted and his head dipped forward so that his chin rested on his chest.

"Stop it!" I cried, finding my voice. The words rasped across my lips like dry leaves.

Derek stepped into view again and held up a hand to Mark. "Hey…easy there. Dave's had a rough day."

"Let him go," I whispered, the sickness in my stomach rising. "Please, let him go."

Derek folded his hands behind his back and appraised the two of us. "Let him go? Now why would I do that?"

I licked my cracked lips. "He's got nothing to do with this."

Derek stroked his chin. "Hmmm…he's got nothing to do with this. Huh." He walked behind Dave and placed his hands on his shoulders. "I'm afraid I don't believe you, Cole. I think both your brothers had something to do with what went on in this cabin. You know how I know that? I'm not a detective, I'll be the first to admit, but it wasn't hard to miss the three different sets of footprints we found. Footprints soaked in my brother's blood. Look around you. They're still there, plain as the lie on your lips."

"He didn't do anything," I begged. "He's not the one you want!"

Derek remained motionless. "Yeah? And who do I want?" His voice dropped dangerously. "Which one of you killed Leo?"

"I did!" I sputtered, instantly. "I killed him! Dave told me not to. He begged me not to. He said there was another way we could settle this!"

Mark angrily marched to my side. He jerked my head up by a fistful of hair. "There's only one way to settle this. You took something dear to us. Now we take something dear to you."

I stared up at him, head pounding, eyes heavy. "NO! Jesus Christ, you raped our sister! What the hell were we supposed to do?!"

"You killed Leo's dog," Mark sneered. "We were just resetting the scales. Shit, we didn't kill anyone. Not like you."

"You don't have to do this," I pleaded. Mark gripped my hair harder, seething.

Dave sputtered and coughed as he tried to speak, his eyes rising to meet Mark's.

"Get...your fucking hands...off my brother," he croaked.

Mark's eyes went wide and then he laughed maliciously, releasing me. He nodded and held up his hands as a mock sign of surrender. Still behind Dave, Derek patted his shoulder.

"That's good," he said. "Stick up for each other. Help each other. Fight for each other. I can respect that. I really can."

Derek circled around Dave and looked down at the two of us. "Now...I need to know where the third Barker brother is. Where's Joe?"

I couldn't take my eyes off Dave, his bloody, beaten body sagging against the ropes that held him. Our eyes met and I saw despair that cut me to the bone.

"Don't give up," I whispered across to him, my eyes welling, chest heaving. "Don't you give up on me."

Dave's eyes fluttered and he stared at the floor, a bloody strand of drool dripping from his chin.

"Hey, I asked you a question," Derek growled, snapping his fingers. "Where is your brother?"

Slowly, I raised my eyes, contempt slithering across my tongue. "Where's yours?"

Mark balled his hands into fists and I thought he would strike me, but Derek held up a hand, stopping him. He met my gaze and I saw death reflected back at me.

"You kept pushing us," he said slowly. "You just kept pushing us. All we wanted was a fair shake on life, but you Barkers wouldn't even allow us that."

"What you did to our sister—" I started, but Derek cut me off.

"What we did was set things right again. We're not the bad guys here," he leaned down, his shadow consuming me. "You are."

I gritted my teeth, lost in the thunder blasting through my head. "So fucking kill me then."

Derek sniffed and stood back up. "I'm going to. But not before you know what it's like to lose a brother."

Panic seized me once again and I jerked forward in my chair. "NO! I told you he had nothing to do with this! I killed Leo! I buried that fucking hatchet in his head! It's me you want! Not him! Not him, goddamn it!"

Mark shook his head. "You can't stop this."

Derek pointed out of the kitchen and down the hall. "My baby brother is lying in the other room, ruined. Not just murdered, but tortured." He balled his hands into fists. "Killing him wasn't enough...you wanted him to suffer." Derek shoved a meaty finger into my chest. "And you enjoyed it." His finger was joined by the others and he gripped a handful of my shirt. "So stop lying to yourself. You're not a good person."

He stepped away and pulled a pistol out from behind his back. My heart leaped into my throat as he grimly went and stood behind Dave.

"I want you to look him in the eyes," Derek said. "And I want you to know this is happening because you're a malicious person, Cole."

"STOP IT!" I screamed, eyes bulging, terror surging through me. I thrashed about in my chair, heart racing, panic erupting. "KILL ME! JUST KILL ME!"

Dave slowly raised his eyes to mine and I saw he was crying. His voice trembled as he felt the barrel of the pistol press against the back of his head.

"Cole...?"

I leaned forward, drool and spittle dripping from my mouth, my eyes wild. "Dave! David! Look at me! Look at me, David!"

Dave's bottom lip began to tremble and a tear rolled down his face. "Cole, I don't want to die. Help me…"

"I'm right here!" I sobbed, screaming. "I'm right here with you! I love you! Jesus Christ, I love you so much! It's going to be OK!"

"I'm scared," Dave wept, sniffling, chest rising and falling rapidly.

I tore my tear-stained eyes away from him. "Derek! Stop this! I'm begging you, don't do this!"

Derek cocked the hammer back.

"NO!" I howled, looking back to Dave. "Oh, CHRIST! David, I'm sorry! Oh, FUCK I'm so sorry! Don't leave me! I can't do this without you! OH GOD, PLEASE DON'T LEAVE ME! DAVID!"

He held my eyes for a second longer.

And then Derek shot him in the back of the head.

"FUUUUUUUUUUUCK!" I screamed, eyes bulging, throat tearing. Blood splattered across my face and I rocked in my chair, howling, weeping, dying, hands shaking uncontrollably.

"OH MY GOD, NO!" I bellowed, tears running down my face. "OH JESUS FUCK NO PLEASE GOD!" Bile crawled up my throat and I gagged, face wet with sorrow, with horror, as Dave slumped forward, dead.

"I'M SORRY!" I bawled, croaked, screamed. "DAVID, DON'T LEAVE ME, PLEASE! I NEED YOU, DAVID! COME BACK! PLEASE GOD, COME BACK!"

I thrashed and jerked, begging to be freed. My chair

tilted and then crashed to the floor, my head bouncing hard across the tile. Through blurry, tear-soaked eyes, I watched blood pour down the front of my brother's chest.

Mark leaned over me, his voice a low hiss. "It hurts, doesn't it?"

I gagged and shivered violently, my howls of sorrow deafening.

Derek stepped around the chair and stood over me. "Now you know what it's like."

I squeezed my eyes shut and shuddered as sharp, hoarse sobs wracked my body.

Not this…oh God, please, not this…

"And now it's your turn," Derek said gravely. A shadow rose across my face and I knew I was about to die.

At the very moment before Derek pulled the trigger, the front door exploded inward in a flurry of violence. Derek and Mark leaped up, spinning around in a panic as the heavy wood thudded into the living room.

From the darkness, Joe emerged, shotgun raised.

Without hesitation, he pointed it at Mark and blew his head off.

The report cracked the air and gun smoke wafted overhead. I heard bits of Mark's skull splatter against the wall. The mangled corpse dropped to its knees and blood streamed from the gore.

Still moving, Joe pumped another round into the chamber and trained the gun on Derek. Crying out in shocked fear, Derek stumbled backwards and tripped over me. As he went down, Joe fired. The buckshot whistled overhead as Derek thudded onto his back, onto the floor behind me. His pistol went skidding across the tile and disappeared beneath the fridge.

Cursing, Joe advanced, cocking the shotgun once more. But he froze when his eyes fell on Dave. Vision blurred, I saw my brother's face go pale, his jaw clench, and shock rattle through him like dynamite.

Derek took the opportunity to scramble to his feet and bolt for the back door. Joe ignored him; he had to, his attention was absorbed by the horrific scene.

My head pounded with an insistent, merciless beat. Snot dribbled down my face, tears mixed with blood, and my throat screamed raw. I could hear Derek outside, starting his truck, followed by the roar of the engine. Any bloodthirst Joe had felt drained instantly out of him as he took in the body of our brother.

I struggled away from Mark's corpse that lay next to me, a pool of blood inching its way toward my face. I weakly struggled against my restraints, the ropes having loosened from the fall.

Joe walked into the kitchen, his gun lowered. His eyes were wide and despite my pitiful pleas for help, he never looked away from Dave.

"Oh, my God…" he whispered.

"Joe!" I begged at his feet.

He suddenly looked down and realized I was still alive. Like a zombie, he knelt, taking the knife from his boot. He cut the rope that held me and then stood back up, still staring at Dave's dead body.

Crying, I snatched the knife from Joe's hand and went to my dead brother. Gritting my teeth and choking back sobs, I cut him free. With the ropes gone, Dave tumbled into my arms and onto the floor. I knelt, holding him, squeezing my eyes shut as the world shuddered and throbbed around me.

"I'm so sorry," I choked, staring down into his still face. I could feel my arms dampen with blood. He looked so horribly...absent.

"Oh, God, I'm so sorry, David," I wept, bringing him into me and hugging him fiercely.

"C-cole..."

I tore myself away from Dave and looked up at Joe.

He shifted his weight from one leg to the other and looked sick. "I-is he dead?"

"Yes, he's dead!" I yelled, throat burning. I couldn't seem to stop crying as the weight of the night crushed me with murderous claws.

"Fuck...oh fuck..." Joe whispered, shaking his head.

I gently lowered Dave out of my arms and onto the floor. He left a river of blood across my body.

"Forgive me," I sniffed, wiping my eyes.

Joe licked his lips, unable to comprehend what he was seeing. "H-how...who...which one did it?"

"Derek," I said weakly, my stomach spinning, ears thundering.

Joe tightened his grip on the shotgun. "Derek..."

"Where were you?" I growled suddenly, dragging my eyes over to meet Joe's.

"What are you talking about?" Joe asked. "I came as soon as you called! Jesus Christ, it's a miracle I even found you! When I arrived at the wreck, you were gone! All of you! I figured the only place they'd take you is up here! I searched the woods first, just to make sure you weren't still hiding, but then I hauled ass up the mountain! Christ, Cole, this isn't my fault!" His voice shook by the end.

My chest filled with sorrow like ocean water into a sinking ship. And in that sensation, in that overwhelming moment, I felt something else pour in as well.

Fury.

Tears still drying on my face, I ground my teeth together. "This is *all* your fault."

The words seemed to drill a hole in Joe's heart. "Cole…"

I advanced on him, a snarl on my tongue. "Everything we've done has stemmed from your bullshit. First the garage, then the dog, then Tammy…and now…" I stood nose-to-nose with him. "And now this. Our brother is dead." I choked on sadness, felt it filling me up, consuming me.

And then came the burning. The fire. My lips pulled back and began to tremble.

The rage.

"Derek doesn't get to see the sun rise," I whispered,

the words rolling past my gritted teeth like burning coals.

Joe gripped the shotgun with both hands and nodded wordlessly. His face was a blanket of disbelief, hurt, and anger. I could see him struggling behind eyes that dripped with dreamlike paralysis.

Bleeding blood that wasn't my own, I turned around and went to the fridge. With a strained grunt, I pulled it forward. With a crunching gush of gore, it collapsed on top of Mark's body. Joe jumped, the sudden sound startling him beyond his shock. I didn't even look at the ruin the fridge left. I bent down and retrieved Derek's pistol. I curled my fingers, stained a wet crimson, around the grip.

"Let's go," I said, driven by the ache in my head. It was almost overwhelming in its constant strain on my mind. It pressed against the inside of my skull like the fingers of a skeleton.

Joe pointed down at Dave, his voice shaking. "But...what about..."

"He's getting away," I growled, pointing outside.

"Dave..."

I took three quick steps over to Joe and backhanded him across the face hard. "Wake the FUCK up, Joe!"

Startled, Joe stepped away from me, his cheek glowing.

"There's nothing we can do for him right now," I said, the words like razors across my tongue. "And we WILL be back to lay him to rest. But right now I'm soaked with Dave's blood and I'm not letting the fucker who put it there just drive away from this. So pull yourself together, because you're the only brother I have left." I stepped forward and gripped him by the back of the neck, pulling his forehead against mine, my voice softening. "And I need you right now."

Color swarmed back into Joe's complexion and edges sharpened along the creases of his face. "OK, Cole. OK. I'm with you."

I released him and pointed to the door. "You have your truck?"

"Yeah, out front."

"Then let's go kill that motherfucker."

Together we left the house. I spared one last look at Dave's body and I felt like I was leaving a part of myself with him. The overwhelming surge of pain and sadness returned and I whispered quietly back into the house.

"I love you. I'll see you soon."

And then we were running for the truck, a mental clock ticking away in the back of my head. The night sky pressed heavy upon us, the black canvas a low ceiling that burrowed into my mind and spread its inky tendrils.

I welcomed it. I drank it down. Anything so that I wouldn't be forced to confront the staggering loss I felt with every labored, ragged breath.

We reached Joe's truck and began the descent down the mountain. Derek didn't have much of a head start and I knew we could catch him. If we hurried. The road bumped beneath us as Joe roared down it in pursuit of the murderous monster who had killed our brother. There was only one road up to the cabin and I could practically smell the desperation left behind in its tracks. I squeezed the pistol so hard that my knuckles cracked.

"Where would he go?" Joe asked, bouncing in his seat as we tore around a corner and continued down the long tongue of road.

"I don't know," I whispered hatefully. "But if we hurry, maybe we can run him off the road. If not..." I closed my eyes and pictured Derek's face, summoning the source of my fury. "Maybe his house. Maybe the police station. I don't know. Just drive."

Joe sped up, accelerating to a dangerous speed. His shotgun bounced against his leg. It silently begged to vomit its death upon someone. I watched it, eager to comply.

"Are those taillights?" Joe asked after some time, breaking the murderous silence.

I pulled my eyes from the shotgun and squinted ahead. The road had opened up into a long straight stretch, the last trek before leveling out and turning back toward Mill Valley. Two red eyes blinked ominously in the far distance, a driver feathering the brakes.

"It's him," I muttered, the sound coming from deep within my chest.

The taillights disappeared from sight. Joe rounded a

corner, tires screeching, and we bumped down onto the main road again. I quickly jerked my head left and then right, trying to decipher where our aggressor had gone. As I looked to the right, I spotted a streak of red tearing down the road and around a bend.

"He's headed for his house," I said darkly.

"Damn it," Joe muttered.

"Better than the police station, right?"

Joe said nothing and I let it go.

As we ripped through the darkness, I looked at the dashboard and saw that it was a little after three in the morning. I felt like I had been awake for days, the weight across my eyes matched by the anchor in my chest. The muscles in my shoulders tightened as we pursued Derek. I looked down at my hands and saw they were stained a dark red. The swath of color ran up to my elbows and painted my shirt. A shudder ran through my body, a jolting shiver of exhaustion, anger, and suffocating grief.

The woods continued to blur outside as we drove. After a couple minutes, we spotted Derek's truck. It was turning down a side road a couple hundred yards away. It was headed exactly where we hoped it was. Derek was going home. But why?

I realized I didn't care and motioned for Joe to slow a little.

"We'll have him trapped," I said as my brother eased on the brakes. "No need to give away the element of surprise."

"What is he doing?" Joe asked as the speedometer dropped.

"I don't know."

"You think he called the sheriff yet?"

"Of course he has."

We could see the distant lights of Mill Valley as we continued to slow. They illuminated the night sky with muddy color, a dim glow that hung above the town like a fog. If Derek had gone to the police station, he would have had us outnumbered. So why was he headed home to his isolated house in the woods?

"Do you think the police are already waiting for us?" Joe asked, reaching the side road and turning down it.

"It's too soon," I muttered, casting a watchful eye out the window toward Mill Valley. I didn't see any flashing lights.

"I don't like this," Joe whispered.

"Turn off your lights," I instructed. "We need every advantage we can get."

Joe did as he was told. "Can barely see anything."

"Just go slow. We know his house is at the end of this stretch. He can't get out, at least not by road."

We rumbled down the single lane. Joe leaned forward in his seat, squinting. I tightened my grip on the pistol. We were close. We were so close. Derek was just ahead, unaware just how near we were. Maybe he planned to leave, pack up his things and flee. It didn't make sense, but it was the only logical explanation I could think of. Regardless, I knew he must have spoken to his father, informing him of what happened. We were hunted criminals, murderers, and the mental clock in my head continued to tick down. Just how long could we stay ahead of this? How much time did we have before the inevitable hammer of law enforcement shattered us for good?

The forest pressed close to the road, a silent observer to our ill intent. The sky overhead continued to churn with thick clouds, the aftermath of the storm still bleeding across the heavens.

My shirt stuck to my skin, soaked. I pulled at it absently, the smell of blood reaching my nose. My bones rattled with every beat of my heart, my skull seeming to expand with pain. I blinked wearily and reached for the fury I knew was there.

It came easily and I let it consume me with new energy.

"There's his house," Joe whispered, slowing even more.

Derek's truck was parked out front and the lights were on inside. The woods crowded around the small cabin, a shroud of oppressive black that dripped from all directions.

"Stop here," I said.

Joe pulled off the road and turned off the engine. We were about fifty yards from the front door. I couldn't see any movement from the windows, but we knew he was inside. I turned around in my seat and stared at the empty road behind us, checking for anyone who might be following us. There was nothing.

Joe picked up the shotgun, his voice grave. "You ready?"

Without answering, I opened my door and stepped out into the night. I held the pistol loosely at my side as my boots crunched over gravel. A warm wind blustered through the surrounding woods and I felt it ripple across my bloody shirt.

Joe exited the truck and came to my side.

"Hey, Cole?" he said quietly.

I looked at him.

"Whatever happens…just remember why we're here."

"I don't need a reminder," I muttered, walking forward. "Come on. Stay low."

Together we crouched and approached the house. My heart drummed wearily, a low throb that I felt extend throughout my entire body and push against the back of my eyes.

I was so goddamned tired.

We crept to Derek's truck and peeked through the window to find it empty. The keys were still in the ignition, which told us he was leaving again soon. Satisfied, we slowly skirted around it to the side of the house, Joe behind me. The windows were too high to see inside, but I could hear hurried footsteps racing across the floor.

I nodded to Joe and we slunk around toward the

front door. My boots silently ascended the three steps to the rickety porch and I cast my eyes to ground. Tarp, rope, woodpile, axe, chainsaw, broken chair, old tire…

I hugged the wall by the door and Joe took a place at the other side. Our eyes met.

It was time to end this once and for all.

Taking a deep breath, I spun and booted the front door as hard as I could. It splintered inward in an eruption of noise, the hinges cracking from the force.

As one, Joe and I rushed inside, guns raised.

We found ourselves in the living room, a simple arrangement of old furniture, dirt, and disarray.

Standing in the middle of the room with a bag slung over his shoulder was Derek. He froze mid-step when he saw us, the blood draining from his face.

But he was not alone.

A woman stood at his side, a frail thing with wide, terrified eyes. Behind them both was a boy, no more than five years old. He squeaked with fear as Joe and I piled into the room, bringing the night with us.

The child was the spitting image of Derek.

I pointed my gun directly at them, a smile blossoming from my lips that twisted into a snarl. "Well, well, well," I said grimly. "Derek…you didn't tell me you had a family."

Chapter 13

No one said anything for a moment, the five of us locked in place. Derek, weaponless, wrapped his arms around his wife and son and pulled them close. His eyes were frightened and a vein pulsed along his neck.

Finally, Joe broke the paralysis.

"Sit down," he commanded, motioning to the couch with the shotgun.

Derek licked his lips nervously. "Now hold on—"

"SIT DOWN!" Joe screamed. The young boy whimpered and buried his face into Derek's leg. He looked like he had just been woken up. His hair was tousled and he wore thin pajamas. The woman, who I assumed was Derek's wife, clung tightly to her husband.

"Calm down, let's just be reasonable here," Derek sputtered, not moving.

I trained the pistol at his head, a burning hatred rising in my throat. "Reasonable? You stupid fuck…we are way beyond."

"Daddy?" the boy cried weakly into Derek's pant leg.

Derek looked down, concern filling his face. It looked alien on him.

"It's OK, Adam. Dad's not going to let these men hurt you."

I felt rage wrap itself around my throat, my voice low and dangerous. "Your daddy's lying, kid."

Derek looked up at me, a ghost. "Please…don't scare him. He's got nothing to do with this."

I stepped forward. "Shit, now why does that sound so familiar?"

Derek swallowed hard and pulled his family away from me. "Cole…"

The barrel of my gun stared him down. "Shut the fuck up."

The woman clutched Derek's shoulder. "Are these them?"

"Hush, Ann," Derek hissed desperately.

Joe circled around them, shotgun raised. "Yeah, Ann…it's us."

I glanced at Joe. "Why don't you go get that rope we saw out on the porch? I think we're going to need it."

Joe nodded and backed away, his gun still trained on the terrified family. I didn't move, my eyes boring into Derek's. I felt my mind unlocking. I felt every ounce of hatred I possessed pour through my eyes and crash over the frightened hostages. My finger twitched to pull the trigger, but I resisted the temptation.

Derek deserved so much worse.

I heard Joe behind me, returning with a length of rope in his arms.

"Tie him up," I said, motioning toward Derek. "Tie him to that chair there."

The child, Adam, began to cry.

"Shut your goddamn kid up," I growled.

Joe pointed at Derek with his gun. Derek gently, lovingly, pulled his son away from his leg. He did so with great tenderness and I saw pain fill his eyes.

"If you make any sudden movements, your family dies," I threatened as Joe pushed Derek toward the high-backed chair across from the couch.

"Please," Derek begged. "Just…just let them go."

I swung the pistol over and pointed it at his chest. "If you don't shut your fucking mouth, I'm going to cut your goddamn tongue out."

Derek clamped his teeth shut and sat down heavily. Under the paralysis of my pistol, he remained silent and motionless as Joe tied him to the chair. When he was finished, he stepped away, bringing the shotgun back up.

I looked at Derek's wife and child, Ann and Adam. "Go sit down on the couch. And don't do anything that's going to piss me off."

The boy was lost in his mother's skirt, his face riddled with fear. Together, they obeyed. The wife looked petrified, her eyes darting between Joe and me and then back to her husband.

"He can't help you right now," I snarled. "So sit the hell down."

Trembling, they sat. Ann pulled Adam's head to her chest and cradled him like a toddler. I could hear him crying, the sound muffled now.

Joe leaned into my ear. "Hey, let's let them go. They got nothing to do with this. It's Derek we want and we've got him."

I slowly turned to my brother. "They stay."

Joe seemed to struggle, his voice lined with careful reason. "I get it, man. But they didn't do anything to us. The fucker who did is sitting right here. We have him. Let's let the wife and kid go."

"They stay," I hissed quietly.

Joe stole a quick look at Derek, his voice low. "Cole, what are you going to do?"

I ground my teeth together. "I'm going to break his family like he broke ours."

Joe quickly licked his chapped lips. "He's just a little kid."

"What are you two whispering about?" Derek stuttered, afraid.

"SHUT THE FUCK UP!" I screamed, turning on him.

My head thundered.

My blood boiled.

I shook beneath it all, losing myself to the rage. I clutched my temples and took a long, pained breath.

Joe appraised me with concern. "Cole?"

I shut my eyes, the sickness in my stomach heaving into my throat. Sweat stood out on my forehead and I tasted bile on my tongue. Thick clouds of exhaustion fogged my head and filled my mind. It felt like my skull was alive with sparking, burning wires. My chest heaved and I fought to breathe.

Christ.

Where the fuck was I?

I buckled beneath a sudden gasp of dizziness, the darkness behind my eyes filling with memory.

Maria…Tammy…Dave…

So many loved ones hurt because of the cruelty of others. So many unchecked acts of shocking violence. How could these monsters get away with it all? Why should they? Why should they be spared the agony I felt with every fucking beat of my worn-down heart?

I pulled my eyes open.

"Look at her," I instructed Derek, my voice a cold, hateful exhale. I pointed to his wife.

Derek shook against his restraints, eyes bulging. "Stop this! Please! You don't have to do this!"

"Look…at…her," I said slowly, each word like a hammer.

Lip trembling, Derek looked at his wife. "Honey, it's going to be—"

I shot her in the head.

The noise split the air like cracking wood. Blood exploded out the back of Ann's skull and dripped down the wall, her body spasming beneath the force of the bullet. Adam, the boy, screamed hysterically and pulled himself away from the grisly corpse.

"JESUS FUCKING CHRIST!" Derek screamed, lunging against the ropes.

I lowered my smoking pistol, the air singed. I watched the child scream for his mother, his mouth a wailing oval of sorrow and fear.

"Goddamn it," I heard Joe whisper at my side, taking a hesitant step back. "Goddamn it, Cole."

"WHY DID YOU DO THAT!?" Derek screamed, tears rolling down his face. "OH CHRIST, WHY DID YOU DO THAT!?"

I watched the blood pour from Ann's head. It ran down across the back of the couch, staining the filthy fabric. The boy was hysterical. He huddled against the couch's arm, his face in his hands. His little shoulders shook as he cried. The sound pierced me and fueled the acid in my skull.

Slowly, as if in a dream, I walked forward and grabbed Adam by the shirt.

"Get your hands off him! Don't touch him!" Derek howled, the ropes digging into his arms and chest.

Adam tried to jerk away, but my grip was like frozen steel. I pulled him off the couch and together we stood in front of Derek.

I placed the gun to Adam's head.

"No! NO! STOP IT! PLEASE!" Derek shrieked. It was odd to see him in such a state of panic. I didn't think he had it in him. I didn't think he had the capability to love someone like this.

Adam pissed himself, his body shaking uncontrollably beneath my grip. The barrel of the pistol dug into his ear. I stared at Derek, emotionless, my head splitting with a mountain of pain. My body begged to vomit, a gnashing, poisonous sensation that churned my stomach.

Suddenly, a rough hand reached out and pulled the gun away from the boy.

I turned and looked at Joe, my eyes rimmed with darkness.

"Stop this," Joe hissed quietly. "This isn't what we came to do."

"Yes, it is," I whispered, my breath hot.

Joe's grip over my hand remained. "We can cut Derek into little pieces for all I care, but the kid is innocent. I am not going to stand here and let you do this. We are not that kind of men."

"And what kind of men are we, Joe?" I growled. "Look around. Look at where we are. Look at what we've already done."

Joe didn't move, his jaw set. "We're not killing a kid."

Our eyes clashed and I felt the fury return. Not at my brother, but at the circumstances that led us here. The death, the violence, the fucking senselessness of it all. And the man who had orchestrated it was sitting before us, bound and at our mercy. Every part of me wanted to make him hurt in the worst ways imaginable.

I wanted to rip out his heart before I ripped out his throat.

I looked down at the kid, a shaking mess of absolute fear. His pants were stained with urine. The sound that escaped his lips wrapped around my head and pressed into my ears. I closed my eyes against the noise, the sobs mixing with the thumping chaos in my skull.

"Jesus Christ," I whispered, releasing him. Immediately, he ran to his father and clutched him, called to him.

"Be brave, Adam, please be brave for Daddy," Derek sobbed as his son crawled up onto his lap and clutched him tightly.

Joe let my hand go and suddenly the pistol felt very heavy.

I looked at him, my eyes bloodshot.

Joe nodded.

Before we could decide what to do next, the house was bathed in red and blue light, a swirling, pulsing intrusion that froze the blood in my veins.

"Oh, shit," Joe whispered.

Outside, we heard a sudden swarm of screeching brakes and rumbling engines. The room blinked with the telltale colors of law enforcement.

"You called them?" I growled, slowly turning back to Derek.

"Of course I did!" he answered, without looking up, his voice rising. "Soon as I left the cabin. My dad is out there with a whole host of officers and he's not going to let you out of here. You and Joe are fucked."

I didn't like the sudden defiance in his voice. It brought back the rage, brought it bubbling up from my beaten, fatigued mind.

Joe quickly went to the front door and locked it. After a second, he went to the windows and shut the blinds. He moved with a sure step, a precision and energy that had abandoned me hours ago. I watched as he marched across the house and locked the back door, a fragile thing leading outside from the kitchen. When he came back into the living room, his face was burning.

"I have an idea," he said, breathless.

"Fuck you and your ideas," Derek said, now glaring up at us with tear-spotted eyes. "You can't get out of this. Better to turn yourself in. Or don't and die. Either works for me. But if you touch me or my son, you better believe my dad is going to make things very, very bad for you."

Without speaking, I thundered over to him and pistol-whipped his face.

Adam screamed and clawed at his father as blood sluiced from a newly formed gash along Derek's cheek.

"Keep talking like that and I'll put a bullet down your boy's throat," I said, voice rumbling like crumbling iron.

Derek spit a wad of blood onto the floor but closed

his mouth. Adam balled up on his lap, lost in his grief and fear.

I turned back to Joe, my shoulders heavy. "What's your idea?"

Outside, we heard car doors slamming and instructions being shouted. Boots thudded beyond the walls and I knew we were being surrounded.

Joe leaned into my ear. "Trade the kid for the sheriff. Get him in here with us."

"And then end this, once and for all," I said weary, furious.

Joe nodded. "Exactly."

"And then it'll be over. Finally...it'll be over."

"At least for them."

More shouting from outside, urgent and hurried.

I looked into Joe's eyes. "There's got to be twenty cops out there, Joe."

"I know."

I turned the pistol over in my hands, dried blood cracking across my knuckles, and sighed gravely. "I don't think we're making it out of this one, man."

Joe gripped my shoulder. "Tammy is safe. Tammy is alive. I want to make sure she stays that way. That's all I care about anymore, Cole."

Someone was on a bullhorn outside, calling to us. I wasn't ready to listen.

"This really is a mess, isn't it?" I said quietly.

Joe tightened his grip on my shoulder. "It isn't over yet. Not quite. We have one more thing to do."

"I'm not going down without a fight," I whispered. "I won't let them have that. I will not go quietly."

Joe suddenly snorted, a smile turning the corners of his mouth. "Who the hell said anything about that?"

"Let's get it over with, then," I muttered, turning to Derek and his son.

The bullhorn outside was still shouting out to us and I finally started listening. Whoever was on the other end was instructing us to come out with our hands up. I almost laughed. And then I almost vomited. I stood in front of Derek and pulled his kid off his lap. Crying, tripping, stumbling, the kid had no choice but to be jerked away from his father. Derek roared in his chair, unable to stop me.

Joe went to the front door and I met him there with Adam. Slowly, my brother unlocked the bolt and peeked out. I watched Joe's face illuminate with color, pulsing blue and red. Immediately, the bullhorn went silent.

"We have a child in here!" Joe yelled out to the sea of officers. "And we're going to kill him unless the sheriff gets his ass in here! If he comes, then we'll let the boy go! You have thirty seconds!"

Joe slammed the door closed and looked at me. I nodded, tightening my grip on the young boy.

I looked at Derek. "You think he'll come?"

"Of course he'll come," Derek barked, his eyes brimming with hateful tears.

Joe held the shotgun loosely at his side and counted

under his breath. When he reached twelve, we heard heavy boots ascend the porch. A knock at the door came next.

"It's the sheriff! Don't harm the boy!"

Adam lunged forward. "Grandpa!?"

I pulled him back and retreated to the opposite end of the room, my eyes meeting Joe's. When I was a safe distance away, I placed the pistol to the boy's head once more and waited. Derek snarled at me from his chair. I ignored him.

Joe used the door as a shield and slowly opened it a crack.

"Throw your gun inside," he instructed.

"I left it on the hood of my cruiser," the sheriff's voice responded. I couldn't see him, but he sounded shaken.

I adjusted my grip on Adam and called out loudly. "If you're lying, I'm going to kill your grandson!"

The sheriff's voice shook now. "For Christ's sake, I don't have it!"

I gave Joe the signal and he opened the door enough to allow the sheriff to slip inside. As soon as he was through, Joe closed and locked it. He stood beside the big man and trained the shotgun on him.

The sheriff looked pale, his shirt wrinkled and damp. His eyes were wide, like he couldn't believe where he was.

"There, I'm here, just like you asked," he said breathlessly. "Now let Adam go."

I didn't move. Joe glanced at me over his shoulder.

"Let him go! I did what you asked!" he pleaded. I sensed fear for his grandson pooling off him like gun smoke.

"What are you waiting for?" Derek yelled. "Let my son go!"

My grip on Adam never loosened. "I don't think so."

I saw Joe's eyes harden for a second, a frustrated, dark dread.

"What the hell you mean!?" the sheriff exclaimed. "I'm here, ain't I? You telling me you ain't going to honor the trade?"

"Stop talking," I said darkly.

"This is BULLSHIT!" Derek screamed.

"Shut the fuck up, Derek," I said without looking at him.

The sheriff took a tentative step forward. "This ain't right and you know it. He's just a child!"

"I noticed," I said flatly.

"You cock-sucking liar," Derek rumbled.

I eyed him. "You're playing a dangerous game with me right now."

The sheriff held up his hands. "Look, we can discuss this. We can settle down and talk this out. But first, please, let my grandson go. I'm begging you, man to man."

I squinted at him. "Are you fucking delusional?"

"I just want everyone to walk away from this. All of us."

"Just how full of shit are you?" Joe asked, still at the sheriff's side.

"I'll admit, things have gotten a little out of hand," he said weakly.

"People are dead," I growled, pressing Adam against me. "Including two of your children."

The sheriff's chest hitched, and he fumbled to speak. "I know that...goddamn it, I know that. But I still got one of them that's breathing and I want to make sure he stays that way, along with my grandson. So please..."

I glared at him, my eyes chips of ice.

"Why don't you go sit down on the floor next to your son?" Joe said dangerously. "And remember, you do anything stupid and everyone here dies."

"I ain't going to do anything foolish," he assured us. "I swear on my life, I ain't."

"Then sit down," I commanded.

The sheriff looked at me and his eyes widened further. "If I do, will you take the gun off my grandson?"

"You don't make the fucking rules," Joe snarled, jabbing him in the shoulder with the shotgun. The sheriff stumbled forward and walked over to Derek, keeping his eye on me. With great effort, he took a seat on the floor next to Derek's feet.

Without Joe blocking his view, his eyes found Ann, dead on the couch.

"Oh, my God," he gasped. "Oh, my shit, what have you boys DONE!?"

Joe glanced at the still-bleeding corpse. "It looks like we killed her."

"Kill these assholes," Derek growled, twisting in his restraints. "Just send everyone in and kill them both."

"That wouldn't be a good idea," I said quietly, tapping the barrel of my pistol against Adam's head. I could feel the boy shaking beneath my firm hand, his shoulders quivering with fear. To his credit, he didn't move.

Joe kept the shotgun trained on the sheriff. Slowly, carefully, he pulled his knife out as well.

"How is this going to end?" the sheriff asked, somber and in pain. He continued to stare at Ann's body in shocked disbelief. His skin had gone pale and a sheen of sweat stood out on his brow. Concern folded itself along his face, and the gravity of the situation seemed to sink deeper into his eyes.

"How do you think this ends?" Joe asked, skirting around Derek and the seated sheriff. He stood at their backs and tapped the knife against the barrel of the shotgun. The noise made the hair on the back of my neck stand up.

"They're going to kill us," Derek said miserably, his eyes alight. "Just send in the troops. We're all going to die anyway." He looked at his son, his face softening. "I'm so sorry, Adam. I never meant for you or your mother to get mixed up in all this. I wanted to get you out of here before this happened. I thought I had a little more time. But I want you to be brave and stand tall, OK? Just like your old man. Just like your grandpa here.

We Morrisons aren't going to die with tears in our eyes. None of us. I'm proud of you and I love you more than you know."

"Daddy," the boy pleaded against me, "I don't want to die, though…I'm afraid."

Derek nodded, his face full of compassion now. "I know. I am, too. But that's what makes us brave. So bite your lip. Stand tall. I'm right here with you."

"Why are they doing this?" Adam choked, crying.

Derek's voice strained. "Because they're evil. Because they want to hurt me to by taking you and your mother away from me."

I snorted. "Don't listen to your old man, kid. We didn't even know you were here."

Derek's head snapped up. "What the hell are you talking about?"

"I didn't know you had a family," I spat. "But it sure was a pleasant surprise."

Derek's face drained and he turned in his ropes to stare at Joe. "But…you knew, though. You knew I had a family. Surely you were coming to kill them, to get back at me."

Joe avoided my eyes. "Yeah, I knew. But they don't have anything to do with this. This blood is between you and me. You ran, we followed. And you took us right into your living room."

"You were going to kill them, though," Derek stuttered. "I know you, Joe. After Dave…"

"You don't know me," Joe said darkly. "You don't know anything about me."

I looked at Joe. He clutched the knife tightly, now directly behind the sheriff.

"You knew about them? And you didn't tell me?" I asked quietly.

Joe didn't answer.

"Please," the sheriff mumbled suddenly. "Don't do this."

"Shut up," I ordered, still looking at Joe.

"I was just looking out for my boys," the sheriff said, putting his face in his hands. His bulk heaved as he shook with emotion. "I promised their mother on her deathbed that I'd do everything in my power to keep them out of trouble. And I've tried. Goddamn it, I've tried. I didn't mean for things to get so tangled up. I didn't mean for things to get so nasty. Damn it, Derek, how the hell did we end up here?"

"You've done right by me," Derek said softly, looking down at his father. "I'm proud to call you Dad."

Joe tapped the tip of his knife against the top of the sheriff's head, his voice a guttural rumble.

"Oh, cut the shit, you corrupt fuck. You hand-delivered that tape to us. You saw what was on there. You knew what your boys were doing. And instead of repairing the situation, you dug the knife in deeper. So don't sit here and drool all over yourself thinking you're on the right side of this."

The sheriff flinched under the blade, his voice shaking. "I was just doing what my boys wanted."

"What a coward you are," I spat. "Even here, at the very end."

The sheriff looked up, his eyes suddenly ablaze. "Coward? You're calling me a coward? You've got a gun on my grandson. The hell does that make you?"

I leaned over Adam, toward the sheriff. "It makes me in control."

Movement around the back of the house drew my attention, a clatter beyond the walls.

I looked back at Derek and the sheriff. "Seems they're getting anxious out there. I don't blame them. The man who's paying them is sitting in here with two murderers. Or maybe they're waiting for some kind of signal? What was the big plan coming in here?"

"I just want to keep my family alive," the sheriff said openly. "I swear that's all I want."

"And then you'd just let us go?"

"I can't promise what would happen after, but yes. If that meant getting my son and grandson out of here, then I'd let you two walk away."

I closed my eyes and exhaled wearily. "I swear, sheriff, I don't think I can keep up with the bullshit you're feeding us tonight. Between the hat-in-hand routine and the loving-father sob story, you almost had me feeling sorry for you. But if you think for a second that I buy any of it, you're sadly mistaken. Sure, I believe you were looking out for your sons, but you also played a part in what they were doing. You probably even encouraged it. I know Derek hates Joe. I know you're aware of what Joe did to your family name. Frankly, I don't give a fuck about that. Because at the end of the day, you made a choice. And then you made another one. And here we are."

Something drained from the sheriff's face and I saw red-hot rage begin to rise in his cheeks. "Fuck you. Fuck you and your miserable family. I hope—"

Joe rammed his knife down into the sheriff's head. The blade sank deep into his skull, bringing with it a splash of blood.

"No!" Derek screamed, eyes wide. "Dad! Oh, Christ, Dad!"

The sheriff shuddered violently and his eyes rolled into the back of his head. Trails of oozing blood leaked from his mouth. And then he slumped forward, dead.

Joe yanked the knife out and surveyed the carnage.

He looked up at me and our eyes met. I nodded.

"FUCK YOU!" Derek screamed. "FUCK YOU BOTH! YOU FUCKING MONSTERS!"

"Goodbye, Derek," I said darkly, still clutching the weeping boy against me. I felt the child's tears run across my hand as I pressed it against his chest.

"HELP!" Derek suddenly screamed. "HELP, THEY'RE KILLING US!"

Joe grabbed Derek by the hair and yanked his head back. I heard feet thudding toward the house. Any second now.

Joe leaned down into Derek's ear, his voice an angry whisper. "This was always how it would end."

I covered Adam's eyes.

Joe slit Derek's throat.

Blood gurgled from the parted flesh and Derek squirmed in pain, his eyes bulging as Joe stepped away. His feet kicked against the chair, his hands writhing in their restraints as the life drained from his body. His face went ghostly white and he coughed and sputtered, spraying the floor with his own blood.

After a couple seconds, he slowed. And then he died.

Joe stood behind the dead man, his chest rising and falling rapidly. Slowly, he craned his head back and closed his eyes.

"Fuck," he muttered. When he opened his eyes again, they were bloodshot and heavy with exhaustion.

A weighty blow rattled the front door, shaking it on its hinges.

They were coming.

"Get behind me, Joe," I said, gripping Adam tight against me. The boy was a mess, his chest rising and falling rapidly as croaking sobs rattled his body. I placed the gun against his head once more. Joe stuffed the knife in his boot and stood behind us, his shotgun raised toward the shuddering door.

"They want to flush us out back," I said, heart racing as I watched the door begin to give under the drumming thunder of a frantic boot.

"They got men out there, just waiting. They'll shoot

us on sight," I continued, stepping back into the kitchen, pulling Adam with me.

"What's the plan here?" Joe asked, his voice weary and calm.

The door splintered.

"They're not going to do anything with the boy in here," I said, still retreating into the kitchen. "There's woods ten yards out the back door. We use the kid to get to them. It's the only chance we got."

"Then we let him go," Joe said.

"Sure, Joe."

The front door imploded and the living room flooded with officers. Guns raised, they fanned out and began shouting orders at us, faces red, spittle flying. I stared them down, my eyes cold, temples throbbing. I felt sweat slick the grip of the pistol I had to Adam's head.

"Jesus Christ, they killed the sheriff!" one of the officers yelled, his eyes wide as the grisly scene entered the chaos of their vision.

"They have a hostage!"

"Release the boy!" another shouted.

"Put the gun down!"

"Step away from the child!"

Still walking backwards, I felt the heel of my boot connect with the back door. Joe was at my side, his shotgun pointed at the crowding police.

I cleared my throat and raised my voice. "Everyone

SHUT UP! If anyone fires on me or my brother, I'll kill the kid! There's three dead already; don't make it four!"

The police officers formed a line in front of us, sweaty, tense, furious. Their guns remained raised.

"You're dead," one of the officers snarled, taking aim at Joe's head.

"No!" yelled the one at his side, alarmed. "Not with the kid here!"

"They killed the sheriff!"

"And they'll kill his grandson, too! Do not fire, goddamn it!"

Growling like a deranged animal, the officer's eyes clouded with hatred. He kept his gun trained on Joe's head. My heart roared in my ears and sweat plastered itself to my skin.

"We're going out the back door!" I announced, feeling Joe unlock it at my back. "And we're taking the kid with us! I know there's men out there and if they so much as blink in our direction then you're going to have a dead child on your hands! I'M NOT FUCKING AROUND HERE!" I screamed, tendons standing out along my neck. The drum in my head had started again, a maddening, painful beat that hurt my eyes.

"Let the boy go!" one of the officers, an older man with heavy bags beneath his eyes, commanded. I wondered how long he had been on the sheriff's payroll.

"I'll let him go when we get to safety!" I shouted back. "Now all of you BACK UP!"

The officers shifted uncomfortably before us.

"BACK UP!" Joe suddenly roared, shoving the shotgun against the kid's face. Immediately, the men retreated a few steps.

"Tick-tock, Cole," Joe whispered, a trickle of sweat running down his face.

"Open the door," I whispered.

Joe turned the knob and pulled the door open a crack. Warm night air swirled inside and blew across my damp face and through the death-stained house.

"Tell the officers out there to stand down," I growled, addressing the older cop again.

The man didn't move, hard edges pulling at his face. "You can't run away from what you've done here."

"I'm not trying to," I snarled. "I'm trying to get away from you. Now do as I say. You know what? Get over here. You're walking out that door first."

Joe waved the older man over with his gun. Slowly, the cop complied. I stepped away in case he got any funny ideas. I kept waiting for someone to shoot me. Adam whimpered against me. His body was an oven against mine. The arm I had wrapped around his shoulders was slick with sweat.

"Got any snipers out there?" Joe asked almost casually as he grabbed the older officer by the arm. He reached down and yanked the revolver out of his hand and stuffed it into his waistband.

Joe pulled the kitchen door open. "Alright, out you go." He shoved the man in the back and out into the night.

Instantly, the cop raised his hands. "Don't shoot! NO ONE SHOOT!"

I waited, listened, for the crack of gunfire, but none came.

I edged Adam and myself over to the door, keeping my back to the wall. Joe raised his shotgun to the wall of cops in front of us.

"You go first, Cole. Make sure they can see the kid. I'll be right at your back watching these assholes."

I stood beside the open door now. "Remember, anyone shoots, I shoot."

And then I marched the kid out the back door. My heart thundered in my chest and my head throbbed. My pulse thudded in my ears and sweat ran down the back of my neck. My throat was dry and I felt naked as I pushed the boy ahead of me. I kept my pistol locked against his head. A breeze rose around us and I smelled urine.

I heard Joe follow behind me, just a few steps away at my back. He was breathing heavily.

"Anyone fires and I kill the kid!" I yelled to men I didn't see. My eyes skirted the tree line I staggered toward, desperately trying to spot movement or signs of life. I didn't see anyone and yet I knew they were there, watching me. I could feel their guns on me.

"Keep going," Joe whispered behind me. "The cops in the house are following us out."

My boots dampened in the grass as I pressed forward through the meager backyard, the looming trees ushering us closer. We just needed to get to them. Just get to the woods.

And then run.

"Steady, kid," I said as he stumbled and choked out a cry. "We're almost there."

The older officer stood off to the side, watching us with hateful eyes. I glanced behind me and saw Joe, his back to mine, shotgun aimed at the house as the police from inside filed out.

One mistake, one slip, and Joe and I were dead.

I blinked the stinging sweat from my eyes. A couple more steps and we would be at the tree line. As we approached, I saw the first of many hidden officers. He was pressed against a tree, ten yards to my right. He had a hunting rifle trained at my head.

"Take it easy," I ordered. "My trigger finger is a little slippery right now." The cop didn't move.

I reached the first row of trees and slipped between them, my boots crunching through the underbrush. Slowly, I rotated myself and Adam so that Joe was in front of us. I continued to backpedal, carefully watching my brother. I saw his shirt was soaked with sweat as he pivoted his head left and then right, all senses on high alert.

The woods grew around us and my vision filled with swaying trees. The unseen leaves above our heads rustled in the night wind, filling my ears and washing away any sound of approaching footsteps. How many police were in these woods with us? How many were watching us right now?

"Stay away!" Joe bellowed toward the house, past the tree line. We were about ten yards deep now, the light from the house winking between the dark trunks. I swallowed hard and glanced around quickly. I expected to see guns pointed in my direction, the woods filled with angry cops just waiting to take a shot. But there was nothing but claustrophobic night and still woodland. I wasn't sure what was worse.

Joe took a few steps back and reached my side, his shotgun still pointed at the fading house lights.

"You think they're going to follow us?" It was a question he already knew the answer to.

"Of course they are," I said, blinking sweat away. My throat felt tight. I felt like I would die at any second, a sudden surge of nothing that would swarm me entirely too fast.

"We need to run," Joe urged, his eyes rapidly scanning the tree line. We continued to back away from it carefully.

"I know."

"They're not going to hold back much longer, Cole."

"I know, Joe," I said, taking Adam and myself further into the woods. Branches clawed at my back and my shoulder brushed a tree, knocking my pistol into the kid's head. He whimpered pitifully, his chest deflating beneath my constant grip. Just keep walking…we had to just keep walking...lose the police...get to safety...get away from this place...

You don't seriously think you're getting out of this, do you?

I shoved the thought away. There was no time for it.

"Cole, we need to go. Now," Joe said, adjusting the shotgun in his hands. Sweat ran down his face in dirty streaks, a dim, dirty display in the pressing darkness.

I continued to backpedal into the tightening woods, my eyes locked onto the now barely visible house. Despite the warm night, a chill ran up my spine. I ran my tongue over my lips and tasted salt and grime. My head roared with that insistent, hellish throb.

Joe stopped suddenly and lowered his gun. His voice was grave. "Cole. It's time. Let the boy go."

"Not yet," I whispered, stopping, staring at my brother with wide eyes.

"It's not going to make a difference," Joe said, stepping toward me.

"Just a little further."

"I'm not asking, Cole," Joe growled.

Our eyes clashed and I felt sick.

"They're going to kill us," I whispered.

"I know."

"Then how am I supposed to let him go?"

"Because we have to," Joe said quietly. "We did what we came to do."

I looked down at the top of Adam's head, my heart hammering.

"Come on, Cole. They're going to be right behind us," Joe said, reaching out. He gently pulled Adam toward himself and away from me. Adam, shaking, looked up into Joe's face with big, watery eyes.

Joe placed a hand on the boy's shoulder, his voice soft. "Go on. Get back to the house. You're free now."

Blinking back tears of disbelief, Adam turned to go, a sudden surge of life and survival rippling through his small body. Just as he was about to run, Joe caught him by the arm.

"Hey," Joe said gently. "When you grow up...don't turn into men like us."

And then he let the boy go. Adam tore through the woods crying, running back to the house as fast as he could.

I looked at Joe.

Joe nodded. "Run."

Together, we crashed through the underbrush, pressing deeper and deeper into the dark forest. It wasn't long before we heard yelling as the pursuit began.

They were coming.

And they were bringing hell with them.

Chapter 14

We hadn't gone far when the first gunshot cracked across the night sky. My breath came ragged and my lungs burned, pain flaring through my battered, exhausted muscles. Trees rose quickly from the mass of black before Joe and me. We bumped, crashed, and thudded into them as we fled, the darkness not allowing us to correct our route. Rocks and reaching branches tried to slow us, tearing across our skin and slowing our urgent escape.

Another gunshot rocked the world and I heard a tree to my left absorb the bullet. My hair hung down in wet clumps across my eyes, my shirt stuck to my shoulders, and death followed on my heels.

Joe, panting, spun around and emptied two rounds into the forest behind us. I followed his lead, blindly firing my pistol dry in the direction of our pursuers. When it clicked empty, I discarded it. I could hear them, feel them racing closer. The woods at our backs splintered with their urgency. Angry voices echoed in the air above our heads, bouncing off the looming trees and soaring down around us.

I ducked as another gunshot whistled by. And then another. And another.

You're going to die.

"Move! MOVE!" I pleaded with Joe, my brother sucking air at my side.

He tripped, caught himself on a tree, and lunged after me. His face was pale and his eyes dark. He wheezed and pushed himself to run faster.

I didn't know where we were going or what we were running toward. The world pressed in close and the severity of the moment threatened to drown me. My ears screamed with the beat of my heart, and my head felt like it would crack open.

Another gunshot came at our backs and I suddenly felt searing pain flare across my hand. Screaming through clenched teeth, I shook the burning sensation away as best I could, but it refused to lessen. A moment later and I felt blood flow between my fingers.

Joe looked at me as we ran and took a split-second assessment of my injury. I didn't slow, didn't even look at him, the rising pain in my hand spurring me on like gasoline.

Distracted by the biting discomfort, I failed to see the tree flying toward me. Grunting, I collided with it and crashed into Joe. The breath left my lungs for a moment and I wheezed desperately as stars exploded across my vision.

Joe caught me and hauled me back to my feet, gasping. "Shit, come on, man, we can't stop!"

I didn't have the energy to respond. I forced my legs to move. They were getting closer now, the police swarming at our backs. I could hear them snapping through the underbrush, yelling, snarling, hunting.

My heart leaped into my throat as two more gunshots exploded behind us.

This time, it was Joe who grunted.

I saw him stumble, trip, and then catch himself on a tree, clutching his thigh.

"Oh, shit," I cried, digging my heels in. I sprinted back to him and pulled his arm over my shoulders so that he could lean on me.

"It's not…bad," Joe gasped. "Think it just…grazed me."

"We have to keep moving," I begged, wrapping my arm around him. Gritting my teeth, I dragged us forward. Joe ran as best he could, a hopping, uneven gait that I knew wouldn't be enough to rid us of our pursuers.

After a couple steps, Joe's breathing became labored. "This isn't…going to work."

"Yes it is," I cried. "We can lose them!"

More gunfire peppered the night and I heard trees splinter all around us.

"I'm just…slowing you down…" Joe gasped, sagging against me.

"Shut up," I pleaded. "I'm not leaving you."

We stumbled awkwardly through the woods, tears beginning to blur my vision as a horrific understanding began to reveal itself to me.

Joe slumped against me and I found myself taking most of his weight. I heaved him up, my voice a trembling cry.

"Come on, buddy, just a little further, I promise!"

Joe's voice blew heavy from his lips. "You've…already taken me…far enough, Cole."

I suddenly felt my arm dampen, the one clutched around Joe's ribs. A warmth spread over my skin and I felt a sob crawl up my throat.

Still running, dragging my brother along at my side, I looked at Joe's back with prayer on my lips.

A bloody bullet hole gurgled just below his right shoulder blade.

"Oh, fuck, oh Christ, no," I whispered, panting. I readjusted my grip around Joe, refusing to let him go. My feet tangled with his, the forest a malicious monster that battered our desperate flight.

"Come on, Joe," I cried, gasping. "Just stay with me, please!"

Muscles burning, I looked into my brother's eyes as I heaved him through the dark woods.

But Joe had already died.

"No," I shivered, lip trembling. "Oh, no…"

I slowed, letting Joe drag me down. "Oh, Jesus, please, no…" Tears ran down my face as Joe's head slumped to his chest.

Panting, crying, blinded by my own tears, I lowered him to the forest floor. As I laid him on his back, I pulled my arm out from under him. It came away soaked in blood. Angry shouts rose all around me. My heart counted the beats, each one growing heavier than the last.

Kneeling, knowing I had only seconds, I closed his eyes and choked back a rattling sob. In that moment, I wanted to just lie down next to him and close my eyes, never to open them again. I clenched my fists, listening to the approaching police, now dangerously close.

"I love you," I whispered, placing a hand on Joe's chest, sniffling, biting my lip. "I don't think you'll have to wait long for me."

"THERE HE IS!" a voice cried at my back.

The sound was like lightning to my senses. It brought with it the last of my reserves, a deep-seated fatigued rage that roared out from the depths of my chest.

I grabbed the revolver sticking out of Joe's waistband and rolled onto my back, aiming for where the voice originated.

An officer stood, gun raised, a dozen feet away.

I shot him in the throat.

Blood vomited from the wound as the officer pressed his hands to it, a shocked, horrified look on his face. I scrambled to my feet, wiped my face, and turned my back to him.

I began to run once more. Beams of light swept the

crowded landscape at my back, casting shadows over everything. Everyone was shouting and rushing toward my position, a cataclysmic charge that thundered nearer.

My hand burned as I sprinted into the woods. I knew I had been shot, but I didn't want to look at the damage the bullet had left behind. I felt dizzy and my throat was dry. My chest crumbled beneath the sorrow I breathed, the pain I felt. My eyes blurred with tears and I hated myself for leaving Joe behind. Despite the hopelessness, despite everything I had gone through, there still remained a single thought that burned through it all.

I wanted to live.

I held onto that, filled myself with it, allowed it to fuel my churning feet through the dark underbrush. It gave me the push I needed, but it also filled me with the deepest shame, a shadow that threatened to overwhelm the drive to survive.

The ground began to slope sharply downward and I slowed, ever so slightly. Bullets whizzed overhead and long arcs of white light washed through the trees, searching for me.

Gasping, ears ringing, I bolted down the long descent. I tripped once, twice, steadied myself, and then my boot caught a rock. Crying out, I braced myself as I fell to the ground. My shoulder slammed into the earth and I went spinning, tumbling over myself, lost in my own momentum. My bloodied hand connected with a tree and I clenched my teeth together, reaching out for something to slow my fall.

I suddenly felt myself plunging through mid-air, a horrible, almost dreamlike sensation. I had only a moment to realize I had just dropped off an embankment before freezing water exploded around me.

Gasping, I surged for the surface, panic erupting in a great storm cloud. I found my legs and struggled to gain my footing in the swirling waters. My terror subsided slightly when I discovered the water only reached my knees.

I fell into a creek.

Shivering, I turned to look at where I had fallen from. A small embankment stood within arm's length. I followed the slope of earth up the steep incline, back to where I had come from. Flashlights hovered near the top of the slope, their sweeping beams swatting aside the darkness. And they were drawing closer.

I looked around for something, anything to get out of this hellish situation. Teeth chattering, I wrapped my arms around myself and felt pressing claustrophobia swarm my aching head. My stomach burned with nausea and I realized I didn't have the energy to continue. The flashlights were getting closer, the men holding them sensing my fatigue.

I sloshed two steps forward through the creek and pressed myself flat against the embankment. I withdrew into myself as best I could, the low lip of the bank brushing the top of my head. Freckles of dirt spattered my face as I pushed my back against the muddy wall. The creek lapped at my knees as I drew them into my chest. I shivered violently and willed my breathing to steady.

The cops were almost on me. They called to one another, sliding, sprinting, running toward the creek. I had no idea if they had seen me curl into my meager hideaway, but at that moment I couldn't move even if I had wanted to.

I jumped in the shadows as the first of the officers splashed into the creek to my right, a dozen yards away. His flashlight lit the waters as he waded across to the other side, pistol raised.

Another followed, a determined, furious spout of water springing from the surface as boots met the creek bed. They were so close, the two cops lit up by the flashlights at their backs.

Don't turn around, please don't turn around.

I huddled into myself, making myself as small as possible. To my left, another two leaped into the water and angrily marched the ten feet across to the other side. More followed, some further, some closer, each one catching my heart in my throat. But none turned around, none slowed, and none saw me.

I watched, miserably wet and cold, as the last of the hunting party reached the opposite embankment and tore into the woods, searching for a ghost they would not find.

I counted to sixty in my head. Then I did another

thirty. Convinced it was clear to move, I braced myself and tensed my leg muscles to stand. A split second before I did, one last cop splashed into the water, directly in front of me. The sweeper. The clean-up man.

He turned, sensing me, and his flashlight caught me full in the face.

His eyes went wide and he raised his pistol, shocked, reacting on pure instinct and training.

My boot shot out in front of me and connected with his kneecap, blowing it out the back of his leg. The cop crumbled into the water, a scream rising as his face hit the surface. Hands shaking, alarms screaming in my head, I lurched for him and plunged his head deep beneath the swirling current, drowning out any sound he might make from the crushing blow.

Face-down, the cop reached backward, trying to claw me away. Panting, I pressed my body over his, using my weight as an anchor. He tried to buck me off, sensing my hold over him, but his shattered knee wouldn't allow it.

"Shh," I whispered frantically, water splashing into my face. "Shh." Tugging in air through my quivering lips, I watched as the cop slowed, his hands sank, and his body stilled. I kept him underwater for another minute just to be safe.

Finally, I dared to let him go. My hands shook violently as I released my grip on his neck. The current collided with the corpse and gently goaded it downstream. I watched it go, my eyes dark and heavy. I needed to get up. I needed to move. They would come back, they would do another sweep after they realized I wasn't ahead of them anymore.

Wincing, I pulled myself into a standing position. I glanced down at my hand for the first time since getting shot. Blood oozed between my thumb and index finger. A deep gash filled the space. A graze. The bullet had just grazed me.

Still hurt like all hell.

Every part of me hurt like hell.

I heaved myself up the embankment and barked a short cry as something dug into my stomach. I looked down and saw the revolver tucked into my pants. I didn't even remember putting it there. I stripped it out and shook water from it. I had no idea if it would even still fire.

I scanned the opposite bank for signs of movement and when I saw none, I headed down the creek, parallel to the water and away from the path of pursuit I had scorched. My teeth chattered as I trudged forward, my bones creaking with every step. The pain in my head flared brilliantly and the fog of deep exhaustion joined the cacophony of discomfort. My feet hurt, my hand howled, my shoulders cramped, and worst of all…worst of all was the guilt and unrelenting sorrow.

Joe…Dave…

I don't know how long I walked down that creek. At some point the sun began to rise, a sickly purple bruise on a beaten, blood-red sky. Birds began to chirp. Squirrels conversed with one another. The clouds from last night's storm scurried away as a new day began.

And with every passing moment, my heart grew heavier. With every step, my shame deepened. If I hadn't been so tired, I would have wept bitterly. But I barely had the strength to keep moving. My body pulled toward the earth, begging me to stop, to rest, to sleep. My feet plodded over uneven ground, a tired, worn march toward inevitable doom.

And still, like a madness…

I didn't want to die.

I hated myself for that.

Chapter 15

I was still walking. The afternoon sun trickled down to me from between the trees. The woods seemed endless, and yet I had no desire to leave them. I knew the police were still out there. I had heard them, multiple times, far off in the distance. I didn't know if they had caught my trail yet or not.

I just knew I had to keep…walking…

Dark circles had formed beneath my eyes and the twisting sickness in my stomach had gotten worse since sunrise. I was bone-tired, worn out, horrifically isolated, and suffocatingly miserable. I couldn't stop thinking about my brothers. I couldn't stop replaying how they died.

I couldn't stop hating myself.

I mentally retraced my steps for the hundredth time, cursing every choice I made along the way. Why hadn't I stopped this? Why hadn't I been a better brother? Why did I let my own rage and anger consume me, drive me, use me?

"Goddamn it," I muttered, lips numb, voice shaking

with grief. The creek gurgled to my right and I wandered closer. My throat was dry. My head was splitting. My legs trembled.

Somewhere in the distant woodland, I heard yelling.

"Goddamn it," I said again, slumping to the water's edge. I lowered my hands into the cold current and drank deeply. Exhaling, I splashed some on my face.

Allowing myself a moment I couldn't afford, I stared into my rippling reflection, droplets of water dripping from my nose. I looked like hell. I looked like I had died.

A sudden pressure sank down over me and I bunched my hands into my eyes, shoulders shaking. Feeling hopelessly alone, I began to cry. It was the sobbing of a child, a raw exorcism of frustrated, all-consuming grief. The rattled weeping trembled through my body, and tears left trails down my cheeks.

After a second, I felt the sensation lessen and I forced myself to stand. I looked behind me, listened for sounds of pursuit. I could still hear the yelling.

Move, Cole. Keep walking.

I obeyed.

I vaguely knew which direction I was headed, not that it made much difference. I didn't have a plan. I didn't have an escape route. I didn't have anything.

Just stay alive.

I marched, dead leaves and underbrush crunching beneath my filthy boots. Every joint ached, every muscle burned, and every heartbeat brought dizziness. I had torn part of my shirt away and wrapped the cloth around my wounded hand. Not that it made much difference. I just didn't want to see any more blood.

The sun climbed the sky and then began to sink once more.

Night approached.

I needed to stop. I needed to sleep.

Where the hell was I going?

Would I ever leave these woods?

The evening air chilled slightly and the moon peeked curiously over the horizon. I stared at it, a blinking beacon between the swaying trees, as I trudged forward.

Christ, I was hungry.

The thought of food sent my stomach plummeting and I immediately rejected the idea. I wouldn't be able to hold anything in even if I did get the chance.

Where are you going, Cole?

I blocked out the thought once more.

You know where you're going...

I sighed, blinking heavily.

Yes...subconsciously, I think I did...

I knew I shouldn't, but I had to. I needed to. Before this was all over, I needed to see them one more time.

I needed to see Ma and Tammy.

Ma's house isn't too far away from here, is it? But you already knew that, didn't you?

I did. And so I walked.

You're going to get caught. They're going to get caught

with you. You're going to drag them into this shit. You can't go to them.

"I have to," I growled to the night.

You selfish fuck.

"Shut up," I hissed, stumbling.

I walked faster. I felt like I would fall down. I felt like every step was an impossibility. My feet felt like concrete. My head...oh God, my head...the aching...

I pushed ahead, deeper, further into the woods, keeping the creek to my right. I began to close my eyes for a second or two at a time, allowing myself to relieve the weight upon them, if only for a moment. I wanted nothing more in the world than to lie down and go to sleep. Simply the thought of sleep loosened a choked sob, a longing that I knew I couldn't afford.

Twigs, rocks, branches, trees, leaves, dirt, discomfort...they all blurred together in the growing night, one long stretch of repeating misery.

I didn't know how many more miles I had to go before I reached Ma's house, but I knew I was headed in the right direction. These woods ran past her house, across the road. At some point, she would be on my left. Through the tree line. Wherever that was.

I needed to move away from the creek. Find the edge of the forest. Get my bearings.

The tree line runs parallel to the road...the road will have cops...

"I'm not leaving...until...I see...my family," I spat, gasping.

Why? What good will it do?

"I need…"

Yes…tell me what you *need, you bastard.*

My eyes welled up and my voice quivered. "I need to tell them I'm sorry."

The voice in my head silenced.

Sniffling, I took one last look at the creek and then turned to my left. Keeping the sound of running water at my back, I waded into the rolling woodland.

The night grew thicker. The moon rose and then began to fall.

I was getting closer.

Where were the police now?

At some point, more dead than alive, I realized the sun was coming up again. I watched it through squinted eyes, a smothering of color across the sky. I didn't know how I was still awake or moving.

Fall over. Just fall over and don't get back up.

I pressed on.

Not long after I noticed the new dawn, I heard something. A rumbling ahead of me.

A road.

I quickened my step, a pinprick of hope piercing the eternal darkness of my thoughts. If I could just see the road, I could get to Ma's house. Only for a moment. Only for a second.

Only so that I could beg for their forgiveness.

I was crying again.

"God…oh God…" I sobbed, wiping my eyes with a

grimy hand. The sorrow pressed in, rising up off the back of my exhaustion like great wings that beat against me. I was helpless against it and so I cried.

I staggered toward the sound of the road. I filled my head with it. Close...I had to be close.

How long had I been walking now?

Hours?

Days?

Weeks?

My thoughts slithered through my head like slugs beneath mud. Every time I blinked, I thought the sun had gone out. Every lungful of air tasted like my last. Almost...there...

Light filtered through the trees ahead. I squinted and lurched toward it. Yes. Please, yes...

Panting, I stumbled the remaining distance and found myself looking out of the tree line onto the main road. To my left I spotted the outline of Mill Valley. To my right...

Ma's house.

It sat alone against the countryside, a tiny smudge that filled me with purpose. I just had to get there. It couldn't be more than a couple miles. I just had to walk down the tree line and across the road. I could make it...

Don't do it.

"Shut the fuck up," I growled, my voice like chafing rock.

I sunk back into the woods and began the hike along

the edge of the forest. I kept my eyes on Ma's house. I watched it grow closer with every step, with every labored breath.

I fell into a state of dreamlike exhaustion those last couple miles. It was as if I was watching myself from above, a beaten, filthy survivor clinging to the last ghost of redemption. My mind emptied and my consciousness drifted. I could still see, I could still hear, but my overwhelming fatigue numbed my body through the final stretch.

My eyes fluttered and I was suddenly standing directly across the street from the house. Had I fallen asleep? Had I passed out? Where had I gone?

I didn't care.

I looked out across the road. I didn't see any police. I didn't see anyone. Maybe they had closed the roads? No...there was a car coming now. It was headed for Ma's house...

I recognized that car.

"Mama," I croaked, heart surging. I staggered from the tree line, a lump forming in my throat. My feet passed empty grassland, my eyes trained on the approaching car. Yes...it was Ma's car...she was coming home...

Tears filled my eyes as I watched it pull into the driveway a hundred yards away. I pressed myself to go faster. I hurried into a lumbering jog, my vision blurring with relieved sorrow. She was right there...

I reached the road and saw Ma get out of the car. She

hadn't seen me yet. She walked around to the passenger's side. I stumbled into the driveway and then skidded to a halt.

Ma was helping Tammy out of the car. My sister looked exhausted, her skin pale, her hair ratty. I cried out to them, my voice a sobbing plea.

"Mama!"

Tammy and my mother turned to me, suddenly alert. I staggered down the driveway, tears flowing across my face, my arms outstretched to them.

Ma pulled Tammy away from me, fear rising in her eyes.

I slowed a dozen yards from them. "Ma? Tammy?"

Tammy's eyes widened. "Cole?"

"Oh, my God," Ma whispered.

I wept as I went the final distance to them. "Oh, Ma…Tam…oh, God…"

They embraced me fiercely and pulled me into a circle. Ma's arms found my back and Tammy pressed her cheek against my shoulder. I choked back wet cries and hugged them close.

"I'm sorry," I sniffled. "I'm so sorry…"

Ma squeezed me harder, her voice soft, shaking. "Shh, it's OK, Cole. It's OK, baby. Mama's here."

"Oh, Jesus," I wept, my shoulders trembling as a hoarse cry rattled from my lips. "Oh, Jesus, we did a bad thing, Ma…"

Tammy gently pulled away, her eyes wet. She looked into my face. "They're dead, aren't they? Joe? Dave?"

Tears streaming down my cheeks, I looked pathetically at Ma and then back at Tammy. Lip quivering, I nodded.

Ma bit her lip and closed her eyes, sorrow consuming her. "Oh, my dear boys…"

Tammy's face twisted with grief. "Who's left, Cole?"

I wiped my nose with the back of my hand. "They're dead. Everyone's dead. It's just me…it's just…me…" I pressed my hands to my eyes.

Tammy took me by the shoulders, her voice firm. "Look at me, Cole. Look at me, please."

I obeyed, my eyes bloodshot.

"Thank you," Tammy croaked, a wash of sadness overcoming her. "For what you did to get me back…I can never repay you. Don't turn away; look at me, Cole."

I did, eyes brimming.

"You're the best brother I could ever ask for," she said softly.

"You didn't back down to those bastards," Ma whispered, her face molded with grief. "You stood shoulder-to-shoulder with your brothers until the very end." Ma embraced me in a hug. "I'm proud of you. My heart breaks, but I'm proud of you, son."

"The Morrisons aren't going to bother you," I whispered into her shoulder. "Not ever again."

Tammy hugged me as well, the three of us holding one another for as long as we could.

Finally, I pulled away. "I have to go. The police...they're looking for me."

Ma took my hand. "I know...they were all over the hospital. We heard they were pursuing someone and I just knew it was one of my boys. I managed to sneak Tammy away. I had a feeling you'd come here. We needed to see you. Help you. But Cole...you can't leave..."

"I have to," I said quietly, weakly.

"Where?" Tammy asked gently. "What are you going to do if they catch you?"

My hands formed fists. "I'm not going to jail."

Ma squeezed my hand. "But if you're not going to let them take you in..."

"I gotta go," I whispered, a swell of emotion rising in my chest.

Ma just stared into my eyes, helpless.

Tammy took Ma's hands and gently removed them from mine. "Then you go, Cole. You run until they can't find you. You get away somewhere and start a life of your own. Away from this place. Away from us. Away from all the heartache. You go and have a good life. For me, Cole. Do it for me."

I nodded, lied, and hugged them both once more.

I knew it would be the last time I ever did.

When I pulled away, Ma handed me her keys. "Take the car."

I pushed them back into her hand. "No, I couldn't. What if they think you helped me?"

"I'll report it stolen tomorrow," Ma said, fighting against another wave of tears. "But you take the car. Get as much of a head start as you can. I won't have you leave here without helping you. I won't do it, Cole."

Gratefully, I took the keys.

"Goodbye," I whispered to them both.

"I love you," Tammy breathed.

"I love you," Ma cried.

I walked around to the car and opened the driver's door. I smiled at them, tears running down my face. "I love you, too."

I got in the car and started it up. I took the revolver out of my waistband and placed it on the passenger's seat. I took a shuddering breath and backed out of the driveway.

I chanced one last look at Ma and Tammy. They clung to one another, grief-stricken, like statues. Ma waved to me.

Gripping the steering wheel, tears flowing down my face, I gunned the engine and took off down the road.

At my back, I began to hear sirens.

Trembling, I checked to see how many bullets I had left.

About the Author

Elias Witherow lives in New England and continues to explore new ideas and ways to disturb people. But if you ever run into him, he'd be more than happy to buy you a drink and talk writing. With each new book, he strives to grow and provide increasingly entertaining fiction. Find him on Twitter @EliasWitherow and on Facebook at facebook.com/Elias-Witherow-831476890331162.

ALSO BY ELIAS WITHEROW

The Third Parent

The Black Farm

The Worst Kind of Monsters

THOUGHT
CATALOG
Books

THOUGHT
CATALOG
Books

Thought Catalog Books is a publishing house owned
by The Thought & Expression Company, an indepen-
dent media group based in Brooklyn, NY. Founded
in 2010, we are committed to facilitating thought and
expression. We exist to help people become better com-
municators and listeners in order to engender a more
exciting, attentive, and imaginative world.

Visit us on the web at
www.thoughtcatalogbooks.com and *www.collective.world.*